BOOK THREE: UPHEAVAL

THE BEGINNING OF SORROWS

MARK GOODWIN

Technical information in the book is included to convey realism. The author shall not have liability or responsibility to any person or entity with respect to any loss or damage caused, or allegedly caused, directly or indirectly by the information contained in this book.

All of the characters, places, and incidents are products of the author's imagination or are used fictitiously. Any resemblance to actual people, places, or events is entirely coincidental.

ISBN: 9798664511604

ACKNOWLEDGMENTS

I would like to thank my Editor in Chief Catherine Goodwin, as well as the rest of my fantastic editing team, Jeff Markland, Frank Shackleford, Stacey Glemboski, Sherrill Hesler, and Claudine Allison.

CHAPTER 1

And when he had opened the fourth seal, I heard the voice of the fourth beast say, "Come and see." And I looked, and behold a pale horse: and his name that sat on him was Death, and Hell followed with him. And power was given unto them over the fourth part of the earth, to kill with sword, and with hunger, and with death, and with the beasts of the earth.

Revelation 6:7-8

Joshua Stone walked by his wife's grave early Friday morning. The air was muggy already, and the sun had yet to clear the tree tops. He knelt and straightened the simple wooden cross which served as a marker alongside the others. "I miss you, baby. But I have a feeling that it won't be long now." More than two years had passed since her death, and he still felt incomplete without Stephanie.

"Those weeds in the garden aren't going to pull themselves. I best get to work before the day gets any hotter." He felt sure that she couldn't hear him, yet he longed to have her there to talk to. His few words spoken over her burial site were more cathartic than anything else.

Josh watched Micah come out of the travel trailer that he shared with Lindsey. He was laughing and tugging at his arm which Lindsey was pulling in an attempt to bring him back inside. Micah gave her a long passionate kiss, then insisted that he had to go. Lindsey caught Josh watching and blushed. Her long tee-shirt provided adequate coverage, but she pulled it down with her hands nonetheless. "Good morning, Mr. Stone."

"I told you—call me *Dad*." Josh waved at the girl who'd blossomed into a woman.

"Okay, *Dad*." She smiled and went back inside.

Likewise, Micah looked more and more like a man with each passing day. He slapped his father on the arm. "Did you sleep well?"

"Yeah. You?"

Micah glanced back at the trailer. "Yeah, once we finally went to sleep."

Josh shook his head. "I don't need to hear about all of that."

Micah walked briskly. "No, not that, well—yeah, that too. But we talk… after, you know."

"Glad to see married life is treating you well." Josh let a slight smile creep over his face. "I'm happy for you."

Micah grinned. "Thanks. Lindsey wants me to bring some more green tomatoes from the garden today. She's going to can a batch of that salsa that you like."

"It's good stuff," said Josh. "Goes a long way in making those dried beans not taste so bland."

Micah said, "I was listening to the news last night. They claim Australia is having another outbreak. Even people who have been vaccinated are getting sick."

"The scientists and epidemiologists have been expecting the Red Virus to mutate," Josh replied. "Jesus called this period, the beginning of sorrows. The Greek word used for sorrows there is the same word that's used for labor pains. So, we should expect all these calamities to keep getting more intense and closer together—just like labor pains for a pregnant woman."

Micah asked, "What do you think about the locusts in Africa and India? Do you think they'll start spreading to other parts of the world? The news said it's really bad there. The WHO estimates that 5,000 people a day are dying from starvation in eastern Africa and about the same amount in India."

Josh felt sad for the people losing their lives on such a massive scale. "It's terrible, but whether the locusts migrate or not, things will certainly get worse. If this is the Pale Horseman of the Apocalypse, he has the power to kill a quarter of the global population through war, famine, and the beasts of the earth."

"I suppose locusts could be considered beasts," said Micah.

"Yeah, I suppose so."

Micah added, "The news also said that the drought could make the locusts worse. For one, they're desert locusts, so they thrive in dry environments. And if they can't find adequate forage in East Africa and India, they'll look elsewhere."

"Like a caravan of death." Josh paused when he heard the sound of a vehicle. He drew his pistol and nodded at Micah to do the same. "Let's get back to the house and get the rifles."

Micah drew his sidearm and then removed his walkie-talkie from his belt clip. "Lindsey, we've got company. Get dressed, grab your rifle, and go to the farmhouse."

"10-4," she replied.

Josh sprinted to the house and through the back door. He yelled up the stairs, "Emilio, Nicole, look alive. We've got visitors!" Josh shouldered his AR-15 and rushed to the front window.

Micah took a second rifle from the downstairs bedroom and followed behind him. "Who is it?"

Josh let the curtain fall away and lowered his rifle. He let out a despairing sigh and glanced toward the old wooden floor. "It's Solomon."

"That's good news, why so glum?" asked Micah.

"He's come to collect. I knew this day would come, but I'd always hoped it wouldn't," said Josh.

Emilio arrived wearing only his jeans and holding his M-4. “False alarm?”

“Yeah, you can go back to bed,” said Josh. “You were on watch all night. I’ll fill you in when you wake up.”

“If I can go back to sleep,” grumped Emilio as he headed back toward the stairs.

Lindsey was next to show up. “It’s Solomon!” She was much more excited to see her old family friend.

“Is everything okay?” Mackenzie’s voice came over the radio.

Micah lifted his walkie-talkie to his mouth. “All clear.”

Josh opened the front door and tried to look more cheerful than he felt about the unannounced social call. “Solomon, good to see you.”

Solomon exited the passenger’s side of the small Ford Focus, which made him appear even taller than he was. “Glad to see you folks have survived.” He hugged Lindsey when she came to greet him.

Dana, the rugged warrior who’d assisted Josh’s team against the marauders’ compound, stepped out of the driver’s side of the vehicle. She offered the closest thing to a smile that her stern face would allow.

Josh held the door open. “Come on in. We’ve got sweet tea if you don’t mind the fact that it’s sweetened with honey.”

The two visitors followed Josh, Micah, and Lindsey inside and to the kitchen.

Nicole came in. She embraced Solomon and Dana. “Can I make you guys something to eat? I’m sure you're hungry. You've been on the road all morning, I'm sure."

"I could eat." Solomon took a seat.

"We've got rabbit rillettes with cornbread pancakes. We've even got real maple syrup, thanks to Micah—got butter, too." Nicole began retrieving dishes from the cupboard.

"Butter? I'm impressed. I didn't see any cows," said Solomon.

"We trade with some of the local farmers around here." Josh pulled out a chair and sat next to Solomon.

"And you still have electricity?" Dana sat on the other side of her companion.

"For now," Josh replied. "We've been able to sell some silver, having the marks direct-deposited into my alias account. We use it to keep the lights and the internet going, but not much else."

"That's good," said Solomon. "It beats having to cook outside."

"Especially in this torrid weather," Dana added.

Solomon thanked Lindsey for the Mason jar filled with sweet tea, then redirected his attention to Josh. "I suppose you know why I'm here."

Josh swallowed hard and nodded. "Yeah, I guess I do."

"We're planning an operation, next Thursday."

"The fourth of July?"

"Just kind of worked out that way," said Solomon.

"What's the mission?"

"We're going to kill Alexander."

Josh's heart stopped. He had to remind himself to breathe. He looked around at Micah, Nicole, and Lindsey. With mouths open in shock, all stared at Solomon as if they'd misheard him.

"Lucius Alexander?" Nicole asked.

"The Secretary-General! You're going to kill the Secretary-General?" Lindsey seemed to not understand the absurd concept.

"The anti-Christ—you think you're just going to walk right up and shoot him?" Micah inquired.

"Not me," said Solomon. "We. Indianapolis is to become the fifteenth OASIS city in North America. The official opening ceremony will be on the fourth. It will be followed by a huge fireworks display."

"Celebrating Independence Day? America isn't even a country anymore," Josh stated.

"No. The fourth has been co-opted. It's going to be called Global Unity Day," Dana replied.

Solomon continued, "Alexander will be giving a speech from the stairs of the Scottish Rite Cathedral downtown."

"Scottish Rite Cathedral? Is that like a church or something?" asked Lindsey.

"It sure looks like one," said Solomon. "But you won't catch anyone worshipping God there."

"Then who do they worship?" asked Micah.

"Good question," Solomon replied.

"Is Alexander a Mason?" Josh tried to put the pieces together.

"Not that I know of." Solomon took a sip of his tea and continued speaking. "But right over the entryway where he'll be speaking is a relief of a huge two-headed eagle. It's a symbol of worldly power and empire.

"But back to the mission. They'll have a grand gala inside the cathedral after the ceremony. That's where we'll make our move."

Nicole placed some food on the table. "How do you think you're going to get inside? That place is going to be like breaking into Fort Knox."

"Will you pose as part of the catering staff?" Lindsey asked.

Solomon shook his head. "Not a chance. Anyone allowed within a hundred yards of Lucius Alexander will be vetted by a very thorough examination. Not the kind of thing any of our people could hold up to."

"So what's the plan?" asked Micah.

Dana said, "The venue is rented out for special events. A big wedding is being held there this Sunday."

"So you'll get on the catering staff for that event?" Lindsey inquired. "Do you think there will be less scrutiny for this wedding?"

"I doubt it. This is a pretty high-end facility. Anyone getting married there has big bucks and will probably want background checks on all the staff."

"Sounds like you're out of luck," said Nicole.

"Maybe not. While they're very picky about who serves them, they don't much mind who sweeps up afterward. We've got a guy on the janitorial crew who will be cleaning the cathedral after the wedding Sunday night."

"That's four days early." Josh fidgeted with the bill of his ball cap.

"Yep. We'll camp out inside the building until it's time to make our move."

"You don't think they'll search the premises before Thursday?" Josh imagined the scenario.

Solomon nodded. "I'm sure they will. Probably look through the building Monday or Tuesday, then lock it down. But they've got a lot of ground to cover. This place is a maze. The staircase which leads up to the bell tower is behind a false wall. The entire building was designed to be intentionally surreptitious. It has secret passages throughout the structure. Remember, this place was constructed by Masons. All the dimensions of the building are divisible by the number three, and many by the number thirty-three."

"How did you get the skinny on all the trap doors?" Josh asked.

Solomon looked at Dana. "It wasn't easy. Let's just say we know a guy who knows a guy."

Dana corrected, "Knew a guy."

Nicole wrinkled her nose. "In other words, your information source is no longer with us."

"Those people take their oath to secrecy pretty serious," said Solomon.

"Until you bring in the power tools, at least," added Dana.

Micah shook his head. "Dad, doesn't the Bible say something about killing the anti-Christ? Like it's impossible, or something?"

Josh picked up the worn Bible he'd inherited from Rev. He opened it near the last pages. "Revelation 13 says, 'I saw one of his heads as if it had been mortally wounded, and his deadly wound was healed. And all the world marveled and followed the beast. So they worshiped the dragon who gave authority to the beast; and they worshiped the beast, saying, "Who is like the beast? Who is able to make war with him?"'

"If you were able to actually kill Alexander, you'd be playing right into his hands." Josh placed the Bible back on the kitchen table.

Solomon stared into Josh's eyes. He seemed unpersuaded by what he'd just heard. "Even so, I need your help with this."

"Are you not listening?" asked Josh. "He's going to come right back to life. We'd be risking our lives for nothing. Have you considered how much security this guy has around him day and night? Even if you happen to be the chosen one who gets to put a bullet in his brain, in all likelihood, you'll be captured before you can get away. Plus, imagine having to look at his resurrected face on television while you're in a prison cell waiting to be executed."

Micah nodded. "Zombie apocalypse. That's what I've been calling this thing from the beginning."

Josh had no patience for the jest. "This is serious, Micah."

"What did I say?" He looked around at the others. "I'm sorry, is there a more PC term for a reanimated corpse than a zombie? I didn't mean to offend anyone."

Josh waved his hand to dismiss the line of conversation. He looked at Solomon. "I know that I owe you one, but I can't be a part of this."

Solomon was quiet, then said, “It’s not a request, Josh. Like you said—you owe me.”

“I committed to providing you with like-kind tactical support. What I asked of you was assistance with a reasonable, well-planned assault against an unorganized group of drug addicts and low-level thieves. You can’t possibly equate that with a direct action against the most powerful man on the earth. It doesn’t even come close to being the same thing. What you are asking is suicide!”

“It’s not suicide. We have a plan,” said Solomon. “A plan that will work.”

“It won’t work!” Josh stood up and shouted. “The man is going to come right back to life! No amount of planning and execution is going to change that. It’s written in the Bible. Maybe you don’t believe in this book, but I do. Anyone who has read through it can’t deny the events contained in these prophecies are playing out precisely the way they were predicted.”

“I’m a believer,” said Solomon calmly. “It took me a while to come around, but I’m a born-again believer now.”

Josh shook his head in utter frustration. “Then how could you possibly think this will work?”

“It’s more complex than what I’m able to tell you right now.”

“What’s that supposed to mean?” Josh demanded.

“If I could read you in on the whole thing, I would. But you understand that information has to be passed on a need-to-know basis.”

"If you expect me to jeopardize the lives of my people, I need to know."

Solomon bit his lip then looked up at Josh. "I need you to trust me. And I need you to do this. You owe me. Your entire group owes me. It's a favor that you can't refuse. It's what you agreed to."

"What are you going to do? Are you going to compel me at gunpoint to go along with this asinine scheme?"

Solomon stared long and hard, as if debating his response to Josh's challenge. "No. I won't force you. But if you back out on your obligation, your word is absolutely worthless, and I don't ever want to hear from you again. Do you understand?"

Josh nodded. "I'll hold up my end of the bargain, but what you're asking for is outrageous. I won't do it."

Solomon pushed away the plate that Nicole had just served him. "Dana, we should be going."

She said nothing but got up from her place at the table and followed Solomon out the door.

"You made him a promise," Lindsey said to Josh.

"She's right, Dad. You did," Micah echoed.

Josh tightened his jaw as he watched Solomon and Dana walk away. "I never promised to participate in a suicide mission. And that's exactly what this is."

CHAPTER 2

Eventually we will have digital certificates to show who has recovered or been tested recently, or when we have a vaccine, who has received it.

Bill Gates speaking on the COVID-19 Pandemic

Josh had no assistance with weeding the garden Saturday morning. Lindsey and Micah were giving him the cold shoulder. Mackenzie mostly kept to herself. Emilio was sleeping since he was pulling night shift for security, and Nicole was busy taking care of the house, laundry, and cleaning.

Josh heard the door of Rev's old RV open. He tossed a pile of weeds away from the bare earth and looked up to see Mackenzie walking toward him. "Good morning."

"Good morning, Josh. I have something I want to talk to you about."

"Sure. Go ahead."

"The San Francisco OASIS zone has been extended to include Berkeley. They'll be reopening the college in the fall. I'm heading back."

Josh felt his stomach knot up. "Heading back? I thought you were going to be a permanent member of our group."

She crossed her arms. "I appreciate the hospitality. I really have no complaints about anyone here, but it's obvious that I don't fit in. My ideas are very different from everyone else's here."

Josh considered the implications. If she suddenly popped up on the radar, the GU would have questions. They'd want to know where her father was since Rev had been a connected member of Patriot Pride. They'd want to know where she'd been and if she'd had contact with any of the other members of the group. However, Josh did not want to lead with that card in the negotiations.

He said, "We all have different ideas. Emilio is my best friend, but he's not even convinced God exists. My sister knows I don't agree with her and Emilio sharing a room. And forget about Micah, he has his own theory about everything. We all sort of agree to disagree. Or, you might say, we disagree without being disagreeable."

She forced a smile. "I know. And no one has made me feel shunned or anything. But I feel like I'd be happier with…forgive the terminology, but—

my own kind. You folks are great. I know you have differences, but at the end of the day, you're all conservatives. That guides the decision-making process around here. So it's also about me feeling like I have a voice—and I don't."

Josh certainly wasn't about to hand the compound over to Marxism and atheism to appease her. He felt trapped by the situation. "But everything your father believed in, he taught you about the events of the last days before he died. Don't you think that explains a lot of what's in the world?"

Her face softened, as if she were speaking to a naïve child. "I think the Bible can be interpreted to help people make sense of what is happening. But I also think it could have been applied to other chaotic periods throughout history. I'm happy that it gives you comfort."

Josh nodded. "Opium of the people, huh?"

"Those are your words, not mine."

"No, they're actually Marx's words. And his utopic vision for the planet has failed miserably in every instance where it was implemented. But that's not going to stop the GU from trying it once more—and this time with the entire world at once."

"Capitalism doesn't seem to be fairing much better," she said.

"We haven't had capitalism anywhere on the planet since FDR." Josh stopped himself. "But I didn't intend to turn this into a debate."

Mackenzie smiled. "I know. And neither did I, but it's sort of what happens around here when *I* get involved in a conversation."

"If you go to Berkeley, you'll have to take the Red Virus vaccine. And you'll have to take the digital-certificate implant chip to prove your immunization is up-to-date."

"I don't see that as a bad thing," she replied. "It's part of being a responsible citizen. You were immunized, and I don't see any ill effects."

"Yeah, well. I got one dose. And, I got the unadulterated dose. They gave me the same thing they were giving all of the politicians and the elites. I'm not opposed to vaccines. I'm opposed to being shot up with mercury, which is added to all the consumer-level vaccines."

"That's just a myth."

"Google *thimerosal*. Then tell me it's a myth."

"Just to humor you…" She took out Rev's burner phone.

Josh watched her facial expression change as she read the information. "Next, why don't you read what effect mercury has on the human body?"

Her brow lowered as she received the results of her new search. "Can cause neurological and behavioral disorders, such as tremors, emotional instability, insomnia, memory loss, neuromuscular changes, and headaches—can also harm the kidneys and thyroid."

"Want to know why everyone is on so much medication, anti-depressants, anti-psychotics, anxiety meds, and a host of other problems? That's a really good place to start."

She closed the window on the phone and put it back in her pocket. "I'm sure they have a good reason for it."

"Yeah, to create a drugged-out, stupefied population that can't think for themselves and will go along with everything the globalists say."

"That's a little more conspiratorial than what I believe, but I can understand why you feel that way."

"It's just a little mercury now, but every time the virus morphs and you have to take a new vaccine, they get another chance to include more chemical additives with the inoculation. Once you start, you'll be stuck. You can never turn down another vaccine. If you don't keep your digital certificate up-to-date, you'll be denied access to groceries, banking, public spaces, and everything else under the auspices of being a threat to the rest of the population."

"Thank you for your concern, but I'm afraid my mind is made up. I have a proposition."

"Go ahead." Josh listened.

She said, "I'll give you my father's RV and weapons for enough gas to get me back to Berkeley. I appreciate all that you've done for me, Josh, but it's time for me to go. I think it's a generous offer."

Josh felt the tightness in his neck over the stress of the situation. He tried to think of anything that might convince her to change her mind. Finally, he looked up. "I'm sorry. We can't let you leave."

Her face quickly snapped into a growl. "What do you mean, you can't let me leave?" She put her hands on her hips and the volume of her voice rose. "Am I some kind of prisoner, or something?"

Josh stood up from the bucket he'd been sitting on. "Calm down." He held his arms out. "It's nothing like that. Let me explain."

Her nostrils flared. "No! You let me explain! I'm leaving! And no one is going to stop me. Tell me you understand!"

"It's not that simple. The GU was looking for us before we ever came to California to rescue you. If you suddenly show up, they'll bring you in for questioning. They'll want to know where we're at, and how many of us are here."

"I'm not going to tell them where you are."

"Once the enhanced interrogation techniques begin, you'll tell them. You'll tell them everything you know."

"I'm a college professor. They're not going to torture me."

"I worked for the system. No one was more shocked by their willingness to use brutality than me. But trust me when I tell you that you are grossly underestimating them. You *will* break. If Solomon hadn't gotten me out, I would've broken. Everyone has a breaking point. And these people are professionals. They will get the information they want."

"I'm sorry, Josh. I have to go."

"I can't help you. I'm not giving you gas or any other provisions."

"Fine. I'll hitchhike if I have to." She turned to walk away.

Josh abandoned his task and marched back to the farmhouse. When he came inside, Emilio greeted him with a perturbed snarl. Nicole stood nearby.

"You're awake?" Josh inquired.

"I am now. What was all that yelling about?" Emilio asked.

Josh explained the conversation with Mackenzie.

Emilio shook his head. "We can't let her leave."

"We can't exactly chain her to a tree," said Josh.

"Why not?" asked Nicole.

"Because, I promised Rev that we'd look after her. And because we're not Nazis."

"She's going to get us all killed. It's her or us," said Emilio.

"I don't think we have a choice." Josh shoved his hands deep into his front jean pockets. "We have to let her go. It's the only Christian or civilized thing to do."

Emilio said, "Why don't you let me put a bag over her face, and I'll drive her out to the state line. Maybe she won't be able to remember how to get here if she doesn't see the roads when she leaves."

Josh wrinkled his forehead. "Yeah, like the guy we interrogated that you were supposed to drop off for the GHS to pick up? You had alternate plans for him before you ever left the compound. I couldn't in good conscience place her in your care."

Emilio looked at Nicole. "GHS would have killed him anyway."

"Still, nothing better happen to Mackenzie!" Nicole scowled at him. "I'll never speak to you again."

"But you'd still marry me, right?" Emilio asked.

Josh lifted one eyebrow.

Nicole slapped Emilio on the shoulder and hid her face, as if desperately fighting a smile.

However, she lost control. She beamed as she looked up at Josh. “I was going to tell you, but I was waiting for the right time.”

“Oh. Okay,” said Josh.

“Aren’t you happy for us?” she asked.

“Sure.”

Emilio put his arm around Nicole. “He’s just stressed out over this thing with Mackenzie. He’s happy for us.”

“Is that true, Josh?” Nicole looked deeply into his eyes.

“Yeah,” he said.

She slowly began shaking her head. “No. It’s something else. What is it? I thought this is what you wanted, for us to not be living in sin.”

Josh had no mental energy for another heavy conversation. But, he could find no point in delaying the inevitable. “The Bible says not to be yoked to unbelievers.”

“Wow.” Emilio shook his head. “It never ends with you, bro.” Emilio turned to walk away. “I’ll be upstairs.”

Josh felt terrible about alienating his only friend, but he couldn’t deny his convictions.

“I’ve got news for you, Josh,” said Nicole with her hands on her hips. “Emilio and I are already *yoked* together. So to me, this seems like it should be a win for everybody. Why can’t you just accept it and be happy for me? And another thing, he’s your best friend and a member of this compound, so it kind of seems like you’re *yoked* to him also.”

Josh said nothing as his sister walked away and followed Emilio up the stairs. She had a point.

Maybe he should just be happy for them. But it was something he'd have to consider at a more convenient time. He spent several minutes mired in contemplation over what to do about Mackenzie. Then, he heard the engine of Rev's old pickup truck. He ran to the front door and looked out just in time to see the cloud of dust kicked up by the tires speeding across the gravel driveway.

Emilio came storming down the stairs. "She left?"

"Yep. At least I don't have to figure out how to deal with that situation."

Emilio huffed. "But we've got a whole new can of worms on our hands now."

Josh nodded in agreement. "And I don't want to compound the issue by having animosity between us. I'll be happy to have you as my brother-in-law." He extended his hand to Emilio.

Emilio bypassed the handshake and hugged Josh. "Thanks, bro. That means a lot to me."

Josh patted his friend on the back and pulled away. "But I'm still praying that your eyes will be opened—before it's too late."

CHAPTER 3

When you pass through the waters, I will be with you; and through the rivers, they shall not overflow you. When you walk through the fire, you shall not be burned, nor shall the flame scorch you.

Isaiah 43:2 NKJV

Josh and Emilio rummaged through Rev's RV to see what Mackenzie had left behind. "She didn't take any of the guns. I thought she'd at least learned the importance of being able to defend herself." Josh checked the chamber of Rev's AR-15.

Emilio tucked Rev's pistol into the back of his pants. "She can't take guns in an OASIS city anyway."

"Maybe not," said Josh. "But there's a lot of road and a lot of bad actors between here and Berkeley. I would have kept a weapon until I reached the city limits, then tossed it out the window if I thought I was going to be searched."

"You'd have never gone in the first place," Emilio corrected.

A brief knock on the door preceded Micah's entry into the RV. "Mackenzie left?"

"Yeah." Josh paused his search to pay attention to his son. "She took all of the gas."

"But we got this apartment on wheels and some nice firearms out of the deal," Emilio said in a light-hearted tone.

Josh's voice was much more somber. "I'm worried that she'll be questioned by the GU. We'll have to relocate."

"Relocate? To where?" Micah looked upset. "Everything we own is here! And all the supplies back in the cave, that will take forever just to bring them out, much less cart them off to another camp."

"We'll figure it out," Josh assured. "For now, I've got to find fuel. Then, we'll take the trailer, the RV, and the vehicles to somewhere we can lay low for a while. We don't have to move the supplies inside the cave right now. Worst case scenario, we can always access the cave from the park and retrieve the supplies as we need them."

"What's the time frame on relocation?" Emilio asked.

Lindsey walked into the RV. "Relocation? We're leaving?"

"Twenty-four hours." Josh nodded at the girl who'd decided to resume talking to him. "Micah will fill you in on the details."

"I don't know if we should even wait that long," said Micah. "What if Mackenzie has already ratted us out? The DGS could be assembling a team to hit us as we speak."

Josh shook his head. "Mackenzie wouldn't voluntarily give us up. DGS would want to know why she'd waited so long to turn in known terrorists. She could be implicated. She's smart enough to know that.

"On the flip side, she'll cave fast. She'll start talking before they ever get her to an interrogation room. My guess is that she's already flagged for questioning. If she hits a checkpoint or has any contact with law enforcement whatsoever, she'll tell them everything they want to know. The clock is ticking. We need to pack up and break camp as soon as possible."

"What about the food in the garden?" Lindsey asked.

"Harvest everything that's even close to being ready to pick," said Josh. "Since I'm probably inoculated from the virus, I'll take care of relocating the rabbits and the chickens."

"And the bees?" asked Lindsey.

"And the bees." Josh picked up the guns they'd found. "Emilio, come with me."

"Where are you going?" asked Micah.

"To see Hoot. Hopefully he'll know of someone who has some fuel to trade."

An hour later Josh and Emilio arrived at Hoot's farm in the El Camino. Dressed in well-worn denim overalls, Hoot walked out onto his porch carrying a double-barrel shotgun.

Josh stuck his hands out the window. "Hoot, hey, it's me." He had to think quickly to circumvent giving his real name in lieu of the alias by which the country farmer knew him. "Peter Gray."

"Oh, hey! I didn't recognize you with the beard." Hoot lowered his weapon. "Come on up."

Josh and Emilio exited the vehicle. Since the outbreak, the new normal was for people to keep their distance from one another, so they did not approach Hoot to shake hands. "I'm looking for gas."

"Let me know if you find any," said Hoot. "That's somethin' all of us would like to have."

"Even a few gallons would help. I've got guns I'm willing to trade." Josh pointed at Hoot's shotgun. "That's a ferocious firearm you've got there, but times being what they are, it's conceivable that you might want something with a little higher rate of fire."

Hoot gave a disappointed glance at his break-barrel shotgun. "Whatcha got?"

"AR-15. I'll throw in two loaded magazines for twenty gallons of gas." Josh took the rifle out of the El Camino to show Hoot. It was a much higher offer than the going rate for fuel, but he was in a tight spot.

Hoot nodded. "I've got five gallons in a can. Probably got another fifteen in my pickup. I'll siphon it out if you have something to put it in."

"Someone stole my gas cans," said Josh. "That's why I'm in this predicament. You can put it in five-gallon buckets with lids if you have any."

Hoot seemed to be thinking. "Yeah, if you're not too picky, I'll find something to put it in."

Josh glanced at his vehicle. "I can fit another ten gallons in the El Camino."

"I think we've got us a deal." Hoot smiled. "I'll come across more gas before I ever get another chance to trade for a beauty like that. Mind if I check it out?"

Josh placed the rifle on the edge of Hoot's porch. "Go right ahead."

After careful inspection of the goods, Hoot took the rifle and magazines in the house. Next, he brought his pickup around and siphoned out fifteen gallons of fuel in addition to the filled five-gallon gas can. Ten gallons went in the El Camino and five in a plastic bucket with a sealed lid.

Josh and Emilio bade Hoot farewell and headed back to the compound. They wasted no time in hauling all of the supplies out of the farmhouse. Nicole, Lindsey, and Micah assisted with stowing as many provisions as possible into the travel trailer and the RV.

Two hours later, the group paused for a short break.

"We still have a lot of stuff that won't fit into the vehicles." Nicole sat on the back stairs of the farmhouse.

Josh lay on the ground, allowing his back to decompress for a moment. "We'll take the rest into the cave."

"Everything?" asked Micah. "Even the furniture?"

"We'll carry the furniture to the first chamber of the cave. We can't get it much farther back than that. The smaller items will go all the way back to the cache."

Lindsey frowned. "That's going to take all night."

"Do we know where we're going yet?" Nicole stretched out one leg and leaned back on the porch.

Josh still hadn't come up with a solution. "We'll find a place. Everything will work out." He had little confidence in the statement but hoped the others wouldn't see through the façade.

"We could go to Indiana," said Lindsey. "If we honor our deal with Solomon."

Emilio looked at Josh with inquiring eyes. "What do you think?"

Josh glanced at his friend. "Are you serious? That's a death wish!"

Emilio lifted his shoulders and looked away. "The girl's right. We'd have a place to lay our heads."

Josh looked at the other members of his group. Micah and Nicole both stared at him as if waiting for him to approve the motion.

Josh stood up. "Guys, are you thinking this through? No way we're getting out of there alive if we participate in a plot to kill Alexander. And it will all be for nothing. Alexander will be up walking around the next day!"

"We've got nowhere to go, Dad. If we did, you would have thought of something by now." Micah took Lindsey's hand.

"What about you, Nicole? Do you want to sign on as a kamikaze?"

She shrugged. "If we don't have a place to hang our hats, we're as good as dead anyway. At least if we have somewhere to call home, we have a chance."

"I can't believe you people." Josh walked away from them. "Lindsey, see if you can get a hold of Solomon. I doubt he'll even answer the call if he sees the number of my burner phone show up. The rest of you, five more minutes of break time, then we need to start getting the rest of these supplies stashed." He collected his first load of supplies and began ferrying them to the cave.

Sunday morning, Josh awoke feeling as if he'd just run a marathon. His back and shoulders ached. His neck was tight, and his bad knee was stiff. He'd slept little the night before as his bed and mattress had been loaded into the cave. Once the travel trailer was unloaded, he'd have the bunk beds for his sleeping space, but for now, they were stuffed to capacity.

He allowed himself a few moments to stretch and get limbered up. Then, he got up and mentally prepared himself for another tough day.

He took his rifle and backpack out to the El Camino. Next, he loaded the rabbit cages and portable chicken coops into the bed of the vehicle. As he was donning his beekeeper's attire, Micah came out of the house to put some gear in Lindsey's truck, which would be pulling the travel trailer.

"We're going to need more gas to get to northern Indiana," said Micah.

"We'll make a pit stop in Lawrenceburg." Josh removed his Stihl ball cap, replacing it with a wide-brimmed hat and mesh veil, which covered his face.

"That's a good 70 miles out of the way. Besides, we don't even know if that station is still open. Why don't we just buy gas with your bank card?"

"If Mackenzie flips… no—when Mackenzie flips, she'll give them my alias. Then, the DGS can see where Peter Gray's card has been used and pull the footage from the cameras at the filling station. From there, they can determine which direction we were traveling and search traffic cameras to follow us right to Solomon's front door. Then, this really will be all for nothing."

"Oh. I guess I didn't think about all of that," said Micah. "What happens if the pumps are closed?"

"We'll have to figure out something else. It's not a perfect plan. But we don't have many options to choose from." Josh pulled the long, thick white gloves over his hands. "I'm going to get the bees loaded into the El Camino. Tell everyone to load up. I want to roll out in fifteen minutes."

"Yes, sir." Micah returned to the farmhouse to carry out Josh's instructions.

An hour and a half later, Josh pulled into the familiar gas station in Lawrenceburg, Kentucky. He was pleased to see the counter was still manned by the same old man he'd done business with on several other occasions. "Good morning."

The man stared at Josh for a moment. He looked out at the pump to see the black El Camino. He snapped his fingers and pointed at Josh. "I thought you looked familiar. The beard threw me off. Hair's longer too. Hope you ain't turnin' into some kinda hippy."

Josh laughed. "There's no threat of that happening. Pumps look like they're turned off."

"Ain't got no gas," said the old-timer.

Josh felt his stomach sink. "No gas?"

The man looked around. "Not none I'm selling for that stinkin' devil money."

"But for trade?"

"Trade for what?"

"What do you need? Guns? Ammo? Fresh produce?"

"Got produce." The man pointed to a table full of milk crates all filled with what seemed to be home-grown vegetables. "What kinda guns and ammo?"

"AR-15, AK-47, magazines, 5.56, 7.62x39, pistols."

The man looked out at the RV and the pickup pulling the travel trailer. "They with you?"

"Yeah."

"All of 'em need gas?"

"The RV coasted in on fumes," said Josh.

The old man thought quietly for a moment, as if formulating an offer. "Give me an AK, an AR, three magazines for each and 200 rounds of ammo for each."

"To fill up all three vehicles?" Josh looked back out toward the pump. "Sounds steep."

"What'd you have in mind?"

"I'll do one rifle, two mags, and fifty rounds."

"Make it a hundred rounds, throw in a pistol, and you've got a deal."

"Thirty-eight snub nose okay?" Josh would give the man one of the pistols taken in the raid against the marauders' ranch.

"That'll be fine. I need at least twenty-five rounds for it."

Josh replied, "I can do that."

"Good, I'll take an AK. They're less fussy. I get enough fussin' when I'm at the house. Reckon that's part of what keeps me comin' in here."

"Sure thing." Josh looked back at the out-of-order pumps. "Where do I go to get the gas?"

"Have 'em pull up to pump number three." The old man flipped a switch and the lights came on for that particular pump. "If anyone else pulls in, hang the pump back up right away and just act like you didn't see the out of order sign. I'll kill the pump, but you can get right back to it once they're gone."

"Great. I'll be back with your merchandise." Josh left the store to retrieve the AK and the pistol. The trade was made, the tanks filled, and the convoy headed north on US-127. From there, they took I-64 west to Louisville where they went on I-65, which would take them all the way to the rural road leading to Solomon's compound.

CHAPTER 4

By faith Abraham obeyed when he was called to go out to the place which he would receive as an inheritance. And he went out, not knowing where he was going. By faith he dwelt in the land of promise as in a foreign country, dwelling in tents with Isaac and Jacob, the heirs with him of the same promise; for he waited for the city which has foundations, whose builder and maker is God.

Hebrews 1:8-10 NKJV

Josh and the team arrived at Solomon's compound early Sunday afternoon. An armed guard stopped Josh who was in the lead vehicle. "You the new guys?" He was robust with a thick brown beard.

Josh rolled down his window. "Yeah, Solomon is expecting us."

The man let his AR-15 hang from the single point sling around his chest and motioned for a second watchman to move the heavy red combine out of the way. This allowed Josh's team to access the driveway. The man turned his attention back to Josh. "As you can see, we don't have much in the way of trees around here. Your trailer and your RV are going to feel like solar ovens in this heat during the day. I'd recommend parking them on the back side of the barn being used as the barracks. It's the one furthest back. At least the barn will shield one side of you during the day. It will be a symbiotic relationship as you'll be shielding one side of the barn. The folks living inside will appreciate it.

"We've got a mechanic. He can probably convert your vehicles and generators over to run E-85. Might be able to run your AC units then. Flex-fuel conversion, they call it. Motors will run on regular gas or ethanol blend—up to 90 percent, the way he sets it up." The man looked around at the endless rows of corn. "Ethanol is the one thing we ain't gonna run out of any time soon."

"Okay, thanks for the information. I'm Josh, by the way. I'm looking forward to getting to know you better."

"No problem at all. I'm George. Most folks here are pretty friendly. Some might be a little standoffish at first, but they'll come around. We're all in this thing together. Solomon has vouched for you, I reckon you must be good people."

"Thanks." Josh drove past the combine and followed the gravel road past the small farmhouse, a quaint little livestock barn, and three large metal industrial barns. He noticed a few other travel trailers and RVs set up around the property. He pulled behind the third metal building. He called over the radio to Micah and Emilio who were driving the pickup with the trailer in tow, and the RV, respectively. "Pull up as close as you can to the barn. Maybe leave two or three feet."

"10-4," said Emilio.

"Got it," said Micah.

Josh parked and exited the El Camino. He stretched his back and looked out at the greener than green fields flanking the compound all around.

Solomon arrived shortly after the rest of the team had exited their vehicles. He swatted at a bee buzzing around his head. "You brought your bees?"

"Yeah. Where can I put them?"

Solomon pointed to the corner of the field. "Over there. I hope they like corn pollen. Not much else for them around here."

"Thanks." Josh frowned. He suspected they wouldn't be producing as much honey without flowering plants.

"You all get settled in. Eat something and then gear up. You and Emilio will be with me. We're rolling out at 9:00 PM. Wear street clothes that make you look like you could be part of a cleaning crew. And bring nice clothes that will make you fit in at a high-end soirée.

"Micah, Lindsey, and Nicole will be part of the extraction team. They'll be working with Dana, so they'll be staying here until Thursday morning."

Josh hated the situation but had no other alternative. "Thanks for putting Micah on the outside team."

"Oh, I didn't do it as a favor to you. You're a solid operator, and I need your skills. That's why I agreed to give you a place to live. But I'm not over you backing out on me. And it better not happen again—especially while we're in the field."

"It won't. Once I commit to something, I'm in it." Josh had very little leverage in this situation, so he had to put up with whatever Solomon dished out. "But I didn't bring my tux. I doubt Emilio did either."

Solomon stared at him for a moment. "We've definitely got dress clothes that will fit you. I'll have to see about Emilio. He's a big dude. What about black boots?"

"I've got two pair of Coyote. Had some black dress shoes but left them in Frankfort when I had to bug out. I'm pretty sure Emilio has black combat boots. What about our weapons load?"

Solomon shook his head. "I'm taking care of that. We'll be running Glock 18 clones."

"Full-auto?" Josh asked.

"Yeah. We can't exactly walk around a cocktail party with AK-47's tucked under our jackets."

"33-round magazines?"

"Yeah," said Solomon. "We'll start out with 19-round mags. Actually 17-rounds with plus-2 extension plates. Once you burn through that, you'll have six 33-round mags and an extra 19-round magazine. Bring your own backup gun."

"What kind of ammo are we running?"

"Alternating ballistic tip and full metal jacket. Alexander's men are going to be on him like white on rice once the music starts. You might not get a clean shot. You may have to punch through some security personnel to hit Lucius."

"They'll all be wearing body armor."

"Not on their heads, they won't," said Solomon.

Josh pressed his lips together at the thought of hitting a moving target in the head. "This is a pretty sketchy hit."

"Three of us with over 200 rounds each?" Solomon lowered his eyebrows. "It's statistically impossible for us to not kill him."

"Mmmhmm. Except for the fact that we'll be dodging return fire."

"Yeah, well, we just need to take him out before the security detail has a chance to draw their weapons." Solomon pointed at Josh's shaggy hair. "You're going to need a haircut. And you need to lose that beard. Go see Anne Marie." Solomon pointed to one of the other RVs. "She'll get you cleaned up. Tell Emilio to get a shave and a haircut too."

"If we're hiding out in a bell tower for three days, we're going to have razor stubble. Might need a shower by then also."

"The building has restrooms. You can shave and take a cat bath. It's not like you're going to be rolling in the mud while you're there. And we'll have the run of the place once the doors are locked until the security team shows up on Wednesday. Bring a razor and a washcloth. Be ready to roll out at 9:00 PM. We've got about a one-hour drive from here to Indianapolis." Solomon walked away.

***

Later that evening, Josh looked out the driver's side window of the non-descript white van as they drove through downtown Indianapolis. He watched a team of men in a bucket truck placing surveillance equipment on top of a lamp post. "That's the third Omniscience crew I've seen putting up cameras. It's got to be difficult doing an install like that at night."

"They've got plenty of lights set up." Solomon pointed to the top of a building as they passed through a roundabout. "More guys working up there. I'm sure they're with Omniscience as well."

Emilio looked over from the back seat. "The GU is cutting it close with getting the city retrofitted in time for the official launch party."

Solomon shook his head. "They've got this down to a science by now. This is the fourteenth US city they've upgraded in two years. That's in addition to the cities retrofitted in Canada, Australia, South America, and Europe. Alexander plans on adding one new North American city per month from here on out."

Josh looked to his left at the towering Soldiers' and Sailors' Monument in the center of the circle. It reached nearly 300 feet toward the sky. Large spotlights on the ground illuminated elaborate limestone sculptures surrounding the base of the massive obelisk. The carvings depicted Civil War soldiers, cannons, winged beings, and triumphant goddesses. "All the blood that has been shed to defend America, and in the end, we fell without a fight."

"What exactly do you call this little mission that we're undertaking right now?" Solomon asked.

Josh sighed. "A futile sacrifice on the altar of waste."

"Ye of little faith," Solomon scolded. "Like I said, this is all part of a bigger plan."

"Yeah, well, I've read the book and I know how effective our leg of the operation turns out."

Emilio watched a patrol of GU peacekeepers eyeing the van as it continued past Monument Circle on Meridian. "That's if we even make it to our destination without being captured."

"Getting caught isn't an option. If we have to engage, we either shoot our way out or die trying," said Solomon.

They successfully advanced the next few blocks without incident. "This is the place." Solomon pointed forward and to the left at the ornate stone Gothic Revival building.

"Sure looks like a church," said Emilio.

"Oh, they may very well hold prayer services here," said Solomon. "But they sure don't pray to the same God we do."

Emilio laughed, "Yeah, well, your God has been gradually going out of style anyway."

"Not for long," countered Josh.

"So you don't buy into the whole end-times thing, huh?" Solomon glanced at the rearview mirror.

"I don't know," Emilio replied. "I can see why you guys believe it, but it all sounds rather vague to me. What about you? You believe in the Bible, but you don't think Josh is right about Alexander coming back to life?"

"Maybe, but like I keep telling you guys, this is only one piece of the puzzle," Solomon answered.

"I sure would like to know what the big picture looks like," said Josh. "I'd feel much better about risking my neck on a mission that's doomed to failure."

"You'll see in time," said Solomon. "Just be patient."

"Yeah," scoffed Josh. "If we live long enough."

CHAPTER 5

Furthermore He said to me, “Son of man, do you see what they are doing, the great abominations that the house of Israel commits here, to make Me go far away from My sanctuary? Now turn again, you will see greater abominations.”

So I went in and saw, and there—every sort of creeping thing, abominable beasts, and all the idols of the house of Israel, portrayed all around on the walls.

Ezekiel 8:6 & 10 NKJV

Josh climbed out of the van. He opened the side door and retrieved the heavy black duffle bag which contained everything he needed for the mission and the next three days he'd spend holed up in the Scottish Rite Cathedral. "This place gives me the creeps."

Emilio exited the vehicle with his duffle bag. He stopped when he saw a short, dark-haired man approaching.

"Hola, ustedes trabajando conmigo?"

"Si," Emilio nodded and turned to Solomon.

"This is Rodrigo," said Solomon. He retrieved a plastic tube from his front pocket and passed it to Rodrigo.

Rodrigo opened the tube and poured out five gold American Eagle coins into his palm. His eyes glistened as he felt the weight of the gold in his hand. He nodded as if very satisfied by the remittance. "Ah, bueno!"

"Have most of the wedding guests cleared out?" Solomon asked.

"Si. Bride and groom leaved like two hours before. Few peoples still here, pero mucho borracho. No making problems for you."

"What did he say?" Josh asked Emilio.

"Said the guests who haven't left yet are drunk." Emilio gave his friend a scolding look. "I can't believe you lived in Florida your whole life and never learned Spanish."

Solomon pointed to his duffle in the back of the van. "Can one of you guys grab my bag?"

Josh replied, "Where are you going?"

"To ditch the van."

"Ditch as in get rid of?" Josh asked.

"Yeah. The rough end of town is only a couple miles west from here. I'm going to take it across the bridge and then leave the keys in the ignition. It'll be gone before I even make it back."

"Speaking of making it back, how are we supposed to get home?" Emilio asked.

"The extraction team will have plenty of empty seats," said Solomon. "We'll get a ride."

"How are you getting back here?" Josh inquired.

"Walking."

"Through the hood? At night?"

"Nobody's going to mess with a six-foot black man strolling down the street over there. And if they do, I've got something for them." Solomon pulled up his shirt to reveal the butt of his Glock 18 clone.

"Haughville?" Rodrigo shook his head. "It's not so bad."

"You don't think someone will boost a van if I leave it parked on the street with the keys in it?" Solomon asked.

Rodrigo seemed to re-assess his previous analysis of the neighborhood. Finally, he nodded. "Jes, they take it."

Emilio took Solomon's duffle bag from the rear of the van. "Be safe."

Josh held the sliding door of the van. "If you don't come back, does that mean we're released of our obligation?"

Solomon pressed his lips together. "If I didn't think I could make it two miles through the hood, I never would have put myself on this team."

"I don't have the highest confidence in your ability to make those types of judgments. If you don't come back, we're out of here." Josh slid the door closed and Solomon drove away.

"The guy saved your tail," said Emilio. "Twice, actually." He picked up the extra bag. "You should give the man a break."

Josh considered that he probably never would've escaped DGS custody without Solomon. "I know. I suppose I should be grateful for the two extra years he bought me."

"You're not dead yet." Emilio looked at Rodrigo. "A donde vamos?"

Rodrigo motioned for them to follow him. "Sígueme. Te mostraré donde."

Josh trailed behind Emilio and Rodrigo. Two very intoxicated women stumbled out the doors toward the parking lot as Josh was going in. They each leaned on the other to keep from falling. One held a half-filled bottle of Cristal Rose champagne, and the other held two pairs of high heel shoes by the straps. The one with the champagne stopped in front of Emilio. "Are you on the cleaning crew? Why don't you come home with me? My apartment is *filthy*."

The other woman tugged her arm. "Come on, Pam. We don't fraternize with the help."

"I don't wanna marry him." She winked at Emilio as she was dragged away. "I don't even want to fratern-nern—nize."

Josh and Emilio continued following Rodrigo. They passed several people from the catering staff as they carried crates and chafing dishes out of the building. They walked through the ballroom, which was paneled in wood. Josh noticed the white oak parquet floors bordered with black walnut. He guessed each panel to be 33 inches square. He adjusted the strap of his duffle bag and looked up at the huge gilded bronze chandelier decorated with ornate crystal beads and pendants.

"Fine place to throw a party." Emilio took in the elegant surroundings.

Rodrigo led them down a hall that seemed to be a dead-end.

"Now where?" asked Josh.

"I show for you." Rodrigo pressed against one of the wood panels. As he did so, the adjacent panel popped out. Rodrigo pressed the tips of his fingers against the newly revealed edge of the protruding panel. He tugged against it with even pressure and the panel opened up to expose a hidden passageway. "Hurry." Rodrigo motioned for Josh and Emilio to enter.

The two went inside and Rodrigo closed the panel. Emilio turned around. "Think we can get back out of here?"

Josh studied the mechanics of the two panels from the inside of the secret entrance. "Yeah. This one has handles. I suppose you pull this one up and the door pops out."

Emilio pointed to a stone spiral staircase. "This looks like something that belongs in a haunted house."

"Or a temple to Satan." Josh led the way up the winding stairway. The stairs terminated on the second floor. Josh looked up at the interior of the open stone tower above. An array of large bells were suspended overhead.

"Take a look at this." Emilio stood motionless before a stone altar.

Josh shivered as he looked at the red stains on the heavy granite table.

"Is that animal blood?" Emilio inspected the single furnishing in the room but kept his distance as if afraid of touching it.

"I hope so." Josh looked closer.

"Why would you say that?" Emilio wrinkled his brow.

"Because if it's not animal's blood…"

Emilio cut him off. "Okay, okay. Listen, this stuff creeps me out. Some of the old ladies in my neighborhood where I grew up practiced Regla de Ocha. I used to have nightmares about all that when I was a kid."

"Is that like Santeria, or something?"

"Basically the same thing," said Emilio.

"Wait, let me get this straight," said Josh. "So, you believe in witchcraft, at least enough to be bothered by it, but you can't bring yourself to believe in God?"

"I never said I don't believe." Emilio dropped his bag as far from the stone altar as he could get. "I think there's more than this realm, I simply don't think we can know for sure."

"You'll know for sure one day. I hope you figure it out in time." Josh put down his duffle near Emilio's. His first order of business was to remove his suit from the bag so he could hang it up and let the wrinkles fall out. The altar was the only place that would support a hanger, so he made use of that.

Emilio also hung his jacket on the edge of the altar. "Maybe it's not blood. Don't Masons have some kind of thing they do with corn and wine?"

"I couldn't tell you. I don't know much about them." Josh fished through his bag and took out an MRE. "Of course, they're a secretive bunch, so that leaves them wide open for speculation and conspiracy theories."

After hanging Solomon's clothes next to the others, Emilio pulled out a thin blanket from his bag and stretched it out on the floor. "Might as well get comfortable. We're going to be here for a while." He positioned his bag to use as a pillow. "Although, getting comfortable is going to be tough on this travertine floor."

Josh opened his MRE and began eating "We'll go exploring tomorrow once the wedding party is gone and the place is locked up. I don't want to be cooped up in here for three days."

***

An hour later, Josh drew his pistol at the sound of someone entering the bell tower.

Emilio awoke. He sat up quickly. "Did you hear that?"

Josh kept the Glock near his side. "It should be Solomon."

Likewise, Emilio retrieved his weapon. "Let's hope."

"Anybody home?" Solomon's voice called up the stairs.

Josh placed his pistol back inside his bag. "Just us."

Solomon entered the confined rounded space. He stared up at the bells far above. "Wow! This place is something."

"Yeah, complete with a sacrificial altar." Emilio pointed to the gruesome feature in the room.

Solomon took out his phone and typed on the screen. Soon, the sound of monks performing a Gregorian chant echoed up into the hollow stone tower, resonating throughout the chamber. He placed his phone on the granite altar.

"No, man! I was sleeping!" Emilio protested.

Solomon chuckled. "One song! Give me one song."

"How long is a song? Do they even have a beginning and an end?" Emilio continued.

"Five minutes," Solomon countered.

"Starting now." Emilio took out his burner to monitor the time.

Solomon abided by his promise and turned off the music after the stated period. He provided a quick synopsis of his travels around Indianapolis, describing the dire state of poverty most of the people seemed to be living in. He also told of the uneasiness he felt wandering the streets on his way home. Afterward, the team made themselves as comfortable as possible and went to sleep.

***

Early Monday morning, sunlight poured in through the stained glass windows above. Josh stretched out. His neck, back, and joints ached from sleeping on the hard floor. It reminded him of his cell when he was in DGS custody, however, he'd had to endure no blaring music or blinding lights. He stood slowly and continued to limber up.

Emilio looked up to see him making circles with his arms. "Feeling stiff?"

"Yeah." Josh performed a series of toe touches, then grabbed his pistol to tuck in the back of his pants. "I'm going to find a bathroom."

"Hang on, I'll join you." Emilio hoisted himself up from the hard floor.

"I think I can manage by myself. Nothing personal, but I've never been a fan of company in the restroom." Josh went down the stairs and found the men's facilities. He washed his hands and face, taking a few drinks from the faucet before drying with one of the white cloth towels provided for guests.

After leaving the restroom he meandered quietly through the halls, looking around to pass the time. He admired the grand architecture as he walked for the next twenty minutes. He picked up a pamphlet about the building as he strolled through the entrance area, which according to the brochure, was called the Tiler's Room.

"Hey, there you are." Solomon walked over to Josh.

Emilio was right behind him. "What are you looking at?"

"It says the floor in this room is a reproduction of the inner sanctum of King Solomon's Temple." Josh handed the paper to Emilio.

Solomon inspected a brass medallion set in the floor at the center of the room. "Do you think the original Holy of Holies had an engraving of the signs from the zodiac and a two-headed eagle?"

Josh studied the medallion. "It wasn't part of the original plans." He smirked. "But maybe they added it after. Ezekiel had a vision of all kinds of abominations carved into the wall of the Temple. Perhaps that's part of the reason why God turned the Israelites over to be sacked by the Babylonians.

"And, Daniel specifically says that the anti-Christ will set up an abomination in the Temple. I think that will mark the official kick-off party for the Great Tribulation. I'm really hoping to be out of here by then."

"Where are you going?" Emilio asked.

"Raptured, I hope. You better get your act together soon. Otherwise, you're going to get a front-row seat to the biggest fireworks show in history."

Emilio furrowed his brow. He seemed anxious to change the subject and pointed at one of the emblems within the design on the floor. "That's the cross Rev told us about, the one with the roses. Remember? It's when he was explaining the Georgia Guidestones."

"The Rosicrucians." Josh examined the engraving. "I'm starting to understand why Alexander wanted to have his little shindig here."

"Am I missing something?" asked Solomon.

Josh explained the principles written on the Georgia Guidestones and how they meshed so seamlessly with Lucius Alexander's new world order.

"That's pretty wild," Solomon said.

Josh motioned for the other two to follow him. "Come on. Let's try to find more suitable accommodations for tonight."

The group continued the expedition through the eerie halls of the cathedral. Josh came to a pair of double doors. "What's in here?" He pushed them open and gazed at the extravagantly finished room.

"A lounge! Now this is what I'm talking about." Emilio walked across the room and plopped down on one of the oversized sofas. "Have Jeeves bring my bag around, would you?"

"What do you think?" Solomon asked.

Josh nodded. "It could work. One of us will have to keep watch in case Alexander's security team shows up earlier than anticipated. You believe they'll show up Wednesday morning to lock down the area for Thursday, right?"

"That's what I would do. Anything earlier is a waste of resources," Solomon replied.

"Okay then, I recommend we sleep here tonight. Then we can catch a little nap tomorrow night and be out by 4:00 AM Wednesday."

"4:00 AM?" Emilio protested. "Can we at least take some cushions from the couch? Going back to that hard stone floor is going to be like moving from first-class to coach."

"Sorry, big guy," said Josh. "It's just like camping, leave no trace."

The three men retrieved their bags and settled into the more agreeable living quarters.

Josh set up the couch where he'd be sleeping, then opened the World News Network app on his phone to listen while arranging his space to make it more livable for the next day or so.

The reporter said, "After the withdraw of Saudi Arabia, Venezuela, and Ecuador from OPEC, the global oil cartel has completely disintegrated. However, many former members are banding together with China and Russia to form a new alliance, which is being called the Eastern Trade Organization. Unlike OPEC, the ETO will provide for mutual defense and free trade among member nations. Secretary-General Alexander called the ETO a pathetic attempt to recreate the successes of the Global Union. He went on to say the organization is doomed to failure and the best thing the leaders of member countries could do for their people is to join the GU.

"Talks between Secretary-General Alexander and former UN ambassadors representing several African nations, Indonesian nations, and India have stalled. The Secretary-General has pleaded with those nations to become signatories to the GU Charter, however, most have expressed a desire to remain neutral. The GU press secretary issued a statement on the talks saying that the Secretary-General hopes to re-engage those nations in the near future, but for the time being, the GU would be closing its airspace as well as Global-Union-controlled oceans for use by non-signatory countries.

"Since most of the continents of the world are now part of the Global Union, Secretary-General Alexander has declared the Arabian Sea, North and South Pacific, North and South Atlantic, and Indian Oceans to be sovereign territory.

"Pundits expect the declaration to be unpopular with the Eastern Trade Organization as they will be restricted to waters directly connected to their respective countries for shipping and fishing."

Solomon began laughing. "Unpopular! Now that's the understatement of the year."

"Countries will go to war over a single shipping channel." Emilio hung his suit on the back of a chair and smoothed out the wrinkles. "I can't imagine this will end well."

Josh kicked off his boots and reclined on the sofa. "Yep. Alexander is overplaying his hand."

The report continued. "In other news, Dr. Subhash Ahuja from the World Health Organization spoke earlier today about the latest outbreak in Australia, which has already killed twenty thousand people. He warned that previous vaccines for existing strains of the Red Virus are not effective against this latest mutation. He told reporters in this morning's press conference that under the microscope, the new strain looks entirely different from the original pathogen stating that this version has taken on a pale green coloration. Researchers at the WHO are already fast-tracking a new vaccine, hoping to have it in production by the end of the month.

"The new strain has already traveled around the globe with community spread cases in North and South America, Africa, and Europe."

"Behold a pale horse," said Josh.

Solomon spread out his blanket on the sofa he'd chosen. "I have to admit, it fits the timeline."

Emilio arranged his MREs on an end table that he was using for a nightstand. "So this is the fourth one, right? According to your Bible, that's the end of it. There are only four horsemen of the apocalypse."

Josh shook his head. "Not even close."

Solomon ticked off the remaining judgments. "We've still got two more seals, then seven trumpets, then the seven vials of God's wrath."

"Yep," said Josh. "You better get with the program. You don't want to be around for those."

Much of the day was spent listening to the radio about the latest developments with the virus and the new Eastern Trade Organization. They also filled their time by roaming the halls and playing cards. Josh spent several hours reading through the small New Testament, which he'd inherited from Rev.

CHAPTER 6

And then shall that Wicked be revealed, whom the Lord shall consume with the spirit of his mouth, and shall destroy with the brightness of his coming: even him, whose coming is after the working of Satan with all power and signs and lying wonders, and with all deceivableness of unrighteousness in them that perish; because they received not the love of the truth, that they might be saved. And for this cause God shall send them strong delusion, that they should believe a lie: that they all might be damned who believed not the truth, but had pleasure in unrighteousness.

2 Thessalonians 2:8-12

Thursday evening, Josh stood on top of the granite altar so he could hoist himself up onto the stone ledge of the bell tower and peer through the wavy leaded panes of glass.

"What do you see?" asked Emilio.

"They're setting up cameras. We should be able to watch the ceremony on our phones once it starts."

"That's not scheduled to start until 8:00 tonight. Then the fireworks, then the party. We've still got a lot of waiting around to do," said Solomon.

"I don't mind the danger of the actual mission," said Emilio. "In fact, I kind of miss the adrenaline rush. It's been over two years since I kicked in a door or saw any action. But it's being stuck in the bullpen that kills me."

"Normally, I'd agree with you." Josh lowered himself down from the ledge. "But I have to admit. I'm not looking forward to this one."

"Don't overthink it." Solomon sat on the floor with his back against the wall. "We'll walk in the party, get a drink and stroll around until we spot Lucius. Then we take our shot. Once he's down, it's all about making noise and creating panic. We should have plenty of ammo left to do that."

"Easy peasy." Josh frowned. "Then we still have to fight through the security teams on the outside of the building and hope we can get across the park to the getaway van."

"You just have to trust the plan," said Solomon.

Josh peered through the opaque section of orange-tinted glass. "I wish I could."

The seconds crawled by at a glacial pace. Finally, Lucius Alexander's address to the globe began. The group could hear the large PA speakers from outside. The feed on their phones had an annoying five-second delay, so they simply listened to the speech coming from the stairs below.

The Secretary of Religion, Carl Jacobs, was present at the ceremony and introduced the Global Union Secretary-General. "Global citizens, it is my honor to speak to you tonight. Three years ago, our planet entered into the most challenging period in all of recorded history. But with the leadership of our most exalted Secretary-General Lucius Alexander, we've navigated the storms. We've endured a complete failure of the economic system, a massive terrorist attack, which triggered a global pandemic, and all the peripheral catastrophes which sprung up in the midst of the mayhem. Yet, we now stand in a city which is today far more resilient, safe, and sustainable than it was, even before the upheaval of our world began.

"Secretary-General Alexander has taken what was broken and given us something whole. He has given us a crown of beauty for ashes and filled our lives with abundance and joy where once we had only want and despair. Please join me in giving a warm welcome to the benevolent leader of the world, Secretary-General Lucius Alexander!"

The crowd, which filled the street and adjacent park beyond the Scottish Rite Cathedral, clamored in praise and adoration.

"Thank you, thank you," said Alexander. "You're too kind." The applause and cheers continued for several minutes. "Thank you very much, please," he said.

Finally, the praise subsided and Lucius Alexander said, "Secretary Jacobs, thank you for that wonderful introduction. But I can't take all of the credit. This has been a team effort and wouldn't have been possible without the hard work and support of the entire globe.

"Today, Indianapolis will join a host of other metropolitan areas around the globe in becoming an OASIS city. As Carl stated before, the unprecedented challenges of our world can be daunting, but we've proven that through unity and the human spirit, there's nothing we cannot do or overcome.

"Our planet continues to see hardship through famine, violence, and even the recent outbreaks of what appears to be a new strain of the Red Virus. But know that we are working tirelessly to combat these complications. The latest outbreak has been in Sydney, which is an OASIS city. So we have the ability to quickly trace the movement of the infected and quarantine anyone they may have had contact with.

"Furthermore, we already have teams working on an updated version of the vaccine and have the infrastructure to make it widely available to OASIS citizens. If you are listening to this message today and you still have not made the move to an OASIS city, I implore you to take action now.

"It simply isn't feasible for the GU to provide economic assistance, nutritional subsidies, health care, education, and most importantly, vaccines to the massive geographical areas currently within Global Union borders.

"Additionally, it isn't consistent with our goals. By bringing everyone into an OASIS city, we can reduce carbon emissions to near zero. OASIS cities are powered almost entirely by sustainable and renewable energy which is made possible by the close proximity of citizens to work, recreation, goods, and services.

"So if you've been procrastinating, I encourage you to make the leap. Pack a bag and make the move now. We have plenty of temporary housing until we can get you integrated into a new life, a better life, for you and your family. You have nothing to lose and everything to gain."

"Kind of goes against the whole social distancing thing we're supposed to be doing to avoid the new outbreak, don't you think?" asked Emilio.

Josh replied, "This guy has mastered the art of talking out of both sides of his mouth."

"It's going to be nice to shut him up for good," said Solomon.

"I wouldn't count on that," Josh added. The group resumed listening to the speech being given below.

Alexander continued his address. "We've tried to make the transition very comfortable. One of the things that we are asking of new OASIS citizens, is that they take a pledge to adhere to the new global guidelines set forth by the Ministry of Religion. The GU is all about freedom, but we must remember that your freedom ends where the next citizen's freedom begins. Therefore, we cannot accommodate hate and intolerance. The Ministry of Religion has been very diligent in providing new translations for major religious texts. Obviously, some texts have the propensity to be more offensive and dangerous than others. Even the writings from Buddhism and Hinduism can profit from a re-examination of how they are read in the light of our ever-evolving vernacular.

"But more than those, the state-of-the-art interfaith re-translations of the Koran, Bible, and Jewish texts have benefited immensely from the tireless efforts of Carl Jacobs and his team at the Ministry of Religion. Careful attention has been given to the true meanings of the original texts and the result has been scriptures that bring us together rather than push us apart.

"Carl has made a special effort to put together a compilation text, which takes some of the most spiritual teachings from all the major religions of the world. We're calling it the Unity Scriptures. The Ministry of Religion is making copies of the Unity Scriptures available to anyone who wants one. I encourage everyone to take advantage of this offer. We need encouragement in times like these.

"Speaking to the issue of famine, we feel that our efforts to bring citizens together into sustainable cities is already beginning to have an effect on climate change. This is despite the fact that China,

Russia, and many countries in the Middle East have yet to come into the fold of our global community. The damage we've done to our planet didn't happen overnight, and we can't expect to heal it in one day. However, we will persevere and continue the work we've begun, both for ourselves and for the generations to come.

"In the meantime, the Global Union continues to partner with Monsanto in developing crops which can thrive in the harsh environment which we created for ourselves during our planet's period of ecological ignorance. Scarcity will soon be a thing of the past here in Indianapolis as it has become in so many other cities in the Global Union."

"Violence has ceased to be a problem in OASIS cities, thanks to a total weapon ban throughout the Global Union. We still have issues in the hinterlands, but those can be avoided by making the change and moving your family to an OASIS city today.

"I think you've heard enough chattering from me for one day. We have a magnificent firework display and celebration planned for you this evening, not only for Indianapolis but for the entirety of the Global Union. Today marks our first annual Global Unity Day. I do hope you remember how far we've come together not only today but throughout the year. Thank you and goodnight."

Once more, the crowd applauded and cheered their beloved supreme leader.

"Okay, guys. Get your suits on." Solomon began changing into his dress clothes.

Josh slipped a compression brace over his bad knee before putting on his dress pants. "What about our bags?"

"We have to leave them behind," said Solomon.

"They'll pull our DNA and figure out who we are," Josh buttoned up his white shirt.

Solomon put on his jacket. "You're already a wanted man."

"Yeah, but they don't have my face on a deck of playing cards yet," said Josh.

"In for a penny, in for a pound." Emilio stashed two 33-round magazines inside his jacket.

Solomon smiled, "Look on the bright side, if they do put you in a deck, at least you're guaranteed to be a face card."

"Or an ace!" Emilio added.

"That's reassuring. No self-respecting terrorist wants to be relegated to a number card." Josh set the select fire on his pistol, setting it to full auto.

Emilio stuck his pistol inside his in-the-waistband holster. "One man's terrorist…"

Solomon finished the phrase for him, "Is another man's freedom fighter." He buttoned his jacket and looked at his phone. "The extraction team is in position. Sounds like they're having quite a party in the park across the street. It should make it easier for us to blend in with the crowd."

"If we can get out of the building," said Josh.

"Let's go grab a glass of champagne and mingle." Solomon led the way down the stairs.

CHAPTER 7

And I stood upon the sand of the sea, and saw a beast rise up out of the sea, having seven heads and ten horns, and upon his horns ten crowns, and upon his heads the name of blasphemy. And the beast which I saw was like unto a leopard, and his feet were as the feet of a bear, and his mouth as the mouth of a lion: and the dragon gave him his power, and his seat, and great authority. And I saw one of his heads as it were wounded to death; and his deadly wound was healed: and all the world wondered after the beast.

Revelation 13:1-3

Walking through the ballroom, Josh focused on his breathing, hoping not to look nervous as he passed four GU peacekeepers.

Once beyond the guards, Emilio said, “I think we’re good.”

“Why wouldn’t we be?” asked Solomon.

“You’re just as nervous as us,” said Josh.

“Dwelling on it isn’t going to help,” Solomon replied.

“I’m going to get a scotch— to blend in,” said Emilio.

Josh followed him toward the bar. “Stay on your game.”

“It’s going to take more than one drink to cause me a problem.” Emilio stepped up to the bartender. “Johnny Black, rocks, please.”

“Yes, sir,” said the man behind the bar. “What can I get for you gentlemen?”

“Club soda with lime,” Josh replied.

“I’ll have a glass of Champagne,” said Solomon.

The bartender quickly served them their drinks.

Josh watched as a woman next to them at the bar shook white powder from a small vile onto the back of her hand and snorted it. She then passed the vile to her friend who did the same. The second woman noticed Josh looking. She smiled. “Want some?”

“No thanks.” He returned the smile.

“Let’s walk,” said Solomon.

Josh smelled marijuana smoke and turned to see three men passing a joint. One of them coughed violently as he handed the smoldering narcotic to his acquaintance. “The Bible is banned, but drugs are totally legal."

"Hookers also, evidently." Emilio pointed to a woman who was dressed much more provocatively than most of the other attendees. She was approaching a much older gentleman who appeared to have no female companionship.

"There's our boy." Solomon nodded toward the entrance of the grand ballroom.

Dressed in radiant white, with snow-colored hair, and his spectral pale-blue eyes, Lucius Alexander walked through a sea of adoring worshipers. He allowed them to touch or kiss his hand as he passed by. Two bodyguards walked in front on each side of Alexander, and two more trailed close behind. All four wore white suits with white ties so not to clash with the attire of their master.

Josh looked around the room, spotting at least a dozen more white-clad security personnel. "I've counted no less than twenty GU peacekeepers in addition to Alexander's Praetorian Guard."

Solomon sipped his Champagne. "One of us needs to take a shot from down here. The other two can split up and get into position in the balcony. The downstairs shooter will create the distraction, giving the other two an opportunity."

"What about the man on the ballroom floor?" asked Josh. "Is he supposed to be a sacrificial lamb?"

"It doesn't have to go that way. Once the target is down, just start spraying. That will give me a chance to get clear."

"So, you're volunteering to be the guy on the ground?" Emilio asked.

"Unless you want to do the honors," Solomon replied.

"I appreciate the offer, but if you're good with it, I'm happy to let you," Emilio replied.

"Okay then." Solomon looked at his watch. "Three minutes. Get into position and be ready."

Josh and Emilio each checked their watches.

Solomon said, "Starting…now!"

Josh watched the second hand tick past the nine, then headed for the stairs. He walked slowly trying not to draw attention. He finished the remainder of his club soda on the way up the stairs, handing the empty glass to a waiter with a tray filled with other such items. "Thank you," said Josh.

"My pleasure," replied the waiter.

Josh watched Emilio heading toward the right, so he went left. He walked casually along the railing, as if people watching from above.

"Waiting for someone?" asked one of the scantily clad women walking by.

"What?" Josh was caught off guard and did not want to be distracted. "No, I mean, yes. My wife." He pointed toward the restrooms.

The young woman giggled. "Okay, then. Let me know if you change your mind."

Josh quickly turned his attention to the floor below. He watched as Solomon began walking toward the Secretary-General. Josh unbuttoned his jacket and leaned on the thick wooden railing. He checked his watch. *Twenty seconds*.

Solomon drew his pistol and shot the guard between him and Alexander, hitting him in the head. The other three guards sprang into action. One grabbed the Secretary-General while the other two drew their weapons.

Josh pulled his gun and took aim at the melee below. He pulled the trigger and a barrage of bullets streamed in rapid-fire toward the group below. The spent brass popped into the air and rained down all around him like a hail storm. From the other side of the balcony, Emilio's pistol unleashed a similar fusillade of shells.

Between the two of them, they managed to kill the remaining three guards and wound Lucius Alexander. Solomon seized upon the mayhem and ran toward Alexander, shooting him three times, once in the head.

Josh's pistol was empty. He ejected the 19-round magazine and quickly replaced it with a 33-round mag. He looked left and right. Teams of GU Peacekeepers were charging at him from both directions. Josh ran toward the group coming at him from the left. He lifted his pistol and squeezed the trigger, spraying the group of soldiers until the magazine was empty and the top slide of the pistol locked open. He jumped over the bodies of the fallen peacekeepers and quickly changed magazines. He pressed the slide release, racking a fresh round into the chamber, and kept running.

Josh sprinted toward the bathroom. It was the first available option to provide cover. Once inside, he ran to the stall furthest from the entrance and locked the door. Immediately, he climbed on top of the toilet and hunched down, waiting for the next team of peacekeepers pursuing him.

The first one entered and shouted. "Come out

with your hands up."

Josh waited until the entire four-man fire team was inside the restroom. He took a long, slow breath and held it in for several seconds before letting it out at an even pace. He listened.

"Check every stall," called one of the peacekeepers.

Josh heard the sound of each door being kicked open. Anticipating that they would be focused on the next successive stall door and that all four would be in close proximity to one another, Josh stood up on the toilet seat, stuck his pistol over the wall, and began spraying bullets. The four peacekeepers fell to the floor before they had a chance to even see where the attack was coming from.

Josh stepped down from the toilet, opened the door, and tucked the pistol back in his holster. He bent over and pressed the quick release tab on the rifle sling of the first peacekeeper he came to. He removed several magazines from the man's tactical vest and tucked them into his back pockets and the waistband of his pants. He also took a radio from the fallen soldier.

Josh checked the M-4 rifle to make sure it was charged and that the safety was off. He also set the *selector* to automatic. He moved toward the door.

"Bravo, what's your situation?" asked a voice over the radio.

Another voice replied, "I saw Bravo chase one of the shooters into the bathroom on the second floor."

"Take your team and go check it out," said the first voice.

"Roger," replied the second.

Josh pulled the door open just enough to get his foot in the jamb. He pressed the butt of the rifle into his shoulder and got ready to fire. He kicked the door open, raised the barrel of the gun, and took aim at the four peacekeepers headed up the stairs. He fired and killed them all before they had a chance to react. Josh raced toward the stairs and descended them as hurriedly as possible without stumbling. Once on the main floor, he scanned the area for more troops and also his teammates.

Solomon was pinned into a corner by three guards dressed in white. Josh raised his rifle and shot, ending the standoff. The guests were screaming, some running, and others hiding under tables.

He rushed to Solomon's side. "Where's Emilio?"

Solomon was panting for breath. "I don't know. The last I saw him he was running down the stairs."

Josh looked around the room. "I don't see him, but you need a weapons upgrade. Let's get you a rifle."

Solomon nodded and followed Josh toward the stairs. One of the peacekeepers whom Josh had killed lay on his back with his head on the floor and his feet on the sixth stair. A puddle of blood was growing on the white oak floor. Solomon removed the soldier's rifle while Josh collected magazines from the man's vest.

"I've got one sealed off in the theatre," said a voice over the radio. "He's already killed two from my team. I need back up."

"I guess we know where Emilio is," said

Solomon.

"Yeah, let's go!" Josh dashed toward the hallway but stopped short when he exited the ballroom. He ducked back inside the double doors.

"Is it bad?" asked Solomon.

"Twenty or so," Josh replied.

"I'll empty a magazine through one door. That should have them ducking for cover. You kick open the other and mop up." Solomon raised his rifle.

"Got it." Josh put his foot on the door and prepared for the action.

Solomon began shooting. Josh waited for the first ten rounds before pushing the second door open with his foot. Indeed, the peacekeepers were scrambling and Josh took full advantage of the situation. He walked through the door and picked off every guard he came across.

Solomon changed magazines and jogged ahead. "Come on, this way!"

The two soon arrived at the doors to the theater within the cathedral. Josh located the two peacekeepers standing by the doors. They were focused on Emilio who was inside. Josh nodded to Solomon and both took one of the targets. They fired, killing the guards, then rushed into the theatre.

"Big guy, you in here? We gotta go!" Josh yelled.

Emilio's head stuck up from between the seats. "On my way."

The team sprinted toward the front door where they knew they'd have hundreds of peacekeepers to fight through.

"This place is surrounded by now." Emilio slowed his pace as they reached the exit.

Solomon looked around. "Quick, strip off the clothes from these peacekeepers."

"They're all covered in blood! The guards outside won't buy that for a minute." Emilio shook his head.

Josh suggested an alternate plan. "Let's strip off Alexander's personal guards' clothes."

"That's an even worse idea," said Emilio. "The blood shows up more on the white suits than the gray peacekeeper uniforms."

Josh hurried back to the dead bodyguards and began removing the jacket of one of them. "That's not a problem if we're moving a casualty."

Solomon quickly found a guard about the same size as himself. "That could work."

Emilio located the largest of the guards and began taking off his jacket. "So we're going to grab a random corpse and waltz right out the front door?"

Josh looked at Alexander's dead body. "Not just any corpse."

Emilio continued exchanging clothes with the deceased guard. "I hope you're wrong about this guy coming back to life."

"And if you are right," said Solomon as he pulled on a pair of blood-stained white trousers, "I hope he doesn't wake up while we're packing him."

Josh didn't bother with the tie. He forced his feet into the man's white shoes which were about two sizes too small. He changed over to a 19-round magazine for his pistol then tucked the Glock into his waistband. “We need to hurry. They’ll be storming the door any minute.”

Emilio still didn’t have his shirt tucked or his jacket buttoned. “Two seconds.”

“Don’t bother with the details.” Solomon bent down to lift Alexander by the shoulders. “Grab his feet.”

Emilio followed Solomon’s instructions and Josh pressed the talk key on the radio. “We’ve secured the Secretary-General. He’s bleeding badly. Bring an ambulance to the front stairs.” Josh tossed the radio to the side and pushed the doors open to reveal row after row of heavily armed peacekeepers all with their rifles trained on Josh and his team.

“Come on guys. Act like you care about him.”

The peacekeepers and the remaining onlookers gasped at seeing their leader in his vulnerable state. Josh commanded the peacekeepers as he walked through. “Move back! Out of the way!” He escorted Solomon and Emilio to the nearest ambulance. Peacekeepers charged past them up the stairs into the cathedral.

Josh addressed the EMTs in the ambulance. “He’s bleeding badly, and I can’t get a pulse.”

The EMT looked at the gaping hole in Alexander’s head, then looked up at Josh as if he’d lost his mind. “The Secretary-General is dead!”

“We can’t announce that,” said Josh. “It will create a panic.”

The EMT nodded. “Yes, sir. I understand. We’ll proceed as if we’re trying to save him.”

Solomon tugged Josh’s shoulder and whispered in his ear. “The time for theatrics is over. We gotta go."

"Yeah, right." Josh quickly walked behind Solomon and Emilio toward the park across the street.

"Faster!" Emilio moved as quickly as possible without breaking into a sprint.

Josh looked over his shoulder to see another member of Alexander's elite personal guard dressed in white and approaching the ambulance. Several other white-clad guards trailed behind him. "Run!"

The three men took off, dodging people to get through the crowd.

"Stop! Right there!" yelled a voice.

Josh felt sure it was the guard but didn't turn to look. Rifle fire rang out behind them.

"Go, go, go!" shouted Josh.

"Where's our ride?" asked Emilio.

Solomon kept running. "Straight ahead. Down this alley."

They ran across Pennsylvania Street and between a pair of brick buildings. The door of a black van slid open and Dana stuck an AK-47 out the side of the vehicle. "Get down!"

Josh tucked low but kept running straight at the rifle pointed in his direction. Dana began peppering bullets overtop of Josh's head. Emilio, Solomon, and Josh all continued on their path toward the extraction team.

Micah and Lindsey exited an old Volvo wagon parked behind the van. They also had AK-47s and fired at Alexander's personal guards as they moved toward the van. Josh, Solomon, and Emilio tumbled into the van with rifle fire zooming past their heads in both directions. Lindsey and Micah also jumped in the van and Dana slammed the door. She slapped the driver's seat where Nicole was sitting. "Get us out of here!"

The tires squealed and Josh looked out the window at the guards who were still in pursuit. "We're leaving the Volvo?"

"Not exactly," said Micah.

Josh looked at the blue wagon out of the back window as the guards arrived to inspect it. "What do you mean?"

Micah held up a black detonator and pressed the cherry-red button. The Volvo exploded into a ball of fire, eliminating the only eyewitnesses who could describe the van.

"Oh. That's what you mean." Josh slumped down against the wall of the van.

Dana passed him an AK-47. "We're not home yet. Don't get too comfy."

Josh nodded and accepted the rifle.

"Blow the lights!" Dana instructed Nicole. "It's a straight shot up Delaware about a half-mile to the interstate. Once we're on I-65, we'll be in a much better position."

Nicole raced the van through traffic and soon pulled onto the interstate on-ramp. "Did you get him?"

Josh looked at the blood all over Emilio's, and Solomon's suits, knowing that at least some of it was Lucius Alexander's. "Yeah, we got him."

CHAPTER 8

For evildoers shall be cut off: but those that wait upon the Lord, they shall inherit the earth. For yet a little while, and the wicked shall not be: yea, thou shalt diligently consider his place, and it shall not be. But the meek shall inherit the earth; and shall delight themselves in the abundance of peace.

Psalm 37:9-11

Josh peered out the van window at the passing signs. "We're off the interstate. That's a good sign."

"I never thought I'd say it, but I'll breathe a little easier once I see corn fields," said Micah.

Josh looked at Solomon. "So, can you fill me in on the bigger picture now?"

He looked down at his burner phone. "Part of it. Junk and Pigpen were successful."

"I'm guessing those aren't the names given to them by their mothers," said Emilio.

Dana laughed. "Good guess. Junk hasn't thrown away an egg carton, an empty yogurt cup, or a dried-up marker since the mid-nineties."

"And Pigpen?" Lindsey asked.

Solomon smiled. "Let's just say his personal hygiene leaves something to be desired."

"I bet they make quite a team," said Josh.

"They seem to enjoy one another's company," Dana replied.

"What was their mission?" Josh asked.

Solomon answered, "They hit a warehouse on the north side of Indianapolis about five minutes after we initiated the assault on Alexander. They're on the road with a semi-truck loaded with provisions. Dry goods that will store well. We were scraping the bottom of the bucket for food—other than corn, that is."

Josh gritted his teeth. "Tell me we didn't just whack the antichrist as a diversion so Trash and Pigpen could boost a truckload of beanie-weenies, dried rice, and canned ravioli."

Solomon said, "No—and it's Junk, not Trash. But we needed the supplies, and this was as good of a time as any. All choppers, patrol cars, and peacekeepers are looking for us. They couldn't care less about that semi. Any other time, a tractor-trailer would be an easy item for law enforcement to locate."

"Okay, so what was the big hit?" Josh asked.

Solomon looked at his watch, then glanced at Dana. "I'll tell you once we're back to the compound."

Josh felt sure he was being led on about the ulterior motive of the mission to kill Alexander. "Nicole, turn on the radio. Let's hear what WNN is saying about the hit."

The radio came on to the voice of a female reporter. "Details are just starting to come in about the terrorist attack in Indianapolis tonight. Secretary-General Alexander was attending a celebratory gathering this evening after his speech to officially designate Indianapolis an OASIS city. Armed gunmen managed to get past security and began killing people indiscriminately at the event.

"Unfortunately, the Secretary-General was among the victims of this horrendous attack. Lucius Alexander was pronounced dead upon arrival at IU Health University Hospital. His body is being taken to a Global Union Air Force facility in Nevada where he will lie in state. A live feed camera will be set up for mourners to view their beloved leader virtually."

"What's in Nevada?" asked Lindsey.

"Isn't that where Area 51 is located?" Micah looked at his father.

"No, no, you're thinking of Roswell, New Mexico," said Lindsey.

Solomon corrected, "Roswell was the supposed UFO crash site. Micah is right. Area 51 is at an Air Force base in Nevada."

"Still, it makes no sense. The GU is headquartered in San Francisco, at the new Globalplex. Why wouldn't they take him back there?"

"Who knows?" said Josh.

The reporter continued her coverage. "The Global Union Charter prescribes that succession of power will be shared among the remaining members of the governing council. While he will not have voting privileges, the governing council has chosen Ministry of Religion Secretary Carl Jacobs to act as the public spokesperson of the GU for the immediate future. An official memo from the council said that the world needs help through this difficult time and that Secretary Jacobs' healing words and familiar face would be like medicine to the souls of the distressed and hurting."

The signal suddenly went out and the radio broadcasted only static.

Nicole fiddled with the tuner. "I can't seem to get anything. Do one of you want to come up front and see if you can figure out what's going on with the radio?"

Lindsey stepped over the console and took the passenger's seat. "I'll fix it."

"Don't bother," said Solomon.

"You're probably right." Lindsey tried powering the radio off and on, then hitting the scan button. "We're lucky this old junker got us out of Indianapolis, it would really be asking too much to expect the radio to work."

"It's not the van," said Solomon.

Josh lowered his brows. "Then what is it?"

"When Alexander was shot, Omniscience went into its highest-level security protocol. It's called Echelon Six. The system executed a hard reboot and logged out all current users. Every credentialed operator will have to log back in with a four-step verification process, including a password reset, text verification, security question, and finally, a biometric authentication."

"I'm guessing this isn't just some random piece of information you happen to know." Josh's eyes narrowed.

Solomon was slow to respond. "It was our desired outcome."

"Now you're just torturing us," said Emilio. "Come on, let us in on the plan."

Solomon glanced at Dana before continuing. "We have a guy at SpaceX."

"What does that have to do with Omniscience?" asked Micah.

Lindsey interrupted before Solomon could reply. "And question number two, what does it have to do with the radio not working?"

Solomon waited as if to see if anyone else was going to bombard him with more inquiries. "SpaceX has the logistics contract for Omniscience, and subsequently, the GU. In addition to satellite delivery, they also take care of maintenance programs and software updates."

"And?" Josh asked.

Solomon continued. "The entire arsenal of Omniscience's satellites just got an upgrade. That's all 14 communication satellites and 66 surveillance satellites."

Micah nodded. "By upgrade you mean…"

"Downgrade," answered Dana.

Lindsey sat turned around in her seat to face the back of the van. "So like a piece of malware or something?"

Dana replied, "Stuxnet source code is available to download online. Anyone fluent in C, C++, and common object-oriented computer languages can use Stuxnet as a template and design their own physically-destructive malware."

"Wait," said Micah. "Did you write the code, Dana?"

She chuckled. "No. We found someone on the darknet and paid them to write it."

"But how did you get it uploaded? Do you know an operator with the necessary level of clearance?" Josh asked.

Solomon shook his head. "Nope. If we had, there'd have been no reason to kill Alexander—other than our general distaste for the man, that is."

Dana finished explaining. "Our guy at SpaceX inserted a jump drive into the mainframe during the thirty-second reboot. Plugging it in while the system was online would have set off all kinds of alarms."

Solomon added, “But when the reboot hit, the system simply recognized the malware on the flash drive as part of the Echelon Six security protocol.”

“So, now the Global Union is driving blind,” said Nicole.

“That’s a good way to put it,” said Solomon. “They’ll have a backup system up and running in a few days, but this hurts them. It allows other Christian and patriot groups to take advantage of the informational blackout. And it sends a message that the GU is not immortal.”

“Until Alexander rises from the dead,” said Josh.

“Even if that happens, people know that they have a fighting chance,” said Solomon.

“And I suspect that you have other plans while they’re in the dark, don’t you?” Lindsey asked.

Solomon smiled. “Let’s get home and celebrate this win first. Then we can talk about what comes next.”

“Speaking of celebrating.” Nicole glanced up toward the rearview to look at Josh. “Emilio and I would like you to officiate our wedding.”

“Me?” asked Josh.

“Yeah, bro,” said Emilio. “You. We want to have a little ceremony. Nothing fancy. But something to make it official. And we should probably get it knocked out before Solomon drags us into another death trap. Maybe like tomorrow morning.”

“Knocked out?” Nicole’s scowling eyes could be seen in the rearview mirror.

“You know what I mean,” said Emilio. He turned back to Josh. “So?”

Josh sighed. "You guys know how I feel about this."

"No, Josh. Evidently we don't," Nicole argued. "The last I heard, we had your blessing."

Josh hated having a close personal conversation like this in front of everyone. "I said I would be happy for you. I told Emilio I'd be glad to have him as a brother-in-law. I never gave you my blessing. You're going against God's plan. Maybe to a lesser degree than continuing to fornicate, but still, it's not God's best. God's not going to bless it, and my blessing wouldn't mean anything, anyway. I'm not trying to talk you out of it, and I'm not standing in the way, but I'm sorry—I can't be the one officiating the ceremony. I'd be compromising my values."

Dana was the first to break the awkward silence. "Craig will probably do it. He's not really a preacher, but he leads our Bible studies back at camp."

"That's fine," said Nicole in a gruff tone. "As long as we're not offending his higher-than-thou moral standards."

"I doubt it," said Dana. "He's pretty easy-going."

Josh loved his sister and his friend. He felt terrible for offending them, but he didn't have the authority or the audacity to contradict God's Word. The rest of the ride back was quiet.

***

Josh awoke early Friday morning, still feeling wiped out from the prior day's mission. He exited the travel trailer, being careful not to wake Micah and Lindsey. Once outside, he stretched and watched the sun rising over the endless sea of corn. He remained in the immediate area behind the last barn for nearly an hour, drinking in the silence and the relative coolness of the July morning. He sat on an old crate and read his Bible, happy to be out of the confines of the Scottish Rite Cathedral. He caught a whiff of coffee, something he'd not had in over a year. His senses tingled, and after finishing his reading for the day, he set off in search of the tantalizing aroma.

The fragrant scent led him toward the first large metal barn, which was being used as a barracks.

"Hey, partner. Good work yesterday," said George, the man who'd been standing guard upon Josh's arrival.

"Thanks," said Josh. "I thought I smelled coffee. I wonder if that was just my nose playing tricks on me."

"Nope." George opened the door to the barracks. "Got a big pot brewing inside. We found a whole pallet of it on the truck we snatched last night."

"You were on the team with Junk and Pigpen?"

"Yeah, you know those two rascals?"

"No, but Solomon mentioned that they were heading up that mission."

George waved for Josh to follow. "Come on in. I'll introduce you before I head off to work. I've got guard duty at the front gate in about five minutes. We'll get you a cup of that coffee, also. You, Solomon, and that other fellow that came with you are heroes around here."

"Thank you." Josh followed him inside. The barn was filled with rows of bunk beds, single beds, and cots. Most were partitioned off from one another with sheets hanging from wires strung from one side of the barn to the other. Several of the small living spaces utilized cardboard for the partitioning material. Many of them were open, as if available to visitors and others were closed off, as if their occupants might still be sleeping. Some were furnished as well as any bedroom while others were sparse with few belongings.

Most were neat and well-kept. However, Josh looked into one of the quarters. Dirty clothes and trash littered the floor. The quarters which resembled a pigsty had cardboard for the partition on one side while the other side was a row of shelves. The shelves were stuffed with every imaginable item; old magazines, newspapers, empty milk jugs, and used plastic containers, which had once held everything from sour cream and peanut butter, to car wax and drywall spackle. One of the shelves hosted an array of glass jars, all shapes and sizes. Some were filled with screws, nails, nuts, and bolts, while still others held rubber bands, paper clips, lengths of string, and pieces of wire.

Beyond the shelves was yet another living space crowded with odds and ends stuffed into cardboard boxes and plastic milk crates, stacked one on top of the other.

George interrupted Josh's gawking. "This is where they live, but I don't see them around. Probably down at the chow hall. It's at the other end of the building. Come on. I'll show you."

Josh followed, noticing the extension cord running along the back wall and supplying power for small electronic devices in the individual accommodations. "Are you guys getting power from the grid?"

"Generators," George replied.

"They run on E-85?" asked Josh.

"Yep. Junk and Pigpen are also our brewmasters. They run the still to keep the ethanol flowing. They're a talented pair, so folks kinda overlook their…eccentricities." George led him past the living quarters to a large open space where a dozen or so people were eating or preparing breakfast.

Next to a large industrial sink was a row of four household cooking stoves. They were all from different manufacturers with two being stainless and the other two white. Wire-frame stainless-steel shelving units flanked the remainder of the wall next to the stoves. Adjacent to the sink, stoves, and shelves were three long, fold-out tables lined up end to end, which served as a food prep and serving area.

"How many people are at the compound?" Josh looked at the dining area where six big circular tables were set up with chairs around each.

"Well, let's see, we've got about fifteen of us in here. Solomon, Dana, and a couple of other people live in the farmhouse. A few others living in the RVs, maybe ten. Then there's another farmhouse on the property. It's right down the road, sets back in the corn, so you can't see it too well from here. Craig and his family live down there." George seemed to make calculations in his head. "That's thirty-three and your group, five more, comes out to thirty-eight. Of course, Craig and his bunch eat down at that house. We don't see them up here much. This farm was his place before everything went to heck."

A group of four men came into the room through the large rollup door at the end. Two pushed dollies stacked with cardboard boxes, and the other two directed them toward the wire shelves. Josh noticed one of the men was short, just over five feet tall with sandy gray hair, and thick glasses, which were held together by a Band-Aid. The man beside him wore greasy denim jeans and a tee-shirt, which may have been white at some point. The cruddy shirt was slightly too short, allowing the man's hairy belly to pooch out from beneath.

"There's Junk and Pigpen. Come on." George led the way to the shelves.

The two men pushing the dollies began opening the boxes and stacking canned goods and dried foods on the shelves while the other two men assisted them.

"Boys," said George, "This is the new guy, Josh."

The four men stopped what they were doing. "Good to have you," said a tall lean man who'd been pushing a dolly. "I'm Tylor, and this is Clint." He pointed to the muscular fellow next to him.

The short one extended his hand. "Folks call me Junk."

Josh shook hands with the man. "Pleasure to meet you."

Using his thumb, he pointed to his soiled comrade. “And this here’s Pigpen.”

Josh held his breath as he shook hands with the man who seemed determined to live up to his moniker. He looked at the fresh supply of goods going on the shelves. “Is all this from the truck you guys took?”

“Yep,” said Junk. “It was going to GU peacekeepers after it left the warehouse. So, not only is it feeding us, it’s not feeding them.”

Josh smiled. “You guys are a regular band of Robin Hoods.”

Pigpen chuckled. “You like coffee?”

“I do.” Josh followed the grungy man.

“We’ve got pancake mix and dried blueberries, too, if you’re hungry,” Junk offered.

“Canned ham, also.” Tylor held up an oblong-shaped can.

“That would be great.” Josh took the warm beverage offered to him by Pigpen and smiled in anticipation of the luxurious breakfast.

Solomon and Dana walked into the room. “I see you’ve met some of our other members,” said Solomon.

“Yeah. George introduced me. Quite a hospitable bunch you’ve got here,” said Josh.

“We try,” Solomon replied.

Dana rifled through the boxes yet to be stocked onto the shelves. “Pop-Tarts? You guys got Pop-Tarts? I could kiss you!”

Junk laughed, “Ain’t nothin’ stopping you.”

She gave him a big smooch on the cheek then opened the case of Pop-Tarts.

"Hey! Where's my kiss?" Pigpen grinned revealing two uneven rows of yellow teeth, interrupted by the occasional void of a missing tooth.

Dana looked at him, then at her cherished box of processed breakfast pastries. She seemed to be considering the gesture. "I tell you what, come see me on bath day. We'll talk about it."

"I just had a bath!"

"That was Monday!" scolded Junk.

"Yeah," Pigpen countered. "Like I said, I just had one."

Everyone chipped in to prepare a nice breakfast. Then they all sat down to eat together.

Josh enjoyed everything, but the coffee made him feel most at home in his new surroundings. "Has WNN been able to resume broadcasting since the satellite outage?"

"Oh, yeah." Solomon drizzled a little more syrup on his pancakes. "They switched over to their terrestrial networking capabilities. But that's not why we hit them in the first place. Omniscience surveillance apparatus relies solely on satellite. They don't have a workaround for that. We need to be able to move freely over the coming days."

Dana sipped her coffee. "By the way, the news said that Patriot Pride claimed responsibility for all of our work."

"Ethan Combs. He's still operating." Josh finished chewing. "So, are you going to fill me in on the big plan?"

Solomon looked at Dana. "Think we can trust them?"

She laughed, then leaned over to kiss Solomon on the lips. "If you can't, you're already in big trouble."

Josh smiled. He'd not realized that Solomon and Dana were an item, although, he'd had his suspicions.

"We'll talk after breakfast," said Solomon.

CHAPTER 9

Their flesh shall consume away while they stand upon their feet, and their eyes shall consume away in their holes, and their tongue shall consume away in their mouth.

Zechariah 14:12b

Josh followed Solomon and Dana out of the dining area after breakfast. They walked toward the farmhouse where a weathered picnic table sat beneath two of the few large shade trees on the property.

Josh took a seat. "You said something about these attacks emboldening other resistance groups.

Is that what this was all about? Are you intending to capitalize on that somehow?"

Solomon sat at the table across from Josh. "That's pretty intuitive of you. When everything started, I was staying in pretty close contact with a bunch of guys I knew from the military. We had to cut communications when Omniscience launched their SIGINT surveillance program. It makes the NSA look like a blind substitute teacher. SIGINT scoops up everything. Digital and analog."

Josh folded his hands. "What about encryption?"

Solomon shook his head. "Omniscience is quantum AI. It reads through encryption like it's not even there."

"So have you already reached out to the people you know?" Josh asked.

"Yeah. I sent out an email blast this morning. We're organizing a meet and greet amongst the leadership. Dana and I will be traveling to Idaho for the pow wow."

"Idaho? Why not have everyone come here? Indiana is much more central if you're trying to recruit talent from around the country."

"Maybe so, but if a decentralized militia movement had a headquarters, it would be the panhandle of Idaho. Guys who carry a lot more weight than me are up there."

"Even after killing Alexander and taking down the GU satellites?"

Solomon smiled. "That move just bought me a seat at the table."

Josh lowered his brow. "A seat pretty close to the head, I hope. That wasn't just some schoolyard prank we pulled."

Solomon nodded. "They're ready to listen to what I've got in mind."

"The leadership won't doubt that it was you? If Ethan took credit for the attack, might they think you are lying?"

Solomon replied, "No. I gave them a heads up that we were working on a big firework show for the fourth. I'd also tipped them off about Combs right after you had your little run-in."

"How many people are you talking about?"

"A thousand or more. We know people, and they know more people, and they know even more people."

Josh lowered his brows. "No doubt some of them will be affiliated with Patriot Pride. And I'm sure Ethan Combs wasn't the only ATF agent who put together a fake group of constitutionalists, looking to entrap its members."

"Everyone we know has been as careful as possible through all of this. They'd have been swept up by the GU long ago if they weren't being cautious."

"Evidently Combs is still running his op. I'm just saying, there could be others."

"It's a chance we have to take," said Solomon. "This isn't something that can be accomplished with a couple of fire teams."

"Still, more people means more opportunities for a mole."

"I watched a lot of good soldiers die in Iraq. We were over there costing blood and treasure trying to secure a country most of us knew nothing about. What would that say about me if I was willing to kill or die for those people but then sat back and watched my own country go to heck in a handbasket?"

Josh raised his shoulders. "I understand your reasoning, but it sounds like you may be getting a little too far out over your skis."

"You haven't even heard what we're planning yet," Dana argued.

"No, but I can see the direction this is going."

Solomon continued. "We're going to hit the GU complex in San Francisco—kinetic attack against all of their supporting infrastructure, including the Omniscience supercomputer. This will set them back years. We're going to pull out the linchpin, which this entire utopic fantasy is built upon."

"Attack the Globalplex. Wow!" Josh opened his eyes wide. "You people *are* nuts."

"No we're not!" Dana didn't take the criticism well at all. "We're angry! So what if we get killed? I'd rather die on my feet than live on my knees."

Josh thought about Micah. Perhaps he'd feel the same way if it weren't for his son. After all, he had few other remaining attachments to this world. "You're justified in your views. I'm sorry, I didn't mean to sound so dismissive. However, I can't sign on."

Solomon looked disappointed. "I somewhat expected that you'd say that. We'll be leaving a skeleton crew behind to keep the compound secure. Can I at least count on you for that?"

Josh felt a twinge of guilt for not participating. But he saw the endeavor as a waste. "Absolutely. I'll hold down the fort."

Solomon's radio chirped.

"Top, where are you at?" asked the voice.

Solomon pressed the talk key. "In the yard, by the farmhouse, under the maples."

"Be right there. Don't move!"

Dana looked worried. "That's Tim. Wonder what could have him in such a tizzy?"

"We'll soon find out." Solomon turned to Josh. "Tim is our comms guy. He has a Ham radio set up in the farmhouse."

Tim, a man in his late thirties with a buzz cut and wire-rim glasses came running out. His face was white and his eyes looked worried. "Russia and China have both just launched missiles."

Solomon stood up. "Where are they heading?"

"We don't know yet. They just lifted off."

"Did you get this from WNN?"

"Not quite," said Tim. "A leak inside Global Union Aerospace Defense Command sent a message out to one of the old guys on our net."

"How reliable is the info?" asked Josh.

"The old man used to run the agency back when it was called NORAD. It was probably leaked by someone who worked directly under him," said Tim.

"What are we going to do?" asked Dana.

From his time with DHS, Josh knew the military had some fairly advanced systems for intercepting ballistic missiles before impact. "If it's an ICBM, the GU will probably take it down in flight. The problem with that is that if it detonates, it will generate an EMP. We should try to get everything with a circuit into the metal barns."

"You think that will protect our electronics?" Dana asked.

Josh lifted his shoulders. "Maybe. It's better than nothing. But I doubt they'd hit us with an ICBM anyway."

Tim lowered his brow. "Why? What else would they use?"

"Hypersonic. They carry a much smaller payload, but they're very effective."

"Wouldn't the GU still try to intercept them?" Dana inquired.

Josh nodded. "They'll try. But at Mach 27, that's a lofty ambition."

Solomon narrowed his eyes. "Mach 27? How fast is that?"

"Roughly twenty thousand miles per hour."

Solomon pointed to Tim. "Do you have back up equipment in case your radio gets fried?"

"Most of it."

"Good. Strip it down to just the essential listening equipment. Give everything else to Dana. She'll get it into the barns. Then try to figure out how many missiles are up, where they are heading and whether they are standard ICBMs or hypersonic. Radio me as soon as you hear anything."

"Got it!" Tim sprinted back toward the farmhouse.

"See you when I see you." Dana ran behind Tim to complete her part of the directive.

Josh said, "We should get some vehicles inside the first barn. We've got plenty of room."

"Yeah, okay," said Solomon. "Find George and have him help you with that. I'm going to round up all of the radios and see what we have available that can be used for a faraday cage. We can do without a lot of things, but we really need to be able to communicate."

"Agreed," Josh handed over his walkie-talkie. "I'll find you when I'm done." Josh ran to the large combine acting as the barricade for the access point to the compound.

"George!" he called before reaching the security checkpoint.

George was smiling but quickly took on a grave expression as Josh approached. "What's the matter? What's happened?"

"The GU is under attack." Josh quickly explained what he knew so far. "We need to move as many critical vehicles as possible into the first barn at once."

George turned to Ernie, a thin Indiana farm boy whose skin had been reddened and dried by exposure to the sun. "You heard him. Let's get that combine in the barn. Otherwise, we'll be picking corn eighteen hours a day."

Ernie hurried to get the large machine moving.

"I suppose trucks are the most important vehicles," said George.

Josh nodded. "Yeah, but the metal barns are imperfect shields. We should try to save the oldest vehicles first as they'll have the least sensitive electronics and the best chance of surviving."

"Alright then. I guess the old black van and the Ford are first in line." George stepped at a rapid pace in the direction of the vehicle parked near the farmhouse.

"If you and Ernie can take care of those, I'm going to get my El Camino inside and try to solicit some more help from my team."

"Go right ahead," said George.

Josh ran to the back of the compound, leaping up the steps and into the trailer. "Micah, Lindsey, I need you guys out here." No reply came, so Josh knocked on the door of their quarters before opening it. "Not here." Instinctively, he reached for his radio, but he'd already passed it off to Solomon.

Josh abandoned his mission to inform Micah and Lindsey. He bustled down the stairs of the trailer and sprinted to the RV. Josh knocked. "Emilio, Nicole, are you in there?" He knocked again, harder and more rapidly. Hearing no answer, he let himself in. "Nicole, Emilio."

For a fleeting moment, he had the sensation that the rapture had occurred and that *he'd* been left behind. "No, that's impossible. Emilio would still be here. And Jesus wouldn't forget me," he said aloud to himself to dispel the odd notion.

Josh looked around the RV. He grabbed Emilio's laptop, his AM/FM radio, even his small solar charger, and hurried back out. He returned to the trailer and quickly collected all the small electronics from his quarters as well as Micah and Lindsey's room.

What can I use for a faraday cage? Josh looked around. “Ammo box!” Josh popped the top of the .50 ammo can and dumped the loose rounds out on top of his bed. “I need something to keep the electronics from touching the metal.” Finding a cardboard box, Josh tore out panels which would line the bottom and sides of the ammo can.

It’s not perfect, but it will have to do for now. Josh crammed everything except the laptops into the container and closed the lid. Then, he carried the computers and the ammo box out to the El Camino. He started the engine and drove around to the front barn.

George and Ernie were there with several of the vehicles from the compound. “We should close these doors,” said Josh.

“I need to get the Kubota in here!” Ernie said in a voice that betrayed his almost-unnatural affection for the little tractor.

“I doubt that has any sensitive electronics,” said Josh.

“But you don’t know for sure,” countered Ernie.

Josh waved him away. “Go ahead. But then close these doors and don’t open them again until we get the all-clear.”

Josh darted to the farmhouse. He knocked.

“Come in,” Dana said from inside.

Josh walked in.

“We’re back here,” Dana called from down the hall.

Josh followed the voice to Tim’s small room. A single bed was pushed up against the wall while a desk held a stripped-down Ham radio set up. Empty shelves showed silhouettes in dust where additional equipment had recently been. "What do we know?"

Dana's voice sounded grim. "Twelve missiles went up. All hypersonic."

Josh looked at his watch. "We got the warning 20 minutes ago. A hypersonic missile can hit anywhere in the world in that amount of time. Do we know if they've made impact?"

Tim held up a finger.

A staticky voice came over the radio. "Paris, London, and Rome were hit. Stand by for reports on initial damage projections."

Josh thought about the millions who'd likely died in those three cities alone. His heart ached and he felt a lump in his throat. He looked up. "Dear, God. Have mercy on us."

The voice came over the radio again. "New York and Caracas were both hit."

Josh felt his stomach sink. "Those cities were all OASIS cities."

"Five of the originals," Dana added.

Solomon walked in panting heavily as if he'd been running. "What's happening?"

More gargled reports came over the radio. "Quito and Hamburg have also been struck by hypersonic missiles."

Dana brought Solomon up to speed. "New York, Paris, Rome, London, and Caracas were all hit."

"What's the potential payload on one of these things?" asked Solomon.

"Up to two megatons." Josh felt numb with empathy for the lost.

"Will that destroy an entire city?" Tim turned away from his radio.

Josh gave a hypnotic nod. "Nagasaki was twenty kilotons. Two megatons is one hundred times bigger."

"Oh!" Dana let out a guttural sigh of sorrow.

The reception on the radio got worse. "Jerusalem was one of the targets. The payload failed to detonate."

"Failed to detonate?" Solomon asked.

"I'm guessing that was one from China," said Tim.

Josh added, "Or it was a miracle from God."

"Chicago was also hit," said the voice over the radio.

"That's 150 miles away from us. Should we be worried about fallout?" Dana asked.

"Prevailing winds will probably carry the radiation to the southeast," said Josh.

"We're southeast!" said Dana.

Josh tilted his head to the side. "South-southeast. Even if it brought it straight to us, it would be pretty well dissipated by then. Would it increase your odds of getting cancer in the next ten years? Probably, but none of us are going to be around long enough for that to be a problem."

Dana lowered her brows. "That's reassuring."

Josh turned to Solomon. "San Francisco was one of the original OASIS cities. Maybe you can cancel your mission."

Solomon seemed lost in thought as if he'd not even heard Josh.

"LA and Sydney have been struck," said the voice. "Still no word about the twelfth missile."

George and Ernie arrived but could not fit into the tiny room. Dana walked out into the hallway to fill them in about what had transpired so far.

Josh waited anxiously for more news.

Finally, the voice over the radio returned. "A missile headed to San Francisco was destroyed without detonation."

"Destroyed?" asked Tim. "What can stop a missile going 20,000 miles an hour?"

Josh shook his head. "I don't have any idea. It's already pushing the limits concerning the laws of physics to have a missile that moves that fast."

"Unless it was technology operating outside of the laws of physics," said Solomon.

"What are you talking about?" asked Josh.

Tim stared at Solomon. "UFOs?"

Solomon lifted his shoulders. "Alexander has dropped hints about us not being alone before. In all the footage I've seen of aerial phenomenon, the aircraft don't seem constrained to the known laws of physics."

"How is that possible?" Tim asked.

Josh was at a loss. "Demonic forces from another realm maybe?"

Tim asked, "Isn't there something in the Bible about fallen angels giving technology to humans?"

"No, it's not in the Bible," Josh replied. "The Book of Enoch, which isn't considered canon, talks about the watchers. Supposedly, they were immortal beings that bestowed technological knowledge to humans. Second Thessalonians says the antichrist will perform counterfeit signs and wonders."

"Yeah, well, he's still dead. So, it's going to be kind of hard for him to take credit for this one," said Solomon.

"Unless it ends up being Omniscience tech that stopped the missile headed to San Francisco," said Dana.

The voice came back over the radio and everyone grew quiet. "Preliminary reports estimate the damage to the cities hit by the missiles to be severe."

"How many people are we talking about?" asked Dana.

Josh felt for his burner, but it was in the ammo box, as if any cell phone infrastructure would have survived an EMP anyway. "Does anyone have a burner?"

Tim took his phone from the desk. "No signal."

However, the voice over the radio soon answered their question. "Initial casualty reports are twenty million dead. Another twenty million are likely to die in the coming days and weeks from burns, injuries, and radiation poisoning. Complications from the devastation to power grids, municipal water, sanitation services, and supply chain disruption could possibly kill as many as thirty million people in addition to those lost as a direct effect of the detonations."

"Where is this guy getting all of this information?" asked George.

"He used to run NORAD," Tim said. "Got a guy on the inside passing him intel."

Josh added, “It makes sense. They would run preliminary BDAs based on computer models for the blast size, detonation altitude, wind speed, population density, and location.”

“BDAs?” asked Ernie.

“Bomb Damage Assessments.” Josh thought about the horrendous toll the attacks had exacted on the globe.

Dana said, “We called them Battle Damage Assessments in the military.”

Josh nodded. “Same concept. If you folks will excuse me, I need to go locate my son.”

“Real quick before you go…” said Ernie.

“Yes?” Josh paused.

“Can we pull the vehicles out now?”

Josh shook his head. “We don’t know that the attack is over. That could have been the entire show, or it could have been phase one of a prolonged assault. Besides, the vehicles aren’t hurting anything by staying in the barn.”

“Yeah, I guess you’re right about that,” said Ernie.

Josh hurried out of the crowded little space. He sprinted down the dirt road to the back of the barn.

CHAPTER 10

And I beheld another beast coming up out of the earth; and he had two horns like a lamb, and he spake as a dragon.

Revelation 13:11

Josh arrived back at the trailer.

Micah stepped out with his rifle. Lindsey came through the door right behind him, also looking as if she were ready for a fight. However, Josh was caught off guard by seeing her in a dress. He found this more curious and out of place for the young woman than seeing her geared up for battle. "What? Why are you dressed up?"

"We've been robbed!" Micah interrupted.

"Robbed?" Josh was still trying to make sense of Lindsey's attire. "Of what?"

With red cheeks that matched the poppies on her white dress, Lindsey exclaimed, "These no-good thieving snakes came in while we were gone and took all of our electronics. They took the laptop, battery charger, radio, pretty much everything that wasn't tied down."

"No, no, no." Josh waved his hands. "I took all of that stuff." He provided a short synopsis of what had happened.

"What if they hit Indianapolis? It's an OASIS city now, and it's only 70 miles away."

"It's due south of us. The prevailing winds would carry it out of our direction. But so far, they've only fired on the original OASIS cities."

"I feel terrible for the people who died, but it cost the Global Union big time. People will think twice about moving to an OASIS city now." Micah slung his rifle over his shoulder.

"Yeah." Josh eyed the white button-up shirt which Micah was wearing. "So, back to my question. Where have you guys been?"

Lindsey turned to Micah. She puffed her cheeks and exhaled through puckered lips, as if unable or unwilling to provide a satisfactory alibi.

Micah also seemed to deflect the inquiry. He looked to the west. "We were at the house over on the other side of the field."

The answer made no sense to Josh. "House on the other side of the field?" Josh looked in the direction in which Micah was staring. He fought through the haze of everything that had just happened trying to remember who George had said was the occupant of that house. "Craig's? Why were you at… Oh. Nicole and Emilio eloped?"

Lindsey answered, "It's not like that. They just wanted Craig to read a few verses for them—pronounce them man and wife without a lot of fuss. No one else was even there except Micah and me."

"They didn't think you'd want to come anyway," said Micah.

"Plus we didn't know where you were." Lindsey let her rifle hang from her shoulder and held Micah's arm with her hand.

Josh frowned. "Besides a handful of trailers and RVs, the compound has four metal barns, an animal barn, and one house. It's not like I was lost at Disney World."

Micah looked at the dirt. "They didn't want you to come."

Josh felt a slight stab of disappointment. "I understand. I'm not mad at you guys. I'm not mad at them either. We're just looking at things through a different lens."

Emilio and Nicole emerged from the corn field. They were wearing nice clothes but looked rather frumpy, as if they'd perhaps fallen amongst the ocean of green stalks—more than once. Nicole kissed Emilio and went into the RV without speaking to Josh.

Josh warned her before she got out of earshot. "I took your laptop and electronics."

She stopped before going inside. "What did you do that for?"

Once more, Josh gave the account of the attack.

"There goes my honeymoon." Nicole pressed her lips together and continued inside the RV.

George came around the side of the metal building, behind which the trailer and RV were parked. "Solomon is giving a briefing in the dining facility in fifteen minutes. It's optional, but it would be good for at least one member of your group to be present."

Josh nodded. "I'll be there."

"Good. See you then." George walked away.

"I'm coming also," said Micah.

"Me, too," echoed Lindsey.

"I'm going to let Nicole know, then I'll be right back." Emilio paused before going into the RV. "You know, she's not selfish." He looked at the others. "It probably sounded that way, like she couldn't care less about the 40 million people lost in the attacks. But this was supposed to be the best day of her life—and she's already had a very disappointing wedding." Emilio looked at the ground. "I wish I could have given her something better."

Josh replied. "You don't have to tell me. I've known her all my life."

Emilio went inside and quickly returned.

Josh asked about his sister, "Is she okay?"

"She's crying, and upset. Not just about the wedding, but about everything. I told her I wouldn't be gone long. She'll be okay." Emilio's eyes showed his concern for his new bride.

The group walked toward the barracks. Emilio patted Josh on the shoulder. "Sorry about cutting you out, but we didn't think you'd want to come anyway. And it really wasn't much of a ceremony."

"What's done is done." Josh opened the door and led the group into the back of the metal building where the dining area was. They all found seats and listened to Solomon's address to the compound about what they'd learned in the past hour.

After finishing the update, Solomon pointed to two of the women from the compound. "Anne Marie and Kim lent us the TV from their travel trailer. We're trying to connect via a mobile hotspot using my phone. Carl Jacobs is supposed to address the Global Union. But internet has been strained since the attack. I can't guarantee anything."

Solomon picked up the remote sitting next to the large-screen television on a fold-out table. He attempted to get WNN, but the channel's app wouldn't load.

Tim said, "Try YouTube. They're pretty smart about throttling back resolution so they can still get GU propaganda out during spikes of heavy internet usage."

Solomon took the advice and soon had the live stream from the Globalplex's new GU press room. Modeled after the UN's logo, the red and white insignia behind the podium featured the continents on a polar azimuthal projection of the globe, but with a red dragon eating its tail surrounding the image rather than the traditional flanking of two olive branches on each side.

Emilio leaned over and whispered to Josh, "Ever noticed how the lines suggesting the latitude and longitude divisions end up looking like the planet in crosshairs?"

Josh lowered his brows. "Not so much when it was the blue UN insignia, but it stands out a little more clearly in red."

Finally, Carl Jacobs approached the podium. He'd forsaken his previous casual look of being the relatable people's pastor for a more regal appearance. His distressed denim jeans, comfortable shoes, tee-shirt, and sports jacket had been exchanged for a white suit. The eastern-inspired jacket was long, going far below his waist and ending just above the knees. On his lapel, was the red dragon ouroboros. "Citizens of the Global Union, I come to you this afternoon with a heavy heart. While we were still grieving the loss of our precious leader, Lucius Alexander, we were violently attacked by jealous and hateful foes.

"It is our desire to live at peace with one another as well as the rest of the world. However, we cannot control the ambitions of bloodthirsty villains such as those in the Eastern Trade Organization.

"During an emergency meeting of the governing council, it was decided that we should initiate a decisive counterstrike against our foes. Thirty minutes ago, Global Union Missile Command was ordered to launch a volley of ICBMs as well as trident missiles from our nuclear submarines.

"All the targets identified by the governing council have been destroyed. For each OASIS city that was fired upon, we selected three targets within the ETO. And each Eastern Trade Organization city was struck with no less than three missiles.

"War is not what any of us wanted. But as your shepherds, our priority is to guard our sheep."

"At least they're being honest about how they see us," Micah whispered.

Josh nodded but added no comment.

Jacobs continued speaking. "Bagdad, Tehran, Saint Petersburg, Moscow, Shanghai, Beijing, Tianjin, Shenzhen, Guangzhou, Chengdu, Dongguan, Chongqing, and many other cities, including metropolitan centers in Kuwait, and the United Arab Emirates have been razed to the ground.

"We are so opposed to war that we are willing to take the most extreme action to end this conflict before it can continue any longer. However, we are now engaged in a battle on multiple fronts.

"Unfortunately, the ETO is not our only enemy. Our beloved leader was killed by domestic terrorists. And while Patriot Pride is the group claiming responsibility for Secretary-General Alexander's death, they are only one of many such organizations; all of which will be emboldened by this cowardly act to commit similar atrocities.

"Just as those of us convening at the Globalplex are responsible to keep you safe from the ETO, we must also protect you from radical idealists, hatemongers, violent extremists who want to see our vision of global peace fail at any costs.

"Our first act to subdue this dangerous toxin within our society will be to create a task force working under the Department of Global Security. The objective of this task force will be to root out organizers and propaganda materials responsible for spreading this callous ideology.

"Most of these groups are religious zealots who misconstrue the readings and interpretations of their various texts. The cost of allowing everyone to choose an individualized form of spirituality has become too high. It was adherents to the Islamic faith that released the Red Virus, killing nearly five hundred million people. Then, Patriot Pride, a radical Christian organization took the most precious prize the world has ever been given when they murdered Lucius Alexander.

"For this reason, the Ministry of Religion is suspending our production of individualized religious texts like the Christian Bible, Koran, and Hebrew Scriptures. Instead, we will be focusing solely on making sure everyone has a copy of the Unity Scriptures, which incorporate all the various paths people use to find peace with themselves and the universe. The Governing Council has enacted a new law that prohibits religious texts other than the Unity Scriptures as well as gatherings, services, and studies based on texts other than the Unity Scriptures.

"I understand that this seems like a drastic move, especially if you have been a devout follower of your particular religion, but the toll is too great. The division and tribalism that has been sustained around the world by each person having his own dogmatic view of how the world should be is literally killing the human race. We need to put aside the hurdles that separate us today more than ever before. At no other time in history has the world needed unity like we need it at this moment.

"I think most people in our society understand the necessity for this type of ordinance. However, if you find yourself among the extreme minority who do not, I would encourage you to take a long hard look inside. Why would you want to hold back progress and continue to embrace the animosity that comes from alienating your fellow citizens who do not believe as you believe?

"We're not taking away your right to believe as you see fit. We are offering you a way to believe more, to grow in your faith, to go deeper by learning how others recognize the awesome cosmic energy that many of us call God, albeit with any number of names for the same being or collection of beings.

"As a student of world religions myself, I'll be traveling to Jerusalem immediately following this briefing. While there, I'll be seeking guidance from my own personal higher power alongside many other Christians, Muslims, and Jews. I'll also be asking for a miracle.

"But not just any miracle. I'll be asking for something specific. Many religions around the world have been waiting for a messiah. Many Muslims are anticipating the arrival of the Twelfth Imam, Hindus look forward to the arrival of Kalki, who will end the present age of darkness. Christians are watching for the return of Christ. Buddhists believe Maitreya will appear, achieve complete enlightenment, and teach the pure dharma. Our Jewish brothers and sisters have long speculated that Messiah would come and build the third temple. Tomorrow, I will stand on the porch of that temple, built by a generous grant provided by Lucius Alexander, and offer my prayers.

"I know what you are thinking. Lucius Alexander is gone, taken from us in his prime. He cannot possibly be the one written of in all of these scriptures. Well, before you give up completely, let me read a passage from the Unity Scriptures. It was originally found in the Hebrew Book of Psalms. It reads, *For you will not leave my soul among the dead or allow your holy one to rot in the grave.*

"The implication here is that this very same savior, predicted by many different texts, could very well have the power to rise from the dead. I know it sounds crazy, but I think all of us felt something special when we looked upon the face of Lucius Alexander and listened to his healing words. His voice was like a balm for a hurting planet. And what I'm feeling, what you're feeling, it's more than denial, it's not just a stage of grieving. What we feel is real. Over the coming hours and days, rather than focusing on the pain and heartache going on all around the world because of this catastrophic violence we've had to endure, I want you to look inside yourself, deep inside; ask the universe, or Buddha, or Mother Earth, or whoever it is that you see when you close your eyes to give Lucius back to us. We need him.

"Listen, I get it. You've been lied to about so many things. Stuff you learned in Sunday school that turned out not to be true. Things your parents told you that ended up being lies. Maybe your pastor told you about a God that hates people who, through no fault of their own, feel out of place in their own skin or are attracted to people the church said they shouldn't be. Because of those things, it's tough to have faith. But this time is different. Take a chance. Believe. You'll be glad you did.

"Well, I've been going on and on for too long now. Let me introduce someone very special to the GU. The new taskforce I spoke of earlier acting under DGS will be known as the Unity Enforcement Agency. The Governing Council has tapped a person who has dedicated her life to law enforcement to be the new director of the UEA. After a long successful career with the former FBI, Carole-Jean Harris seamlessly transitioned to the DGS and has been serving the Global Union faithfully for the past two years."

Carl Jacobs turned to his side and the camera panned out to show those standing in attendance next to him. "Carole-Jean, please come say a few words."

CHAPTER 11

And I saw the woman drunken with the blood of the saints, and with the blood of the martyrs of Jesus: and when I saw her, I wondered with great admiration.

Revelation 17:6

Josh shook his head as he watched Carole-Jean Harris walk to the podium.

Emilio pointed at the screen. “Hey, that’s your homegirl from Louisville!”

Josh gritted his teeth. “I can’t say that I’m surprised.”

Carole-Jean had the same short, blonde, bob hairdo, and still wore clothes that accentuated her tall, disproportioned body. Although, her long flowing pants with the flared bottoms and short tight jacket were now all white. She wore a red lapel pin featuring the dragon ouroboros.

Lindsey whispered, "She looks like a pear!"

Micah added, "A marshmallow pear."

Josh nodded. "Don't let that fool you. She's the most brutal woman I've ever met."

Carole-Jean began speaking. "I'm honored to be selected as the Director of the Unity Enforcement Agency. I wish this were a more joyous occasion, but I will pledge to the Global Union to diligently hunt down the members and leaders of Patriot Pride. They will pay for what they have taken from the world by this evil act of violence.

"But for the Unity Enforcement Agency to be a success, I need help from each and every one of you. It's a saying that's been around for a couple of decades, but it has never been more relevant than it is today. If you see something, say something. No matter how innocent a religious activity or meeting may look, it could be harboring or even instigating the very types of radicals who murdered the man our planet needed more than any other.

"And I'm not simply asking that you report suspicious behavior out of a sense of moral obligation, although I hope that is an additional incentive. We will be issuing a 100 mark reward to anyone providing actionable intel that leads to an arrest. The reward is per arrest. So if your tip leads to bringing down an entire cell of let's say, five members, you'll get 500 marks, just for the arrests. Bonuses will be paid for contraband as well. The UEA will pay 25 marks for religious materials, such as Bibles or Korans, and 50 marks for firearms.

"Maybe your neighbor is holding unlicensed Bible studies. If you do your part as a good citizen and provide the time and location of the meetings, you could be very well compensated for your act of civil service. A gathering of eight people, all with their own banned religious text could bring in 1,000 marks; even more if one of them happens to be armed, as they often are.

"Those who are arrested and not deemed to be violent will be sent to rehabilitation facilities, where they'll have the opportunity to examine why they have such a strong affinity for divisiveness. Those who are able, will complete a six-month reskilling program after which they will be gradually integrated with society. Those who cannot, will, unfortunately, have no place in the GU.

"Times are tough, and we could all use a little extra money to help us through. Do your part. Help the UEA, help the Global Union, and help yourself."

Solomon clicked off the television and addressed the crowd. "That's the end of the Stasi propaganda. And for those of you who don't know, this woman probably has lunch with Ethan Combs, the ATF agent who organized Patriot Pride.

"But now with unlimited resources and the ability to turn every GU citizen into an informant, she'll have the funding and the manpower to hunt down groups like ours. We may have to move up the timeline on our plans for San Francisco. I want to hit them while they're still reeling from the nuclear attacks and the death of Alexander."

Solomon turned to look at Josh and his group. "Before I was sent to fight in Iraq, I served one tour in Afghanistan. We went in, attacked training camps, broke some things, and had a really good story about how we defeated Al-Qaeda and the Taliban. We set up Karzai and declared democracy in the country. But the reality is that the insurgency was never crushed.

"The mujahideen are in a sense, immortal. Because it is not a group of guerrilla fighters, it is an idea. It is a mindset of a people who have been invaded over and over, by countries and empires. While I do not approve of what they believe or ascribe to their notion of politics or religion, I do admire their tenacity. These groups of decentralized and loosely affiliated militias have successfully evaded being conquered by Russia, Great Britain, and the United States. Even Genghis Kahn's and Alexander the Great's victories over the region were short-lived.

"These people have always been at a disadvantage when it comes to treasures, available resources, and weapons systems. But they don't stop. Despite what you may think of them on a personal level, as warriors, they are to be respected. And I think we can learn something from their determination. If we can glean nothing else from their struggle, let it be this. The battle may go to the strongest and best prepared, but the war will go to the one who determines in his heart not to lose."

George stood up and began clapping. Anne Marie, Tim, and several others joined in. Soon, everyone in the room except for Josh was giving a standing ovation, including Micah, Lindsey, and Emilio.

Solomon waited for the applause to end. "Dana and I will be heading to Idaho this evening. All of you should be training with your individual squads while we're gone. Work on troop movement, magazine changes, all the essentials. We probably won't have much time when we come back with the final details. George will be in charge in our absence. You're dismissed."

Micah looked at his father. "Did you know about this? We're going to San Francisco?" He sounded excited.

"They, not we." Josh watched as Lindsey made a bee-line to Solomon.

"Why? What are we going to do?" Micah seemed insulted at being cut out of the action.

"Hold down the fort."

"It's a barn in the middle of a corn field! It's not going anywhere. It doesn't need to be held down!"

"They need a secure location to return to," said Josh.

"They don't need five people to guard a barn and a field." Micah walked off toward his wife.

Josh sighed and shook his head.

Emilio patted him on the back. "You shouldn't have raised him to be such a patriot. Should have taught him to keep his head down and go along with the official narrative, no matter how much he disagreed with it."

Josh frowned. "You're not helping."

"I'm just saying, the acorn didn't fall far from the tree."

Josh didn't reply. Instead he watched powerlessly as Lindsey and Micah spoke with Solomon. He was out of earshot, but he could hear the conversation plainly in his head. He knew exactly what was being discussed.

He thought about his options while waiting for the imminent news. He shook his head in silent defeat, knowing he had no leverage with which to prevent Lindsey and Micah from participating in the action against the Globalplex.

Solomon smiled and laughed as he spoke with the impressionable pair. Then, all three of them began walking back in Josh's direction.

Emilio stood to shake Solomon's hand when he got closer. "Idaho, huh? You are brave."

"Why do you say that?" Solomon grinned.

"That place is whiter than the inside of a potato. If you need an extra shooter to attack Frisco, I'm in, but don't count on me stepping foot in that state."

Josh was unhappy about Emilio seeming so eager to jump on board with the reckless plan, but he still wasn't about to let his friend's ill-informed opinion of Idaho go unchecked. "That's a myth, propagated by the Socialist People's Law Center. They claim every patriot group is a bunch of white nationalists, but it's not true. It's just the SPLCs way of spreading fear amongst Hispanics and people of color."

"I don't know," said Emilio. "They had an Arian

Nation training center up there."

"Every state in America has racists," said Josh. "And by the way, they're not all white. But Idaho gets a disproportionate amount of coverage on theirs because it's such a constitutional stronghold. The media and leftist organizations like smearing the state's reputation with political hit pieces."

"Sorry to interrupt, Dad," said Micah. "But Lindsey and I are going on the mission."

Despite knowing already, Josh felt a stab in his gut when he heard Micah say it out loud.

"I got room for one more." Solomon grinned as if he knew Josh's dilemma and was taking pleasure in it.

Josh replied reluctantly, "Micah and Lindsey will be on a fire team with Emilio and myself."

Micah hugged his father as did Lindsey.

"Good to have you as part of the team." Solomon still wore his irritating smile and offered his hand to Josh.

Josh accepted the gesture and shook hands with the man, albeit unenthusiastically. "Yeah. Thanks for having me."

"If you'll excuse me, Dana and I need to be getting on the road. I'll let Craig and George know that your group will be working together before we leave." Solomon waved as he walked away.

"What about Nicole?" Lindsey asked.

Emilio quickly replied for his new wife. "She can stay here. They'll need a couple of people to keep an eye on things."

"Yeah, right. Good luck with that." Lindsey gave an amused smile. "We're going to go see what information we can find on the radio about the nuclear attacks." She and Micah left Emilio and Josh in the dining facility.

Emilio shoved his hands in his front pockets. "You're going to help me out with that, aren't you? Convincing Nicole to sit this one out, I mean?"

Josh patted him on the shoulder. "I've squandered enough time and effort trying to keep our necks out of this noose. You'll have to carry that mission on your own."

Josh left his friend and took a long walk. He walked off the property and down the long, lonely road that went on and on through miles of corn fields. Between the nuclear attacks and being sucked into a mission that he wanted nothing to do with, he felt as if his head was going to explode. The walk didn't provide him any answers or a way out of the unfavorable situation, but it did somehow help him process the dilemma. It helped him deal with the stress by distancing himself from the epicenter of the matter for a while.

CHAPTER 12

That they may know from the rising of the sun to its setting that there is none besides Me. I am the Lord, and there is no other; I form the light and create darkness, I make peace and create calamity; I, the Lord, do all these things.

Isaiah 45:6-7

Josh woke up at 4:00 AM Saturday, unable to fall back to sleep. His mind was racing. His thoughts were filled with the lives lost in the previous day's nuclear attacks as well as the souls who were still suffering, waiting to die as a result of their burns, injuries, and radiation poisoning. Josh knew he could do nothing to help them, but still, the horror haunted his intellect.

He tried everything to go back to sleep, but it was no use. Instead, he remained still on his bunk and prayed that they who had not yet committed their lives to Jesus might turn to Him in this their final hour. The early morning crept by and Josh finally got out of bed at 5:00.

Feeling tired and vexed by lack of sleep, he fought through his morning routine of stretching and getting dressed. He made his way to the back door of the dining facility, hoping that he'd not be the first person awake.

George was there, already sipping a cup of coffee. "Morning. How'd you sleep?" George poured a cup for Josh and handed it to him.

Josh shook his head. "Took me a while to fall asleep. Probably nodded off around 1:00 AM. Then I woke up at 4:00. Couldn't go back to sleep."

George's eyes had dark rings underneath. "I don't know how anyone can sleep after yesterday. Might be as many as two hundred million end up dying from the bombs."

"Terrible, I know." Josh sipped his coffee. "Thanks for this, by the way."

"What do you make of what Jacobs said yesterday?" George took out his phone and sat it by the TV, which was still on the table in the dining area.

"About what?" Josh asked.

George clicked on the television and connected it to the hotspot provided by his phone. "About

Alexander coming back to life. You think he's got some kind of trick up his sleeve?"

Josh watched the feed on the television. It showed Lucius Alexander lying in state, surrounded by hundreds and hundreds of white candles on stands of varying heights. "Yeah. I do."

"Well how do you reckon he'll pull it off?"

"I think he'll come back to life." Josh took a big drink, enjoying the hot sensation of the beverage in his throat.

"Seriously?"

Josh took the small New Testament out of his back pocket and turned to Revelation 13 and handed it to George. "Says it right here."

George pulled out a chair and sat down. He took his time reading the text. "Well, I'll be doggone."

"Are you a believer?" Josh sat next to him.

"Yep. I'd always been taught that we'd be out of here before all of this stuff started happening. I guess it's sort of had me questioning the whole thing."

Josh nodded. "That's understandable, but don't let something as speculative as the timing of end-time events shake your faith on the solid truths of God's Word."

George nodded. "Yeah, thanks."

Josh watched as the morning news program began on the television. The volume was too low to hear as most of the people in the barracks were still sleeping. The scene of Alexander lying in state was minimized and placed in the lower right-hand corner of the screen.

Tim was the next person to arrive. He helped himself to the large pot of coffee then joined Josh and George.

"Get any sleep last night?" George asked.

"Not a wink," Tim replied.

"Join the club." Josh watched the first images coming in of aerial footage over the cities which had been annihilated by the nuclear missiles. The images showed both the OASIS cities within the Global Union as well as those from the Eastern Trade Organization.

"This one is still dead, I see." Tim gestured at the bottom right corner of the screen.

"For now," Josh replied.

"Got the locusts in Nebraska." Tim took a seat at the table.

"Nebraska?" Josh asked. "When did you hear that?"

"Last night. I figured I'd just scan the frequencies last night rather than toss and turn," Tim replied.

"The news hasn't said anything about it," George looked concerned.

Tim pointed to the apocalyptic scene of downtown Manhattan, which was little more than a charred pile of debris and rubble. "I'm not sure a plot of dirt where a soybean field once was could get the same ratings as this."

"You've got a point." George grimaced at the horrific image on the television.

"How bad is it?" Josh asked.

"One county, Custer, I think they said, is completely overrun. But they're spreading fast. They've got 'em in eleven counties so far."

Josh shook his head. "How does a swarm of locusts just appear out of nowhere in the middle of America? It doesn't make sense. Seems like they would have arrived at some coastal location first, then spread inland. It sounds fishy."

"Conspiracy or not," said George. "We depend on this corn. We need to see what we can do before they show up on our doorstep."

Josh said, "I agree."

"I'll go see if Ernie is awake. This is his department." George stood up and walked away.

Josh pulled out his phone while he waited for George and Ernie to return. He searched YouTube with the terms *Nebraska locusts*. He began playing the first video that came up. "Wow! Look at this!" He turned the phone so Tim could look on.

The two watched in anguish as a Nebraska farmer in Custer County lost an entire corn field in a matter of minutes.

"They're all over the place!" Tim's mouth hung open in amazement. "How can you possibly defend against that?"

"You don't. Our only hope will be to harvest what we can before they arrive." Josh scrolled down the page of results on YouTube and watched several other videos from other farms in Nebraska. In some of the videos, locusts could be seen as a light swarm, buzzing over fields and lighting on low trees. In others, they covered fields of soybeans, corn, and wheat like a heavy winter quilt.

George and Ernie arrived minutes later. Ernie looked onto Josh's phone at the scene portraying a smattering of locusts working on a corn field while a determined farmer shooed them away by snapping a towel. "That's not so bad."

Tim replied, "This video is from three counties over. Show him the one from Custer County."

Josh navigated back to the first video they'd watched. "It's been removed."

"That's okay," said Tim. "Plenty more where that one came from. Find the one where they destroyed the soybean field in less than ten minutes."

Josh scrolled through his watch history. "It's gone, too."

"Why would they take that down?" George asked.

Josh turned off his phone. "Information is currency now. The CEO of YouTube's parent company is on the governing council. They decide what we need to know and when we need to know it. But this stokes my suspicion that the locusts' arrival may be more than a natural occurrence."

"You think the GU brought the locusts to Nebraska?" George asked. "Why would they do such a thing?"

"Same reason they released a plague and started a nuclear war," Josh replied.

"The ETO started the war," said Ernie.

"Some would argue that by claiming the world's oceans for himself, Lucius Alexander started the war," Josh said.

"What about the virus? Jihadists connected to the previous Saudi regime took credit for that one," Tim said.

Emilio arrived in the dining room, looking as if he'd slept better than most of the others. "Hey, what's going on?"

Josh patted him on the shoulder. "This guy right here and I have firsthand knowledge that the government allowed that attack to take place, despite having been tipped off about it in plenty of time to stop it."

Tim looked to the television still showing scenes of destruction. "Then, I suppose Ham radio is the only remaining alternative media platform."

"Until they shut that down," said Josh.

"But why would the GU intentionally kill their own citizens?" George asked. "I still don't understand."

Josh replied, "Because, the Global Union is run by a Luciferian death cult that wants to exterminate most of the world's population. It fits right into the whole green movement. Once they kill us off, the planet can heal herself, and they can have it all to themselves."

George looked confused. "But you just told me that you think all of this death is from the seals, that it's God's doing."

"The two are not mutually exclusive," said Josh. "God specifically says in Isaiah 54 that He created the waster to destroy. Through the Old Testament prophets, He warned Israel that He would use the Babylonians and the Assyrians to bring judgment upon the Jews for their disobedience. The

Luciferians running the show right now might think they're in charge, but everything they do is serving God's ultimate purpose."

Ernie's eye showed his perplexity. "Wow. That's deep."

"I'll explain more later, but for now, we need to figure out how we're going to salvage the corn crop." Josh gave Ernie a squeeze on the shoulder to bring him back to the here and now. "What do you recommend?"

Ernie nodded slowly, as if still processing everything, but soon came back to the issue at hand. "The corn is ripe. That's the good news."

"Okay, great!" said Emilio. "What's the bad news?"

"Storage," said Ernie. "We don't have a very large still, so we typically only harvest the amount we need to process. Plus, we're all heading off to fight the New World Order. There won't even be anyone around to keep the regular production capacity going."

George nodded. "I can talk to Solomon about having Junk and Pigpen stay behind. They might be of more use to us here."

Ernie shook his head. "Even so, the corn will spoil before they're able to process it."

"Isn't that part of the process?" Tim asked. "I mean, to convert it into ethanol, don't you want the juice to sour?"

"Yes, but until you've pulled the liquid out of the ear of corn, you've got a number of things that can happen. It could sour, in which it would still be useable, or it might mold, or it could just rot. Trust me, there's a difference between the three."

Josh considered what Ernie was saying. "But sitting in a metal silo, baking in the July heat, mold is a relatively low risk, right?"

Ernie twisted his mouth. "Yeah, I suppose. Might even be able to open some hatches on the silo and cover the openings with screen to keep the bugs out. That could provide enough ventilation to lower the risk of mold, at least for a few weeks."

"What about corn for meal and grits?" asked Emilio.

Ernie exhaled. "Too early for that. We usually leave it on the stalk until it's dried out."

"Isn't there a way to dry it after harvesting?" Josh asked.

"Folks who grow tobacco hang it up in the barn and dry it. Maybe we could do that," said George.

"Yeah," replied Ernie. "They have tobacco barns with rafters set up for just such a purpose."

"But what if we could mimic that setup?" Josh inquired. "Would it work?"

Ernie lifted his shoulders. "I suppose. But you'd need materials to build the rafters."

"Do you have baling wire?" Josh asked. "We could string it across the barn. Tie it off nice and tight. We could probably hang several pounds worth of corn on each strand."

Ernie rubbed his chin. "I have a roll that I keep for repairs and that sort of thing, but not much. We don't produce hay."

"Something is better than nothing," said George.

"What about the metal roof?" Josh looked up. "It's a virtual solar oven. Maybe we could put some corn up there to dry."

"It's pitched. It'd just come rolling right off," said Tim.

"Not if we put the entire stalk up there," George said. We can lay it vertically which will maximize the amount of corn we can put on the roof and give it a better chance of not sliding off."

Josh nodded. "At least until the locusts arrive."

George said, "Josh, Tim, and Emilio, you fellas should start spreading the word. We're going to need all hands on deck for this operation. We'll salvage what we can. Then I guess the bugs can have whatever is left when they get here."

"Sounds like a plan." Josh shook the man's hand and headed back toward the barracks to inform the other occupants of what was happening.

***

An hour later, Josh, Emilio, Micah, Lindsey, and Nicole were all working in the corn field, trying to bring in as much of the harvest as possible before the locusts arrived.

Josh put the old Kubota in neutral and cut the engine. He jumped off the tractor as the others got off the flat-bed wagon being towed behind. They diligently cut stalks of corn with machetes and stacked them on the back of the wagon. Once a section had been cleared, they proceeded to the next portion of the field.

Two hours in, Nicole took a long drink of water and wiped the sweat from her brow with a bandana. She passed the gallon jug to Emilio and looked across the field at the big combine harvesting corn at a blistering speed compared to the progress of their manual endeavor. "Explain to me again how our team got selected to chop corn in the field while that guy is driving in comfort?"

"Ernie was driving a combine before you ever gave your first Zumba class," said Josh. "But I'm sure you could get on his team if you'd like to put in for a transfer."

"Oh yeah? What's the rest of his team doing?"

"Shucking corn." Emilio passed the jug to Lindsey who wiped the top with her shirttail before taking a long gulp.

Lindsey ran the back of her arm along her lips and placed the jug on the wagon. "Nothing attracts flies like a corn shucking. I'll chop stalks over shucking any day of the week."

Nicole looked at Lindsey as if deciding whether or not to believe her. "I guess I'll stay here."

"Speaking of staying here," said Emilio. "Junk and Pigpen are going to be remaining at the compound so they can keep production going on the still. They're up against the clock to get the corn processed before it spoils."

"Why are you telling me this?" Nicole hacked at a particularly stubborn stalk of corn.

"I volunteered you to stay behind." Emilio felled a stalk with each swing of his machete, then tossed them onto the back of the wagon.

"Whoa! Volunteered? I think there might be some problem with your translation from Spanish to English."

Emilio paused from his job. "I was *born* in America!"

"Okay, then." Nicole put her hands on her hips. "You should know that *volunteer* is an action that can only be done by the person obligating themself to a project. I think the word you're searching for is *coerce*."

"I was trying to do you a favor." Emilio let his machete hang from his hand.

"By leaving me all alone with those two depraved men?"

"Number one, they're very decent people—personality-wise, if not from a hygiene standpoint." Emilio put his machete on the wagon and walked toward his wife. "And number two, you won't be alone. Anne Marie and Kim are staying at the compound as well."

"Oh!" said Nicole. "Need some women folk to cook and clean, I guess."

Emilio shook his head. "It's not like that. You'll be providing critical security while we're gone."

"No, I won't, because I'm going to San Francisco—with everyone else." Nicole picked up her machete and resumed her task, as if by so doing, it closed the subject to further discussion.

"You going to help me out here?" Emilio held his hands out to Josh.

Josh swung his machete. "Not my department. Sorry."

CHAPTER 13

And Jesus answered and said unto them, Take heed that no man deceive you. For many shall come in my name, saying, I am Christ; and shall deceive many.

Matthew 24:4-5

After not sleeping Friday night and working in the cornfield all day on Saturday, Josh had no further issues with insomnia. He slept like a rock. His mind was still fogged by dreams when he was awakened early Sunday morning.

"Dad, come on! You have to wake up!" Micah shook the bottom bunk at the front of the travel trailer where Josh was sleeping.

He fought through the haze. "What is it?"

Lindsey was standing behind Micah. "The news feed. It's Alexander. He just turned his head."

Josh climbed out of the narrow bed and slipped his feet into a pair of flip-flops. He pulled a tee-shirt over his head. Still wearing his sweatpants, he followed Micah and Lindsey out of the trailer and to the dining room of the bunkhouse barn. Josh was still unaware of the hour but figured it must be late as most of the other people from the compound were already up and in the dining area.

On the screen of the television, five men stood equidistant around the glass enclosure housing the body of Lucius Alexander. The men wore hooded white robes with red sashes. The back of the robes were embroidered with the red dragon ouroboros. The men chanted in a low whisper with their heads bowed.

Then, Josh saw it. Alexander's hand moved. Chills went up his spine.

Ernie was sitting at a table near the front. He pointed at the television. "I saw it! Right there! He moved. The corpse moved!"

Josh whispered to Micah. "I bet if you drew a pentagram on the floor, those five men in robes would be standing perfectly on the points."

It became apparent that Alexander was breathing. His chest began to rise and fall. Shallowly at first, then the breath became more obvious. Shortly thereafter, the five men in robes moved closer to the glass case. Still chanting, walking slowly and rhythmically in step with one another, they came to the stand where Alexander lay.

Next, Carl Jacobs walked onto the screen.

"I thought this guy went to Jerusalem to pray," Lindsey whispered.

"I suppose he didn't stay long," Josh replied.

"Maybe they built a wormhole portal from Jerusalem to Area 51." Micah looked back at his father. "I told you this was the zombie apocalypse. Alexander is the first zombie, but I bet he won't be the last."

Carl Jacobs signaled with his hands for the robed men to lift the glass case from over Alexander. Continuing their chant, they carried the covering away. Jacobs took Alexander's hand. Soon, Lucius turned toward Jacobs and opened his eyes. Jacobs whispered to the man and helped him to sit up. Lucius looked groggy and tired. Carl Jacobs helped him come down from the stand and supported him as he walked off camera.

"What the heck was that?" Anne-Marie exclaimed.

Josh looked on at the empty platform where Lucius Alexander had been only moments earlier. "I can tell you one thing, Jesus didn't need a helping hand to stand up when he came back to life."

George was sitting nearby. He turned to look at Josh. "I suppose they'll have some kind of news conference or something."

"You better believe it," Josh replied. "They'll milk this for everything that it's worth."

The back door opened and Craig walked in with his wife, kids, and another couple who looked to be in their mid-40s. The man carried an acoustic guitar.

"Good morning." Craig waved to the group. "It's illegal to have church, so instead, we'll just sing a few songs to Jesus with Frank and Mary Beth's help. Then, I'll talk about one of my favorite stories from one of my favorite books." Craig laughed and waved his hand. "I'm sure it's in the Unity Scriptures anyway."

Josh was slow to judge another man's servant, for to his own master he would stand or fall. But he felt a more direct defiance of the order to end religious services would have been appropriate. Craig was doing the right thing by still offering a time of worship, but something about looking for a loophole didn't sit right with Josh, even if it were only meant as a jest.

Craig turned off the television while Frank and Mary Beth got ready to lead the group in song. They sang four songs, then Craig walked to the front with a smile that almost seemed insincere.

He gave an extremely brief sermonette, which ran just over ten minutes, about keeping your chin up during tough times that was loosely based on 2 Corinthians 4:9. Although, he never took out his Bible if he even had it with him. He may have been speaking from memory, could have seen the verse on a refrigerator magnet as he was walking out the door twenty minutes prior, or it very well could be in the Unity Scriptures. Josh doubted Craig would have been able to get his hands on a copy so soon.

Craig said a quick prayer, then dismissed the service. He pointed toward the kitchen. "We're serving ham, baked beans, and my wife, Vivian's famous broccoli and rice casserole. You folks enjoy."

After the minuscule message, Nicole held Emilio's hand and led him up front to speak with Craig.

"What did you think?" Micah asked.

Josh looked down at his own attire. "Considering that I showed up in a tee-shirt and sweatpants, I'm probably not qualified to critique another man's methodology of having church. Besides, we're guests on his property. We had nowhere else to go. I'm very grateful to Craig."

Lindsey looked around. "Yeah, but a little light on the preaching, don't ya think?"

"Especially considering the undead antichrist," Micah added.

"Plus, we're all heading off on a mission that many of us won't come back from," said Lindsey. "I would think he would at least recommend that people spend a little time in prayer."

"Yeah," Micah said. "You know. Make sure you're right with God before you take off running into the fray."

Josh crossed his arms. "An action that I've been against from the beginning."

Micah put his hand on Josh's shoulder. "I know, Dad. But we're not here much longer anyway. Then, we'll have to live for eternity with the decisions that we made here. I'd rather die knowing that I went down fighting than to live on in fear."

"Fear and caution are two different things." Josh pressed his lips together.

Micah hugged his father. "Jesus said whoever wants to save his life will lose it, but whoever loses his life for His sake will save it. Like you said, we're out of here anyway. Might as well go out in style."

It pained Josh to think about such things, but he was happy to see Micah making his arguments with Scripture, even if he didn't fully agree with his son's path of reasoning. "Bravery and commitment are fine qualities, but it's important to be effective also."

"True," said Lindsey. "But we'll get through it. God is watching out for us."

"Come on, let's get something to eat." Micah led his young wife to the tables with the chafing dishes.

"I'll be right along." Curiosity got the better of Josh. He walked toward Nicole and Emilio where they were finishing their conversation with Craig.

Craig shook Josh's hand before heading to the food table. "Hey, good to see you. I'll be praying for you guys when you head off to San Francisco."

Josh asked, "You're not coming?"

"I can't. Someone has to hold down the fort. I'll be helping Anne-Marie and Kim with security. Plus, I'll be working with Junk and Pigpen to keep up ethanol production."

Josh looked at Craig's young children and his wife. "I totally understand. Thanks for the prayers."

"Let's get in line." Emilio headed toward the food.

"Aren't you going to tell him?" Nicole asked.

"Tell me what?" Josh asked.

"You go ahead," Emilio said.

Nicole put her hand around Emilio's arm and beamed. "Emilio accepted Jesus!"

"Oh, really? That's great!" Josh couldn't have been more surprised.

"Yeah," said Emilio.

"Is that what you were talking to Craig about?"

"Yep," Nicole answered.

Josh's mind was suddenly filled with thoughts. "When…I mean, why didn't you come to me? I've been talking to you about this stuff for years."

Nicole answered for Emilio. "You can be a little…"

"A little what?" Josh felt confused.

Nicole answered again. "Pushy. Aggressive. Hard-nosed. Judgmental. Legalistic. Should I go on?"

"No." Coming from anyone else, he would have been insulted. But Josh was used to fighting with his sister. They'd engaged in spats like this since they were children. He still loved her and thought little of it.

Nicole softened her tone. "He just needed someone with a lighter touch, that's all."

"Well, Craig certainly has that, I suppose." Josh looked at his friend. "I just want to make sure the truth doesn't get so watered down that it becomes ineffective. When did you decide that you wanted to commit your life to Jesus?"

Emilio tilted his head from side to side and exhaled as if slightly uncomfortable about the conversation. "Seeing Alexander get up off that slab really got me thinking that there might be something to all of this."

Josh stood behind Emilio in the food line. "Okay. But you understand that a personal commitment is different than just head knowledge, right? James says the demons believe in God, not only that but they tremble in fear of Him."

Nicole stood in front of Emilio in the line. She turned around to face Josh and rolled her eyes. "Can you ever just take a win? Emilio prayed the prayer that Pastor Craig led him in." She held out her open palm toward Josh. "Do you see what I mean?"

"I'm just looking out for my friend. I don't want him to have a false sense of confidence."

Nicole took Emilio's hand and pulled him out of the line. "Come on, we'll just go to the back of the line."

"Wait! Why?" Emilio followed reluctantly looking toward the chafing dishes as if they might be empty by the time they made it through from the rear of the queue.

"Because I don't want to stand in line with Josh or sit at a table with him. I'd like to sit and enjoy my lunch in peace."

Josh watched them walk away. He had a heavy heart for Emilio. He wondered if it was the Holy Spirit who had convinced Emilio that he needed Jesus, or if perhaps it was his sister's nagging spirit who had pressured him to concede.

CHAPTER 14

And the locust went up over all the land of Egypt, and rested in all the coasts of Egypt: very grievous were they; before them there were no such locusts as they, neither after them shall be such. For they covered the face of the whole earth, so that the land was darkened; and they did eat every herb of the land, and all the fruit of the trees which the hail had left: and there remained not any green thing in the trees, or in the herbs of the field, through all the land of Egypt.

Exodus 10:14-15

Josh stretched early Monday morning, attempting to limber up before another grueling day of working in the cornfield. He tapped on Micah and Lindsey's door before leaving the trailer to make sure they were awake. "I'm heading to breakfast."

"Okay," came Lindsey's sleepy voice. "We'll be there in a minute."

Josh proceeded to walk to the barracks. Upon arriving at the dining area, he found Junk making pancakes. "I didn't know you cooked."

"Flapjacks," said Junk. "That's about all I know how to make."

"Well, they look magnificent."

"Getya some," said Junk. "I'm makin' plenty for everybody."

"Thanks." Josh took a stack, drizzled syrup over them, and took his plate to one of the tables.

"Good morning." George joined Josh with his own plate of pancakes.

"Hey." Josh looked up with a smile. "Did you sleep well?"

"Yeah, I did." George began cutting his food into smaller bites. "Which is a good thing. We're going to need it."

"Why do you say that?"

"Just got off the phone with Solomon. Everything is all set."

Josh had managed to keep the mission out of his head. He wished he could have made it through breakfast before having to think any more about it. "Are they heading back?"

"Nope. They're going to meet us in Salt Lake City."

"When?"

"Wednesday morning. The operation is set for Thursday night after sunset. They've got commitments from about six hundred militia members."

"Thursday night." Josh suddenly lost his appetite. "When are we leaving?"

"First light tomorrow morning."

"How long is the drive to Utah?"

"About twenty-four hours."

"Then another twelve or so to San Francisco? Everyone is going to be road weary. We should have set up a camp 100 miles out from the objective rally point and taken a day to recoup from the drive. This is bad planning."

George replied. "It is what it is. We get in, do what we have to do, then get out. Once we're home, we can rest."

Josh poked at his food. "What's he planning to do? Roll 600 militants right over the bridge? That road is going to be heavily guarded."

"Nope. We'll be coming in on an oil tanker."

"An oil tanker. From where?"

"Little town called Martinez. Big oil refinery there on the east bay."

"That's not going to be suspicious? A big tanker rolling right up to the Globalplex?"

"We'll have inflatables, Zodiacs. We'll launch from the east side of the ship so not to be seen by peacekeepers watching the bay."

"Yeah, until we come around from behind the ship."

"They'll have a diversionary force that will already be in San Francisco. Those peacekeepers won't be paying any attention to the bay."

"I thought we were going to have heavy weapons." Josh let his fork drop to his plate.

"We'll have RPGs. Lots of 'em."

"What, like the ones left over from arming the Syrians?"

"Russian. RPG-7s."

"Where are we getting those?"

"Russia," George replied matter-of-factly.

"Russia? As in the Russians are giving them to us?"

"My enemy's enemy," said George.

"Yeah, I guess that makes sense. What about choppers? You know they'll have air support."

"We got some Grinchs. About 30."

"What's that?"

"The latest version of the Igla 9K38."

"Isn't that like a Russian Stinger?"

"Yeah, pretty much."

"Those are great if you can get the helicopters to sit still and not shoot at you long enough to deploy." Josh shook his head. "This sounds like a terrible plan; making a run at the Global Union's headquarters in a life raft with a handful of rocket-propelled grenades."

"Have a little faith." George gave his trademark warm smile.

"It's going to take more than a little." Josh watched Micah and Lindsey walk into the dining room.

Having finished his breakfast, George stood up. "Needless to say, today's corn picking activities have been canceled. We've managed to salvage some portion of the crop. Craig's family, Junk, Pigpen, Anne-Marie, and Kim will keep at it until the locusts arrive.

"Have your team get their gear together. Then try to get to bed early tonight. Like you said, we'll need all the rest we can get. Won't be much 'till we get home."

"Okay, have a good day." Josh watched the man walk away.

Lindsey and Micah joined Josh with their pancakes. "What were you talking to George about?" asked Lindsey.

Josh filled them in on the plan. "But we're going to have our own set of contingencies."

Micah finished chewing. "Like what?"

"Like we're going to drive our own vehicles."

"We can all fit in the pickup," said Lindsey. "You and Emilio up front. The rest of us in the back seat."

Josh took out his phone and opened the maps app. "I'm going to stash the El Camino a few miles out from the objective rally point. I don't want to get stuck out there if this thing goes belly up."

Lindsey looked on at the phone. "How far is the objective rally point from the Globalplex?"

Josh made an estimate from the less-than-perfect distance scale at the bottom of his screen. “By water from Martinez? Looks like a good 40 miles.”

Micah got up and switched seats to sit on the other side of his father so he could look at the map also. “Where are you going to leave the El Camino?”

“Right here.” Josh enlarged an area of the map. “Fairfield.”

“That’s what, twenty miles out from Martinez?” Lindsey asked.

“Yeah, about.” Josh nodded.

“So, if something goes wrong, we’ll have 60 miles to cover on foot?” Micah looked concerned.

Josh lifted his shoulders. “If something goes wrong, it could happen anywhere between the ORP and the Globalplex. We can’t stash the vehicle inside that area. You guys wear clothing that doesn’t mark you as militia. We want to be able to drop our rifles and blend right in with the population. If you have a full-sized pistol for your back-up gun, make sure you also have a compact pistol concealed in your waistband.”

“You’re frightening me,” said Lindsey.

“You should have already been afraid,” Josh replied. “The odds of coming home alive are very slim. This whole thing is rushed, and filled with opportunities for things to go catastrophically wrong.”

Josh stood up and walked to the serving area. He retrieved two large glasses of water, then brought them back to Lindsey and Micah. “Drink up. You need to hydrate as much as possible today.

Tomorrow, we won't be able to stop for very many restroom breaks. Then, once we get to the refinery, you won't have many chances to relieve yourself either. As of tomorrow morning, you'll have to limit your water intake."

Micah looked unhappy about the inconvenience but took a long drink.

Josh noticed his displeasure. "Or, we can stay behind. Provide security and assist with the harvesting efforts."

Lindsey drank her glass with determination. "No. I'm committed. I'll do whatever it takes."

"Okay then," said Josh. "I've got to inform Emilio and Nicole. I'll see you guys back at the trailer."

***

Tuesday morning, Josh looked at the warm pink glow coming over the cornfield to the east. He closed the door of his El Camino and placed the key in the ignition. Micah sat in the passenger's seat sipping coffee from a Styrofoam cup. He passed it to his wife who was sitting in the middle seat.

Josh picked up his radio. "George, our group is rolling out. We'll see you at the first rest stop past Iowa City."

George replied, "Tim, Clint, and Ernie are rolling with your convoy. Keep an eye out for them. They'll be in the white Charger."

"Will do," said Josh.

"Okay, be safe. Text me if you get into trouble."

Josh looked into the rearview. “Emilio, are you ready?”

The lights flashed on the pickup behind him.

“Tim?”

“Let’s go,” Tim replied over the radio.

Josh pulled out of the drive for the long trip to San Francisco.

The only possible location for anyone to steal a short nap was in the back seat of the pickup. So, once they’d arrived in Iowa City, Josh and his team decided that they would take turns getting a little rest. They made eye contact but did not interact with George’s convoy when they arrived at the interstate rest area. None of them wanted to be identified as being part of a large group traveling together.

Micah was the first to try getting some shuteye in the back of the pickup. Lindsey would be the designated driver of the El Camino with Josh riding shotgun for the next leg of the journey. “See you on the other side of Lincoln,” Josh called over the radio.

“10-4,” George replied.

They passed through Des Moines just before noon. Even though they saw few other travelers, Josh breathed a little easier as they drove farther away from the metropolitan area. He glanced into the rearview to see the pickup in the distance and the Charger even farther back. “I might close my eyes for a while if you think you’ll be alright.”

“Sure, go ahead,” Lindsey replied.

The seat didn’t recline, so Josh did his best to get comfortable by leaning his head against the window and stretching his legs toward the floorboard of the center console. Despite the disagreeable position, he managed to drift off.

***

Josh awoke to the sound of Lindsey's voice.

"Josh, I mean, Dad, I think you should see this."

He opened his eyes slowly. It was dark, as if it were late evening. "How long was I asleep?" He took out his phone to check the time.

"Only about forty minutes."

"It's not even one in the afternoon." Josh looked out the window and up at the sky.

Lindsey gave her impression of the cloud above them. "It looks like smog."

Josh shook his head. "No way. We're out in the country."

"A dust storm, perhaps?"

"It's been dry, but nothing like the kind of drought they've had in Africa over the past few months."

"Whatever it is seems to be getting lower," said Lindsey.

"Turn your lights on and drop your speed down to fifty."

Lindsey complied with the suggestion.

"Are you seeing this?" Emilio's voice came over the radio.

Josh pressed the talk key. "Yeah."

Suddenly, a loud thump hit the windshield. Josh called over the radio to relay his directions to the entire convoy. "Slow down. Drop it to thirty-five."

A second thump hit the windshield. Then a third—and fourth in quick succession.

"It's not hail." Josh watched as more objects hit the windshield.

Soon, a barrage of dark objects began assaulting the vehicle. "Bugs!" shouted Lindsey.

"Locusts," Josh corrected.

Suddenly, a swarm of locusts blanketed the windshield and Lindsey slammed the brakes. Josh called over the radio, "Stop! Stop your vehicles! Visibility is about to go to zero!"

"..en four…" The reply was staticky. "…wait…shhhh…nything…"

"What did he say?" In the soft glow of the dashboard lights, Lindsey looked horrified.

"I don't know. We can't even get a signal until these things pass." Josh had to speak loudly to be heard over the incessant buzzing.

"When do you think that will be?" Her voice was anxious.

Josh retrieved his flashlight. "It could be a while. It depends on how large the swarm is and how fast it's moving."

"Should I turn off the engine?" she asked.

"Not yet. Just put it in park and let it idle. We need to keep the lights on so another vehicle doesn't hit us from behind."

"I can't imagine anyone would try to navigate through this." Lindsey hit the shifter, then sat back away from the steering wheel.

"Most people wouldn't, but someone could get claustrophobic. They might panic and try to drive blind. Our tail lights could be the difference in a narrow miss or getting hit."

"Are these the locusts from the Book of Revelation?"

"They're part of the general onslaught of sword, famine, and plague, but no, these aren't the locusts of the Fifth Trumpet. Those will be no ordinary locusts."

"And you think these are?"

Josh shined his light on the aggressive beasts, some as large as five inches long, crawling across the windshield, as if ravenously searching out the smallest morsel of vegetation to consume. "Maybe not. But the ones from the Fifth Trumpet will have stingers like scorpions. So, as bad as this is, it gets worse."

"Great." Lindsey took out her flashlight. She pointed it toward the back window, which was also covered with the loathsome creatures. "I hope Micah is okay."

"They're probably less than a few yards away."

"I hope you're right. And I hope this ends soon. It sounds like we're trapped in a gigantic beehive, and I don't think I can handle it for too long."

Josh put his hand on her shoulder. "We'll get through it."

An hour passed before the first hint of natural light began to come in from outside. Josh turned off his flashlight. The brightness of the exterior light grew gradually. Josh picked up the walkie-talkie. "Emilio, Tim, can you read me?"

"I hear you." Emilio's answer was distorted. "It's broken, but I copy."

"What about Tim?"

Emilio responded again. "I've got him. He says they're a little creeped out but otherwise okay."

"Good. Looks like they might be letting up. I can see sunlight."

"Yeah, same here."

"Can I talk to Micah?" Lindsey asked.

Josh gave her the radio. "Sure."

"Micah?" she called.

"Hey, baby. You okay?" he asked over the radio.

"Yeah!" She smiled at the sound of his voice. "You?"

"Fine. I was asleep when we came to a complete stop. It wasn't the best way to wake up."

She giggled. "I guess not."

Josh watched out the window as the bugs began to fade. The scene was still hazy from the trailing members of the passing swarm, but he could see the landscape all around. "It's the middle of July and it looks like winter." The trees were bare—their branches like dead sticks. The ground was barren, stripped to the earth. "I've never seen anything like this."

Lindsey handed him the radio and put the vehicle in drive. "It looks like a wasteland."

"Apocalyptic." Josh pointed to the shoulder of the road, which was now visible. "Just pull to the side until Emilio and Tim catch up to us."

Minutes later, only a few locusts remained in view. The other vehicles caught up and they continued on their journey. The rest of Iowa was dusty and brown, scraped of vegetation by the bugs.

When they finally arrived in Nebraska, it was worse. Even the bark of the trees had been gnawed off. Trees and bushes looked as though they'd been pruned back, where the locusts had continued chewing after the green leaves were long gone.

"Do you think it will all grow back?" Lindsey asked.

"It doesn't matter. The coming plagues will annihilate most everything," said Josh.

CHAPTER 15

He teacheth my hands to war, so that a bow of steel is broken by mine arms. Thou hast also given me the shield of thy salvation: and thy right hand hath holden me up, and thy gentleness hath made me great.

Psalm 18:34-35

Despite the delay of driving through the swarm, the small convoy arrived on schedule at the rendezvous point outside of Salt Lake City Wednesday morning.

Solomon shook Josh's hand. "Glad you all made it."

Micah stood by his father's side. "I wasn't sure if we were going to for a minute."

Lindsey held her husband's hand and told of the harrowing encounter with the bugs.

Solomon listened with amazement. "Wow! I hope Craig and the others back at the farm can get the crop in before they make it to Indiana. I'm sure you guys are beat. Take a couple of hours before you get back on the road. I'm trying to stagger everyone's arrival at the refinery in California. We have control of the facility and the ship, but I don't want a bunch of cars with out-of-town plates showing up all at once and triggering suspicion by locals in the area."

"Especially with the 100 mark bounty on our heads," said Josh.

Emilio and Nicole walked up to the group. Emilio said, "I heard they busted an underground church in Montana. Brought in over 200 people."

Nicole added, "That's a big reward for someone."

Lindsey asked, "When Carole-Jean Harris said that people who couldn't successfully complete the re-education process would no longer have a place in society, did she mean the GU would lock them away for life?"

"I doubt it," said Josh. "I'm pretty sure they'll execute those who refuse to comply. I can't see them expending the resources to keep prisoners alive indefinitely."

Two hours later, Josh's convoy got back on the road. They continued through Utah, Nevada, and soon crossed the border into California. They made a brief stop in Fairfield to park the El Camino in the back of a big-box store parking lot. Next, they continued to the refinery in Martinez, California arriving shortly after midnight.

***

The next morning, Josh awoke to the sound of someone walking around in the huge industrial building. His back ached from sleeping on the concrete floor with nothing except a thin sleeping bag for padding. The dilapidated building was filled with hundreds of people lined up in rows sleeping on the cold floor. It smelled musty and damp. After a few minutes of stretching out the worst of the stiffness, he quietly crawled out of his sleeping bag and rolled it up. Josh carried his belongings out to the pickup and stashed them in the bed. He took out an MRE from his pack and dropped the tailgate. He sat on the back of the truck and ate breakfast while watching the warm glow of morning coming from behind the giant fuel storage tanks.

Solomon walked by as he was finishing. “Did you sleep?”

“Not much. But anything is better than nothing.” Josh rolled up the trash from his MRE.

“Hopefully we’ll be back in the comfort of the compound by Saturday.”

“That’s optimistic,” said Josh.

“I’m an optimistic guy.” Solomon slapped the side of the truck bed. “Briefing starts at 6:30. You might want to round up your troops so they have a chance to wake up.”

“Yeah, okay.” Josh waved as Solomon walked away. He went back inside the grimy quarters where the others were still sleeping. He went around and gently nudged them all, hating to ruin their much-needed slumber. Once they were all awake, Josh walked back outside and across the road to where the briefing was being held.

Josh found a good spot and arranged some old buckets for his group to sit on. The large empty space would soon be filled with six hundred militia members. Places to sit down would be hard to come by. Tim and Ernie were the first to arrive. George, Micah, and Lindsey came soon after. Emilio, Nicole, and the rest of the people from the compound trickled in one at a time.

Finally, the briefing began. The operation was explained by Solomon, a man from Idaho, and another from Texas. A map had been hand-drawn on several large pieces of poster board, then affixed to the wall behind the presenters.

The man from Idaho explained, "Three diversionary squads will take small strike teams into San Francisco and eliminate the electrical substations providing power to the Globalplex and surrounding areas. Once the facility goes dark, the balance of the fighters will launch an attack against the Globalplex from the tanker." He continued to provide a detailed explanation of the plan.

The man from Texas picked up where he'd left off. "A barrage of RPGs will be launched from the ship as everyone else rappels down the side of the tanker into Zodiac inflatable boats below. From there, we'll take the boats to the shore of the Globalplex and make our main assault."

When the man from Texas finished expounding upon the next leg of the mission, Solomon began the wrap-up. "Our primary goals are to destroy the Omniscience AI mainframe, which is in this building here, farthest from the shore. Our secondary mission is to eliminate all the personnel on the campus of the GU headquarters. The assault will commence around 10:30 at night, so the majority of the personnel will be in the residential building, which is the large glass structure right on the water." Solomon elaborated for a few more minutes.

"We'll have our watches set. Twenty minutes from the time the first Zodiac hits the shore, we'll initiate out retreat. As soon as we finish this briefing, we'll begin ferrying extraction vehicles down to Oakland. We have two locations. One is an industrial complex behind the city landfill and the other is an abandoned tile and marble warehouse about a mile south of the landfill." Solomon wrapped up the briefing.

Josh raised his hand. "If we have 300 people on 40 or 50 boats going to each location, that's a lot of traffic. Easy to pin down by helicopters which will be in the air by then."

"We'll keep a skeleton team on the ship. They'll provide cover for approaching aircraft," said Solomon.

Josh pressed his lips together. "You've got 30 surface-to-air missiles, trying to cover a couple of miles worth of open water from counter-assault by who knows how many choppers. It can't be done. If we had multiple retreat locations, at least we'd have a fighting chance. We'd be like trying to catch a swarm of bees."

Solomon nodded. "I hear what you're saying Josh. But we had to look long and hard to find even two locations that weren't under active surveillance. And besides, the SA-24s can go over three miles."

"Being able to travel that far and hit a target at that range are two vastly different things," said Josh.

"They've got infrared homing, so these are a little better than big bottle rockets," added the man from Idaho.

Josh crossed his arms. "Mmmhmm. Still, it's a lot of ground to cover plus the helos will be shooting back; and probably armed with substantially more missiles than thirty."

"Your concern is noted. But we need to get moving. We have a lot of preparation to get done in very little time." Solomon adjourned the meeting without taking any additional questions or comments.

Josh's further grumblings could accomplish nothing, so he kept them to himself.

After the briefing, the teams were assigned operational code names and tasked with various mission priorities. Josh's team, code-named Neptune, was to carry a load of RPGs to the building which housed the Omniscience AI quantum supercomputer. Tim's team and George's team would provide cover fire while Josh's team focused the RPG fire on a particular location in the side of the building. Once the outer wall was penetrated, another team from Idaho would be responsible for sending a barrage of RPGs through the opening to destroy the computer. All the teams tasked with using the RPGs and SA-24 Grinchs were given an abbreviated tutorial on arming and firing the weapons.

All 600 of the militia members practiced rappelling off the side of the tanker and landing in the Zodiac inflatable boats below. The training was intense and hurried, leaving everyone feeling tired. The force had just enough time to eat before making their final preparations.

At 8:00 PM. The last of the militia members boarded the tanker, and the ship raised her anchors. Moving at 15 knots, the short 40-mile trip would take over two hours on the rusted and weathered vessel.

Josh stood along the railing, watching the refinery begin to creep farther away. He handed two zip-lock baggies each to Micah, Lindsey, Emilio, and Nicole. "Put your phones in one of these and your backup pistols in the other."

They followed his direction. He opened up the map app on his phone. "If something happens and we get split up, the access canal that takes us to the tile warehouse is right before the San Mateo Bridge."

Lindsey said, "We can just follow everybody else. That's where half of the entire force will be heading."

"Unless everybody else is dead." Josh zoomed to another location on the map. "Which brings me to the next point. If this impeccable piece of planning, by some remote chance, happens to go down in a ball of flames, we'll head north instead of south. We'll slip beneath the bridge which connects Bay Farm Island and Alameda. The back side of Alameda is lined with private boat slips and marinas. Plenty of places to lay low if we have to."

"For the record," said Emilio. "The plan isn't all that bad, considering they threw it together in a matter of three days."

"Which is exactly the maximum amount of time one should invest when putting together something this elaborate." Josh frowned.

"Point taken." Emilio looked out at the water.

Josh felt frustrated over the situation. "They should have dedicated no less than two weeks just for recon. Then, another month should have gone into planning."

Micah turned to his father. "The GU is still reeling from the nuclear attacks. Plus, we've got momentum from killing Alexander."

Josh shook his head. "We gave him a nice long nap. If anything, we made him more powerful, at least in the eyes of his mindless followers."

"Micah's right," said Nicole. "Kick 'em while they're down. This is our best shot."

***

Shortly before 10:00 PM, the Golden Gate Bridge came into view. "Wow," said Lindsey. "I wish we could have come here under better circumstances."

Micah held her hand. "It's still romantic—maybe even more so knowing that we're here to take down the New World Order."

Josh failed to see the humor in the statement. He continued scanning the water and the skyline for signs of trouble.

"What's that island there, with the old skeleton of a building on top?" Nicole asked.

"Alcatraz," Josh replied grimly.

Solomon walked by. "That's the San Francisco Bay Bridge up ahead. As soon as we pass under it, we'll begin lowering the Zodiac into the water. From there, we'll have another seven miles until we're off shore from the Globalplex. The inflatables will remain tied off until we drop anchor and load up.

Josh looked at his watch. "So another half hour?"

"That's about right," Solomon replied.

"When will the diversionary teams take out the power?"

Solomon looked at his watch. "In twenty minutes. I've got to spread the word. See you guys on the other side."

Josh didn't like the sound of that. "Come on. Let's get our raft ready to lower into the water. We've got a lot of extra luggage to pass down with the RPGs, so I'd like to get a head start."

The team moved the heavy inflatable with the small outboard motor to the rail of the ship. When they reached the San Francisco Bay Bridge, they used ropes to begin lowering the Zodiac.

Next, Emilio rappelled down the side of the tanker and into the inflatable. Josh and the others lowered the RPGs down to Emilio to stow inside the small boat. After finishing with their gear, Josh's team helped Tim and George hoist their Zodiacs over the side. Emilio worked from below to make sure the lines didn't get tangled.

"Hey, think you guys can give us a hand?" asked another militia member.

"Sure." Josh waved to his team. "Micah, Lindsey, Nicole, let's help these guys real quick."

Josh and Micah lifted the Zodiac from the rear side, which was heaviest because of the motor. Nicole and Lindsey assisted from the front while the team assigned to this particular inflatable held the ropes ready to lower it over the side of the tanker.

Once it was in the water, the man who'd asked Josh for help extended his hand. "Thank you. I appreciate that."

"Glad to help. We're all in this together." Josh lost his smile as he noticed a morale patch on the front of the man's plate carrier. It was the head of a lion colorized with the stars and stripes of the American flag.

Josh walked away and pulled Micah to the side. "You and Lindsey get two of those SA-24s and lower them down into our Zodiac."

Micah shook his head. "Those are surface to air. We're only supposed to have grenade launchers."

"That guy has a Patriot Pride patch. I don't have time to explain, just do what I asked."

"Maybe it's just because they believed the news," Micah argued. "WNN gave Patriot Pride credit for killing Alexander."

Josh nodded. "Yeah, and the fact that no effort was made to communicate to everyone involved in this mission that Patriot Pride is a GU plant means this operation is compromised."

Lindsey joined the conversation. "If that team we just helped was working with the GU, don't you think they would have pulled their Patriot Pride patches?"

"They probably don't even know," said Josh. "But more than likely, they've passed critical information to Ethan Combs. We're sailing straight into an ambush. Now please, do what I've asked! And as soon as you're finished, get over the side and into the Zodiac."

Micah took Lindsey by the hand. "Come on. Let's just do what he says."

Josh found Nicole and said, "I need you to go ahead and rappel down. Get in the inflatable with Emilio."

"We've got another three miles," she countered.

"I know, just do it. Please."

"Okay." She checked her harness and clipped onto the rope while Josh helped her over the railing.

Josh quickly found Tim and George. He explained what he'd seen and pleaded for them to start evacuating the ship.

"You feel pretty strongly about this?" Tim asked.

"Absolutely," said Josh.

George seemed hesitant to follow his advice. "You sorta had cold feet about this thing from the beginning."

"Yeah, and this is why!" Josh felt incensed that George still refused to face the facts. "But I don't have time to argue. Do what you want. I've got to find Solomon and try to warn him."

Josh ran behind the various militia teams lined up along the rails of the tanker. Most were still in the process of lowering their inflatables. Josh could not locate Solomon. He called over the radio. "Solomon, where are you?"

His voice came back, "In the tower. We're supposed to be keeping radio silence unless it's an emergency."

Standing near the bow, Josh looked back toward the cabins which were more than two football fields away. It would take too long to cross the distance and get back to his team. "This is an emergency. The mission is compromised. You need to abort!"

"Josh! You're spreading fear!" Solomon replied. "Get off the radio and meet me on the bridge."

Josh hustled back toward the ropes leading down to his Zodiac. "You've got people affiliated with Patriot Pride on this ship. I'd say fear would be a very appropriate response. You need to call for an evacuation right now!"

"Where are you at? I'm coming to you!" Solomon sounded furious.

"I'll be the guy on the little boat getting out of Dodge." Josh placed his radio back on his tactical vest and ignored Solomon who seemed determined to lead the mission into a trap.

Josh finally reached the rail where the ropes to his inflatable were tied off. He heard the blades of a helicopter in the night sky above. "No! It's too late!"

CHAPTER 16

I will say of the Lord, He is my refuge and my fortress: my God; in him will I trust. Surely he shall deliver thee from the snare of the fowler, and from the noisome pestilence. He shall cover thee with his feathers, and under his wings shalt thou trust: his truth shall be thy shield and buckler.

Psalm 91:2-4

Josh looked up into the darkness but could see nothing. If the aircraft were here for any other purpose than to attack the tanker, the navigation lights would be on. Suddenly, Josh caught a glimpse of a rotor blade in the ambient lights of the city. He hurried to where the crates containing the SA-24s were stacked one on top of the other. He quickly released the latches which secured the lid. He removed the launch tube and armed the weapon system.

The helicopter was at least a mile away. "Let's see if these things are as effective as Solomon says they are." He hoisted the heavy tube onto his shoulder.

One of the other militia members saw Josh raising the launch tube toward the incoming aircraft. "Hey! What are you doing? You'll give us away!"

"It's a little late for that." Josh pulled the trigger. The missile shot out of the tube leaving a quick flash of light and a puff of smoke. The missile spiraled toward the helicopter and struck with a blast. Orange flames exploded in the sky illuminating the people on the ship as well as a phalanx of twenty Blackhawk gunships right behind the one Josh had just eliminated. Despite his present action and previous warnings over the radio, most of the militia members on the ship still appeared oblivious to what was about to happen.

Josh clipped his harness onto the rope and climbed over the rail. He called out to George who was staring up at the helicopters in unbelief. "You better get out of here while you still can!"

Josh began his descent down the side of the tanker to the Zodiac. He called out to Micah and Emilio. "Untie the ropes and get the motor going! Now!"

The two jumped into action to follow Josh's directive. Once in the boat, Josh pointed to Lindsey and Nicole. "Throw those RPGs overboard."

Lindsey seemed caught in a state of denial. "We need them for the mission!"

"Do it now! The mission is over. We're just trying to get out of here alive." Josh armed another one of the Grinch surface-air-missiles and rested the weight of it on his shoulder. "Emilio, get us out of here!"

Just then, the helicopters began sweeping over the deck of the tanker, ripping through the militia fighters with deadly six-barreled miniguns. Josh looked around for Tim and Ernie but did not see any other inflatable moving away from the tanker.

Micah turned away from the slaughter on the tanker to look at his father. "Aren't you going to shoot?"

"We can't do anything for the people on the ship. Deploying the Grinch would do nothing except draw attention and ensure that we die with them." Josh pointed at the two RPGs in the Zodiac. "Get those over the side. They're slowing us down."

Micah looked heartbroken but did as his father had instructed.

Josh continued to watch the skyline for any sign that his inflatable was being targeted. In the background he saw some small arms fire flashing from the deck of the tanker as the militia put up a useless attempt. Finally, another of the SA-24s launched but missed its target as the helicopters were now too close. The last Blackhawk swept the deck with its minigun before they all circled around for another pass.

"South! Go south!" Josh pointed for Emilio to change course.

"We can get behind the cover of Alameda faster if we go north," Emilio said.

Josh shook his head vehemently. "The GU Naval Air Base is at the north side of the island."

"Got it!" Emilio quickly turned the outboard motor to change directions.

Josh watched helplessly while the helicopters circled back around for a second pass over the tanker. However, someone on board the ship managed to fire another surface-to-air missile. The lead chopper exploded just before the remaining train of gunships began their assault. They remained high in the air for the second onslaught, releasing a barrage of Hellfire missiles which struck the bridge and cabins of the tanker as well as the deck.

"We should have listened to you," said Lindsey.

Nicole echoed her sentiment. "All of us."

"I'm sorry, Dad," said Micah.

"We'll have plenty of time for regret—if we survive the night, that is." Josh felt a lump in his throat over the hundreds of well-meaning fighters being slaughtered on the ship before his eyes.

The Blackhawks flew around for a third wave of assault on the tanker which now was glowing brightly with multiple fires burning from the bridge tower and the deck. The choppers peppered the ship with their miniguns for yet another round. This time, no one on the rusty old ship put up a fight.

Josh looked at Emilio. "Can you go any faster?"

"It's a single 70-horse-power engine pushing five people. This is the most you're going to get out of it," he replied.

Josh pointed toward the shoreline. "Then at least get us closer to the island. We're way too easy to spot out here in open water. Now that the tanker is finished, they'll start combing the waters for evacuees." Josh looked around for other boats in the water but he could see nothing in the dark.

Micah pointed toward the southwest. "Looks like the lights are all still on at the Globalplex."

"Of course they are. The diversion teams were probably the first to die," Josh said in a bereaved tone.

Nicole's eyes followed one of the Blackhawks. "That helicopter has his searchlight on."

"So does that one." Lindsey nodded toward the north.

"They're looking for survivors." Josh kept the SA-24 ready to deploy. He turned to see how much farther they had to go.

Emilio said, "We should reach the bridge in about five minutes. We can cut the engine and hangout underneath until they give up."

"Yeah, okay. That's our best shot." Josh gritted his teeth hoping that they could reach the cover of the bridge before being spotted by one of the six helicopters which now had their searchlights scanning the bay.

"This one is coming right toward us!" Nicole exclaimed.

Josh looked at the helicopter then the bridge. "We'll never make it." Josh targeted the helicopter and pulled the trigger. POOF! The missile shot out of the tube. Two seconds later, it struck the

Blackhawk which was instantly evaporated in a billowing inferno.

"They know we're here now," said Emilio.

"They know we're somewhere," Josh corrected, "But they don't yet know we're here."

Micah watched anxiously as they approached the bridge. "You bought us some time."

Josh took the rope of the Zodiac. "Quick! Help me tie off on one of these pilings. We'll climb on to the pedestrian bridge and head for those trees."

The team followed Josh's lead. "Leave the rifles in the boat."

"Leave our rifles?" Lindsey asked.

"Our best bet is to get as far outside of the search perimeter as possible and try to blend in. If someone sees us running down the street with AR-15s, we'll get caught for sure." Josh climbed up and over the railing to the pedestrian bridge and held out his hand to assist Micah.

Emilio was still in the boat. He held out his hand for Lindsey's rifle which she was attempting to take with her. "Josh is right. Come on, let's have it."

"But, but, this was my mom's rifle," the girl said.

"And she would want you to leave it behind right now so you could live to fight another day." Nicole gently took the gun from Lindsey and handed it off to Emilio.

Micah reached out for his wife's hand and helped her over the railing. "Easy. You got it."

The team was out of the water and onto the bridge before the next chopper flew over. They found a cluster of trees for cover and hid beneath them while the bright light of a helicopter searchlight illuminated the area all around.

Josh removed his pistol belt and took out the Glock 18 clone which he'd brought for his sidearm. He placed the pistol in his in-the-waistband holster, then removed the two spare clips from his pistol belt and stuck them in his pocket.

Emilio also tucked his Glock 18 into his pants. "It would've been nice to have some of those 33 rounds mags about now."

"Yep, it would have been nice to stay on the farm, too." Josh retrieved his phone and took it out of the protective bag. Josh opened the map application. "We need to get to the High Street Bridge before they lock down Alameda. Once we're in Oakland, we'll have a lot better chance of evading capture. Looks like it's about a mile. Micah, you and Lindsey stay back about twenty or thirty yards. We'll jog ahead. A group of two or three joggers looks less suspicious than a group of five. It's also harder to spot from the air."

Josh began sprinting at a moderate pace. Emilio and Nicole stayed relatively close. Lindsey and Micah followed at a distance. The group maintained a steady pace up Fernside Boulevard for about ten minutes before the sound of the next helicopter grew new. Josh motioned for the team to duck beneath a large fir tree. He, Emilio, and Nicole waved for Micah and Lindsey to hurry before the searchlight found them. They rolled under the cover of the low boughs in the nick of time.

Unfortunately, they'd not escaped the attention of the dog in the backyard. The large animal began barking incessantly despite Josh's attempts to calm the beast. As soon as the light of the helicopter was gone, the porch light came on where the annoyed dog lived.

Josh and the others rolled out from under the tree and resumed their sprint. This time, they stayed as a group and ran as fast as they could. Josh was panting heavily when he crossed on to High Street and saw the steel truss bridge only a few yards away. His side was hurting and his lungs ached, but he felt glad to be escaping the area. The sound of the metal grate floor of the bridge ringing with each step rejuvenated him, gave him an extra push.

Just then, a searchlight from an SUV shined on the group from behind. A voice came over the loudspeaker. "Halt or I'll shoot!"

Josh took cover behind one of the heavy steel beams. Micah and Lindsey were still not on the bridge yet. Josh drew his pistol and fired at the peacekeeper who had exited the passenger's side of the SUV. Josh waved at Micah and Lindsey. "Come on! Hurry!"

The peacekeeper opened fire. Another peacekeeper stepped out of the driver's side. Using his door as a cover, he aimed his pistol and began shooting.

Emilio and Nicole also took cover behind the metal trusses. Emilio aided Josh in laying down cover fire for Lindsey and Micah.

Micah grabbed his stomach and tumbled to the ground just before stepping onto the bridge.

Lindsey stopped in her tracks. "Micah!" she screamed.

Josh replaced the magazine in his pistol and switched it to full auto. He racked the slide and ran headlong toward the SUV. It was a reckless move but the only possible chance he had of saving Micah. Josh pulled the trigger and sprayed ten rounds at the peacekeeper on the left, then redirected his fire toward the one on the right. He hit them both, but in less than two seconds, the 19-round magazine was empty.

Josh hit the mag release and reached for his final magazine. Still running, he released the slide and changed the selector to semi-auto. When Josh reached the peacekeeper on the left, his stomach was bleeding. The man fired at Josh who took aim and quickly shot the peacekeeper in the head. The other was slumped against the driver's seat. Josh took no chances. He shot him in the head twice.

Josh looked around to be sure no other immediate threats were in the area. He waved at Lindsey and Nicole. "Get Micah up and get him into the back of the SUV." Josh went around to the driver's side, pulled the bloody peacekeeper away from the vehicle, then release the back hatch.

Emilio rushed to the SUV. He picked up the pistols from the dead peacekeepers and removed their spare magazines.

Josh helped the girls get Micah into the rear. "You two stay back here with Micah." He rushed to the driver's seat and closed the door. Josh turned to Emilio in the passenger's seat. "Think you can disconnect the GPS?"

Emilio looked through the glove compartment. "Maybe, if I had a screwdriver."

"Here's a small toolbox!" Nicole said from the back.

Emilio reached back to retrieve the kit as Josh raced over the bridge.

Josh turned north to get off of High Street. He weaved through the side roads to evade being seen. "We need a safe place where we can try to get Micah stabilized."

Emilio watched for additional peacekeepers. "We just gave them a new location to set up a search perimeter. We have to get out of here, or none of us are going to survive."

Lindsey spoke through her tears. "There! What about that marina? There must be some abandoned boats. Oakland wasn't even annexed as part of an OASIS city until a couple of months ago."

"That's a good idea, but we don't want to get stuck in this area," Emilio replied.

"Unless they think we're out of the area," Nicole added.

"Explain," said Emilio.

"You guys could take Micah to a boat and try to get him stabilized. I could take the SUV and keep driving. I'll get it out of town and ditch it. Then, I'll wait for dark and hike back. They'll never guess that you guys are still here."

Emilio replied, "Good idea. It might actually work. But I'll drive the SUV. You stay with Josh."

Josh pulled up to the marina. "Lindsey, find us a boat with some space. Emilio, help me get Micah out and carry him to the boat once we know where we're going. Nicole, look for the trauma kit. They have to have one somewhere in the vehicle. Then, collect the magazines, ammo, anything that could be of use and bring it to the boat."

Everyone began their respective tasks. Lindsey came sprinting back. "That cabin cruiser on the end with the aqua stripes."

Josh carried his son by the arms while Emilio took hold of his legs. They moved quickly toward the boat which Lindsey had indicated. Josh guessed the vessel to be nearly thirty years old. They found it vacant and neglected as evidenced by the green film on the plastic sheeting covering the cockpit. It was very likely that the owners had lost interest long before the collapse.

They got Micah down the stairs and into the sleeping cabin. Josh shined his flashlight around the area, then placed it on the nightstand in such a way as to be able to see what he was doing. The bed was dusty but clean. Nicole followed them in carrying a small red zipper pouch. "Here's the only first-aid kit. I'll keep looking and see if there's anything else."

"Thanks." Josh opened it and took out a pair of EMT shears. He turned Micah onto his stomach and cut away his shirt to reveal two bullet holes in his back. His breathing was shallow and Micah was unconscious.

Lindsey located a large 6-volt flashlight on the boat. She turned it on and placed it pointing up to act as a lamp for the room. Emilio put on a pair of nitrile gloves and opened a pack of gauze. He stuffed gauze into the bleeding wounds. Josh breathed hard, his heart wrenched with agony. "The bullets are still in there. We need something to sanitize these forceps."

Lindsey went to the bathroom of the boat. "I found rubbing alcohol."

Josh took the bottle when she brought it. He poured the alcohol over the instrument not caring that it was spilling all over the floor. "Bring me a towel."

Lindsey went to retrieve one from the bathroom. "Here."

Josh pulled the gauze out of one of the holes and began probing the wound. "Got something!" He pulled out a piece of lead. Emilio held out his hand. Josh dropped the object into Emilio's blue nitrile glove.

Emilio frowned as he inspected it. "It's a fragment."

The hope drained from Josh's spirit. "They were running frangible hollow point."

Emilio removed his glove. "Just try to keep him comfortable. I'm going to get the SUV out of here before a helicopter spots it."

"Be safe." Josh could think of nothing more than his dying son.

Emilio put his hand on Josh's shoulder. "I'll ditch the SUV, then head back in this direction. Once daybreak hits, I'll find a place to lay low. I'll wait for sunset to start moving again. But I should be here by midnight tomorrow night. If I'm not, leave without me. I'll see you back at the compound."

Josh knew the extreme risk Emilio was taking. He knew he may never see him again. He glanced up with pained eyes. "Thank you."

Once Emilio was gone, Josh took Lindsey's hand while she cried deeply and mournfully.

Less than a minute passed before Emilio walked back down the stairs of the boat. Josh looked up at his bewildered friend. "What's wrong?"

"Nicole. She took the SUV!" He tossed the magazines on the floor. "She left these in the captain's chair."

Josh felt another stab. He knew his sister's odds of getting back were slim. "She's in good shape. She's strong. She'll make it." He vocalized this bit of theatrics as much for his own benefit as for Emilio's.

Emilio gave him a disbelieving stare but said nothing. Josh gently rolled Micah over onto his back. He held his son's hand, crying silently while Lindsey wailed and moaned to display her agony.

Micah's breaths gradually grew faint, and finally—they stopped.

Josh felt alone.

CHAPTER 17

And the ransomed of the Lord shall return, and come to Zion with songs and everlasting joy upon their heads: they shall obtain joy and gladness, and sorrow and sighing shall flee away.

Isaiah 35:10

Josh barely noticed when the sound of sirens blared in the distance. He took no action. He was content to be shot down, to die beside his son. At least it would save him the pain of having to bury him.

Emilio, however, frantically began loading magazines with the rounds scavenged from the

SUV. “Come on, Josh. Don’t check out on me. You, too, Lindsey.”

Emilio loaded his pistol and continued getting ready for another fight. Neither Lindsey nor Josh reacted. Emilio left the sleeper cabin and looked out the small oval porthole window. He held his pistol tightly. “We need to figure out what we’re going to do if they find us. There’s probably a trail of blood from the parking lot straight to the boat.”

Josh had done all he could. He was ready to give up. The sirens came closer.

“They’re coming!” Emilio loaded Josh’s pistol and pressed it into his hand. Josh held the weapon limply.

“Lindsey? What about you?” Emilio held out a gun for her to take.

Her eyes were red and her face contorted by sorrow. She shook her head and squeaked out a phrase. “I can’t.”

Emilio ceased his prodding. “Okay. I’ll hold them off as long as I can. We did our best.” He continued looking out the porthole. The sound of the sirens reached a deafening crescendo, then began to fade. “They drove right by!” Emilio sounded excited. He repeated the information. “They drove right by.” This time, he said it with less enthusiasm, as if he knew they were in pursuit of Nicole.

Minutes later, a helicopter flew over. The brilliance of the spotlight illuminated the entire cabin. Emilio quickly turned off the flashlights. Soon, the tumultuous racket of the rotors passed over.

Josh looked at the pistol in his hand. He thought about his loss. Lindsey's loss. He knew Micah would want him to care for his young widow. He took a deep breath and searched for the will to continue the fight. He gripped the pistol tightly. "Pass me a spare magazine."

Emilio looked at him as if he'd risen from the dead. "Yeah, okay. You got it." He tossed him a mag.

Josh tucked it in his back pocket and waited for peacekeepers to come storming across the pier to the boat. However, they never came. The hours passed and no other sirens were heard. A few helicopters flew near but never again with the searchlights so close. Eventually, the first hint of daybreak crept into the cabin. Emilio had drifted off, but Josh could not sleep. Lindsey stared at her dead husband with eyes that seldom blinked. Josh thought about how he'd lay Micah to rest. It was something no parent should ever have to consider, especially in such a terrible situation.

Josh reached across the bed and took Lindsey's hand. "When we leave, I think we should douse the boat in gasoline and set it on fire. We won't be in a position to take his body with us, and I can't fathom the thought of leaving him here like this."

Her hand was limp. She didn't look up. Linsey's delayed response was faint. "Okay."

Emilio woke at the sound of the conversation. "That's going to draw attention."

"We'll figure out a way to delay the inferno." Josh hated looking at Micah in his present state, pale and stiff. He stood up and wrapped his son in the cover from the bed. Lindsey didn't object.

Emilio stood up and went into the galley. He rummaged through the cupboards. "I've got four granola bars that expired three years ago and a can of chicken noodle soup." He squinted as he looked at the bottom of the can. "Also expired." He handed a granola bar to Lindsey and one to Josh. Emilio glanced at Micah's covered corpse. "We'll save one of the bars for Nicole—for when she gets back."

Josh ripped open the thin plastic wrapper. The bar was in crumbles. "Did you see any water?"

Emilio poured pieces of the disintegrated cereal bar into his mouth. "No. The faucets have no pressure."

"I saw a hose." Lindsey looked at the porthole window. "At the end of the pier."

Josh was more familiar with the effects of dehydration than he cared to be. He hated to risk venturing out, but even more so, he could not chance having his entire team get sick and disoriented. "Okay. I'll go check it out." He looked out the windows and saw no other people around.

"Maybe I should go," said Lindsey. "People looking for a group of militants might pay less attention to a skinny little girl."

"She's right," said Emilio.

Josh didn't want her to be exposed, but if suspicions were raised, they were likely all doomed anyway. "Okay. Pull your sleeves down over your hands. Look timid. And make sure you can get to your gun quickly if you need it."

Lindsey did as she was instructed.

Emilio pointed toward the galley. “There’s a plastic pitcher under the sink.”

She retrieved the item before ascending the stairs. Josh watched through the portholes while she walked across the pier. She turned the faucet for the hose, but nothing happened. She looked toward the boat and shrugged. She began coming back.

Josh heard a muffled voice from outside. He saw Lindsey turn to look across the pier.

“What’s going on?” Emilio asked.

“I can’t tell. I’m going up top to get a better look.” Josh started up the stairs.

“Keep low,” warned Emilio.

“Yeah, yeah, I will.” Josh looked through the dingy opaque plastic cover. He could make out an old man standing on a nearby boat. He could hear the man offering to give Lindsey water. “Don’t go! Don’t go!” Josh said as if she might hear him through extrasensory perception.

Emilio climbed the steps behind and looked on with his pistol in his hand. “She’s going.”

Josh watched Lindsey walk over to the man. He filled her pitcher and gave her a gallon jug as well. Lindsey carried them both back to the boat.

Josh waited for her to get inside. “You shouldn’t have interacted with the man.”

She carried her plunder down the stairs. “He’d already seen me. It would have been more suspicious if I had ignored him.” She took a drink from the jug, then passed it to Emilio. “Besides, we needed the water.”

Josh took the jug from Emilio when offered to him. He smelled it as if he had the ability to detect any adulterations. Seeing and smelling none, he took a long drink. "What did you tell him?"

"I said it was my uncle's boat—that my boyfriend and I needed some time alone, so we came out here for a day or two."

Emilio looked at Josh. "It's a pretty good cover story. Especially on the fly."

Josh took another gulp, he slumped back down on the floor next to the bed where Micah's body lay. "You're right." He turned to Lindsey. "Quick thinking. Good job."

The day waned on with little sound around them other than an occasional squawking seagull or the creaking noises from the boat when a breeze disturbed the vessel from its absolute stillness. The sun faded and darkness returned. Josh turned on the large flashlight, preferring to drain its battery over his own tactical light, which he'd be taking when they eventually left. He watched Lindsey as she stared at Micah. She no longer held his hand or attempted to touch him. Likewise, Josh had ceased contact with his son's body, which was now cold and hard. He wanted to remember him as he was—as he would be, after they were reunited.

"How long are we going to wait?" Lindsey looked at Emilio.

The big man kept a vigil, looking out the portholes every three or four minutes. "Nicole will be back soon. She'll be here by midnight."

"And if she's not?" Lindsey asked.

"She will be." Emilio craned his neck to look out at the pier.

***

Midnight came and Nicole was not there. 1:00 AM, 2:00 AM, 3:00 AM passed, and Nicole did not return. Josh finished the last of the water from the jug. "We need to move while we still have the cover of darkness."

"Let's give her until 4:00," Emilio said.

"Okay," Josh conceded. "But at 4:00 we have to go."

Lindsey began gathering her belongings. She looked at Micah's covered body. "Where are we going to get gas?"

"I'm sure the boat has some in the tank," said Emilio.

"It's probably as stale as the granola bars," said Josh. "I can't imagine it will even burn."

"I could ask the old man for a gallon," said Lindsey.

"No way. It's after 3:00 AM. He's probably asleep, and we want to keep it that way," said Josh.

Emilio still watched out the porthole. "Those palm trees in the park haven't been cleaned since the world fell apart. Palm fronds will burn."

"They'll burn fast." Josh thought as he looked at the map on his phone. "We've got about a four-mile trek to the Redwoods. If we can jog at an even pace, we should be able to do it in an hour. I can't imagine their emergency response time is very good in this part of Oakland, especially for a fire on an abandoned boat. We should be in the park by the time they've even discovered that there was a body on board, and long gone by the time they've declared it to be a crime scene or connected it to us.

"Once we're in the park, we should at least be able to have fresh water. I've got a few silver coins. We'll try to buy food once we come out the other side of the mountains."

Emilio popped the pull-top on the can of chicken noodle soup. "We'll share this now. If Nicole isn't back, I guess we can divide up her granola bar."

Josh nodded. He also hated to give up on his sister, but he knew she had probably been captured long ago. Once the soup was gone, Josh and Lindsey went out to collect palm fronds from the surrounding trees. They were able to collect a large amount in a short period of time. Upon returning to the boat, Josh opened the top hatch window above the sleeper cabin and removed the plastic cover to allow maximum airflow. He and Lindsey stuffed the main cabin with the fronds with a slow, solemn grace, knowing this would be their last act of service for Micah.

They made several more runs for additional palm fronds and covered the entire lower area of the boat. Afterward, Josh looked at his watch. 4:00. He nodded to Lindsey and Emilio who gathered their belongings, including the empty water jug. Josh bent down with his lighter. "Goodbye Son. My precious, precious son." His voice broke and tears clouded his eyes as he struck the flame. "I love you so much." The first palm frond began to crackle and smoke. Josh collapsed onto the deck of the boat with a woeful cry.

Emilio pulled him by his arm. “Come on, buddy. We have to go.”

Josh wanted to cast himself upon the flames which were already blazing. He so wished he could lie down and be reunited with his wife and son, all the pain washed away. Emilio wrapped his arms around Josh and picked him up to his feet. “Let’s go.”

Lindsey even tugged at his hand. “Please, Dad. Let’s go.”

She’d always been so hesitant to call him Dad. But perhaps that was the gesture that gave him the will to live for one more minute, one more hour, and one more day. Josh pulled his eyes away from the flames. He turned and gave into Lindsey’s and Emilio’s urging. They picked up speed as they moved farther from the pier. Onto the road, they broke into a fast-paced jog. They maintained the steady clip up the overpass which crossed the railroad tracks and the interstate. Josh paused only for a moment once they reached the top. He looked back toward the marina to see the flames now in a brilliant blaze. He felt a certain satisfaction in knowing the fire was burning sufficiently to do its intended task.

CHAPTER 18

O thou afflicted, tossed with tempest, and not comforted, behold, I will lay thy stones with fair colours, and lay thy foundations with sapphires.

Isaiah 54:11

Josh held the water jug down in the flowing creek. He raised it from the water and gave it to Lindsey. She drank deep and passed the jug to Emilio. “Now what?”

Josh looked up into the dark woods. “We’ll rest for a few minutes. Dawn should be coming soon. Then we’ll be able to navigate through the forest.”

Emilio passed the jug back to Josh. “How far to Fairfield from here?”

Josh finished off the water then began refilling the jug. “Forty miles or so.” He looked at the map on his phone. “Trails will take us almost all the way to Valona.”

Lindsey looked over his shoulder. “Any stores along the way?”

“Probably not without getting off the trail. All the development through the hills looks residential.”

“Maybe we should hit that little minimart,” she said.

Josh shook his head. “It’s too risky. Anyway, it isn’t a twenty-four-hour deal. I don’t think they are even open yet.”

Emilio said, “Maybe not. But I bet they’ll be getting bread and bakery deliveries soon. Maybe Lindsey could take a couple of coins and purchase whatever the driver will sell her.”

“If the fire department or the police talked to the old man on the boat, he would have given them Lindsey’s description,” Josh shook his head.

“Okay, then,” said Emilio. “You go.”

Josh thought about the plan. He was smaller than Emilio, which made him less intimidating—especially for approaching a stranger on the street. “Yeah, okay. I’ll go. You guys stay back in the trees but remain where you can see me.”

The group walked back down the hill, staying inside the tree line. Few vehicles passed by. They waited for half an hour, and the first glimmer of morning came from behind the mountain. Finally, a bread truck parked in front of the market. Josh hurried out from cover and slowed his pace as he approached the truck. The driver unlocked the rollup door. The man looked muscular, which put Josh at ease. He figured he was less likely to be skittish about being approached by a stranger than a frailer individual might be. “Good morning,” Josh said.

The man turned to look at him. “What kind of hustle do you got going on?”

“No hustle.” Josh held his hand up. “Just an honest proposition.”

“I can already tell you my answer is going to be no, but you’re the first nutcase to come up to me today, so let’s hear it.” The man waved his hand as if Josh was responsible for providing his morning amusement.

Josh pulled two silver Eagles out of his pocket. “Do you know what these are?”

The man took one and examined it in the soft morning light. “Yep. I do now. Black market money.”

“Or, some people consider them to be collectibles.”

“Yeah, people who are looking for a way around the GU mark.”

“Fair enough,” said Josh. “To get to the point, I’m just looking for something to eat. I’ll give you both of these for a couple of loaves of bread, a bag of donuts, or a package of sweet rolls. Whatever you’ve got.”

“That’s a lot of money for a bag of baked goods.” The man inspected the coin closer. “You sure these are real? Silver was going for 15 marks an ounce last I heard.”

“They’re real, but you can’t eat ‘em.”

He looked at the coin once more. “I’ll take that bet, that they’re real.” The man pulled his cart out of the back of the truck and began loading it with trays of bread, dinner rolls, and cinnamon rolls. “Take whatever you can carry.”

Josh handed him the other coin. “Thanks.” He took two packages of each.

The man replaced them with products from other trays so his delivery wouldn’t be short. “I’ll buy the missing ones out of my pocket when I get to the next store. You in some kind of trouble, or something?”

“Nothing like that. Just a little hiccup with my bank account.” Josh walked away with his loot. “But if the GU were to get involved, they’d want those coins for evidence. Probably question you about why you’d need them in the first place, being a responsible global citizen and all. Could get messy.”

“I won’t say anything if you don’t.” The man pushed his delivery cart with the stacks of baked goods.

Josh walked briskly back up the hill. Emilio and Lindsey looked famished. Josh opened a pack of cinnamon rolls and passed them around. He removed his long-sleeved shirt and tied it off to make a bag to carry the food. The sun was rising and with hiking through the mountains, he wouldn’t be comfortable in anything more than his t-shirt anyway.

After scarfing down two of the breakfast rolls, he started up the incline. “Let’s get moving. We’ve got a lot of distance to cover.”

The trailhead was only a couple hundred yards from the main road. It led the group winding higher and higher up the side of the mountain. Then, a network of trails traversed through the Diablo Range. Lindsey walked by Josh's side on the wide, well-manicured trail. "It's hard to believe a place like this can exist so close to San Francisco and Oakland. Micah would have loved this."

Emilio stayed close behind. "Nicole would like it, too. We have to find her. We have to get her back."

Josh glanced over his shoulder. "We'll do everything we can. But for now, we're in no position to help anyone. We have to get back, nurse our wounds, and regroup."

Emilio replied, "If they have her, they'll be holding her in California, at least for now. We should find a place around here to regroup instead of going all the way back to Indiana."

"We have no weapons except our handguns and almost no ammo. We've been on the run for two days, and we have just enough food to get us back to the El Camino. I'm in no condition to participate in a rescue mission, even if I had the slightest idea of where Nicole is."

Lindsey turned around. "I can't imagine how hard this is for you, Emilio, but Josh is right. Even if we knew where they're holding her, we can't fight. It's all I can do to put one foot in front of the other right now."

Emilio said nothing but followed at a greater distance.

The group took only minimal breaks for the next six hours. Finally, they all gave out under a clump of trees.

"How much farther to Valona?" Lindsey asked.

"We're a little better than halfway," said Josh.

"I thought it was only like 20 miles." She lay back on the ground.

"That's if you're taking the interstate. The trail is, by definition, the scenic route."

"Well, we need to figure something out," said Emilio. "We can't spend three days getting back to the El Camino, then two more to get to Indiana. We need a more aggressive plan."

"Like what?" Josh asked.

"Like jacking a car."

"No! Absolutely not!" Josh scowled. "It's immoral, and it's out of the question."

"Immoral?" Emilio lowered his brows. "We're at war!"

"With the GU. Not with every unsuspecting citizen."

"Those unsuspecting citizens would dime you out in a heartbeat if they knew who you were. They'd take their 100-mark reward and laugh at you while they were spending it."

Josh shook his head. "Some would, some wouldn't."

"Yeah, well, I could pretty much look at their bumper stickers and tell you which ones would. And in this part of the country, they'll be in the majority." Emilio crossed his arms.

"Even so," Josh argued. "I'll not be reduced to a common thug."

“Okay then, be a self-righteous, high-minded thug.” Emilio stood up and started walking. “But it will probably cost your sister her life.”

Josh examined the map. “We can pick up the San Pablo Dam Road. It shouldn’t have too much traffic. Maybe it will cut a couple of hours off of our travel time. It doesn’t wind as much as the trail. We’ll substitute rural roads instead of the trails whenever we can. We should get to the bridge well before evening.”

Josh helped Lindsey up. “Are you okay to keep going?”

“Yeah. I can do it.”

The group soldiered on.

They reached the Crockett Hills Trailhead at 5:00 PM on Saturday. “The bridge is less than a mile from here,” said Josh. “I recommend we rest and try to take a nap. We want to have something in the tank in case we’re spotted by a peacekeeper patrol vehicle. The sun will set in a little more than three hours. We’ll be harder to spot at night.”

“I vote to keep moving,” said Emilio.

Lindsey took her boots off and rubbed her feet. “I can’t. I have to stop for a while. The El Camino is another twenty miles from here. You can’t possibly keep going without a break.”

“Maybe not, but I’ve got a few more hours in me.”

Josh shook his head. “We rest here. We’ll resume our trip at sunset. We’ll try to make up lost time when we get to the vehicle. We can drive non-stop. One person driving, one on lookout and one can rest in the back.”

Emilio huffed in anger. "I guess I'm outvoted."

***

Josh, Emilio, and Lindsey arrived in the parking lot of the big-box store shortly after 2:00 AM Sunday. All were completely exhausted, but Emilio still had the motivation to keep going. Josh retrieved the keys from inside the rear bumper and tossed them to Emilio who drove the first 300 miles. The team rotated positions as planned. They managed to find enough stations willing to trade gas for silver to get them home. Josh drove the El Camino into the driveway of the Indiana compound at sunrise on Tuesday.

The quaint farmhouse, small livestock barn, towering silo, and rows of industrial buildings they'd left days prior looked exactly the same. However, the surrounding landscape looked entirely different—entirely apocalyptic. The cornfields were shorn, only stubs of stalks remained, most less than six inches tall. The few trees that haunted the edges of the fields looked like something from a nuclear winter.

Anne-Marie was on watch at the entrance. She let her rifle rest on the sling and held the radio to her mouth. "Junk, you need to get up here. We've got survivors."

***

Josh woke up to the sound of someone banging on his trailer door. He stumbled out of his bunk and grabbed his pistol. His mind was in a haze. The lack of exterior light made him believe it must have been night time, or pre-dawn, he couldn't tell which. And his complete disorientation from the extended period without sufficient sleep prevented him from discerning what day it was.

He felt dizzy, as if still partially asleep. He steadied himself against the narrow partition walls of the trailer. Lindsey came out of her room with a look of fright and an AK-47. "Who is it?"

Josh crept to the small window and peered out. He let out a sigh of relief followed by a grunt of aggravation. "It's Emilio." He opened the door. "What's wrong?"

"It's 4:00 AM. You guys have been asleep for at least twelve hours, maybe more." Emilio walked up the trailer steps.

"Considering what we've been through, I think that's justified," said Josh.

"I'm still tired, too, but we need to gear up and get back on the road," said Emilio.

"Road to where?" Lindsey asked.

"Back to California. We have to get Nicole."

Josh plopped down at the small dinette table. "We don't even have a plan."

"It's a thirty-hour drive. We've got plenty of time to come up with one."

Lindsey looked at Josh for support. "Every inch of my body aches. I can't imagine we'd be very effective if we ran off half-cocked right now. Shouldn't we take at least one day to recuperate?"

Emilio interrupted, "You don't have to come. Nicole isn't your responsibility, but Josh and I need to get moving. We should be ready to roll by first light. I've already got food, fuel, and ammo in the El Camino." He glanced at Lindsey's rifle. "I packed 7.62 since I assumed we'd all be running AKs."

Josh yawned. His brain slowly came back online. "Lindsey is right. We need a strategy before we redeploy. We'll be much more likely to succeed if we have a well-thought-out scheme. We don't even know where Nicole is at this point. Setting out completely uninformed and totally unprepared is the worst possible thing we could do for Nicole."

Emilio looked unhappy with Josh's response. "Okay then, let's start brainstorming. What's the plan?"

"Meet me at the dining facility in an hour. We'll get something to eat, have some coffee, and be in a better position to come up with an idea." Josh stood up from the small table. "I need to stretch, get a shower, and spend some time in my Bible. Not only am I physically exhausted, I'm mentally and emotionally beat also. I want to bring Nicole home. But, you're going to have to be patient with me."

"I want to help, too," said Lindsey. "I don't want to lose another member of our group. But like Josh said, I'm still mourning Micah, and I've got nothing left inside to keep me going. Please, Emilio, just give us a little time to heal and recharge. We're not giving up on Nicole."

Emilio let himself out the door. His voice was gruff. "One hour."

CHAPTER 19

And such as do wickedly against the covenant shall he corrupt by flatteries: but the people that do know their God shall be strong, and do exploits.

Daniel 11:32

Josh felt much more awake and ready for whatever came next after praying in the shower and reading a few Psalms. The simple effort of putting the things of the Spirit before the things of the flesh gave him a sense that the weight of the universe was no longer on his shoulders and that God was still in control. He looked up for one last quick prayer before walking into the dining facility. "God, please, I really need your wisdom, comfort, and guidance right now."

Emilio was waiting inside. "I couldn't sit still, so I made breakfast. Coffee, eggs, pancakes, and more eggs."

Lindsey walked in right behind Josh. "Why so many eggs?"

"Looks like the thirty-plus chickens on the property are laying more than the few residents of the compound can consume." Emilio sat down and began eating.

Lindsey took a seat next to him. "Can we pray first?"

"Oh." Emilio paused. "Sure."

"Would you like to do the honors?" Josh folded his hands and looked at Emilio, who claimed to now be a child of God.

Emilio looked uncomfortable. "Why don't you go ahead?"

Josh closed his eyes. He asked for God to protect Nicole, to grant them all peace through this difficult time. He thanked Him for the opportunity to be Micah's father, and for the hope that they'd all be reunited soon.

Lindsey reached over after he'd finished. She took Josh's hand with tears in her eyes. "That was beautiful."

Emilio resumed eating. "I've identified three women's incarceration facilities in proximity to San Francisco. They were previously state and local, but now all three fall directly under GU jurisdiction. They've got the county jail, obviously, downtown. Then, the old state facility in Dublin, which is about fifteen miles south-east of Oakland. Then the Central California Women's Facility in Chowchilla, which is about 120 miles southeast of Oakland. They have two facilities across the street from one another. One is for males and one for females."

Josh asked, "San Francisco County only has one facility? I find that hard to believe."

"All the women are kept at jail number four, which is downtown."

"Prior to the GU takeover," Josh added.

"Yeah, but I can't see why they'd change it," said Emilio.

"Alright, assuming that's true, we still have three possible locations." Josh swirled his coffee in his cup as he thought.

Lindsey looked at the map on her phone. "What about San Mateo County? They have a large women's facility. Since jurisdiction isn't an issue anymore, she could be there."

Emilio scowled at her as if she were complicating the program. "Okay, four possible locations."

"Yeah, four." Josh looked up. "We need to narrow it down to one, with a zero margin of error."

"I don't know how we can do that. It's not like we can call and ask for her location." Emilio pushed his half-eaten plate of food back on the table. "She's a high-risk detainee. The GU won't even acknowledge that they have her."

Lindsey looked like she had something to say but was hesitating to speak.

Josh looked at her. "What is it? We need your input. It's as valuable as anyone else's."

She glanced at Emilio then back to Josh. "They didn't keep you at a standard detention facility. They had you in an interrogation cell in the basement of an FBI field office. Who knows how many black sites the Unity Enforcement Agency has around the country?"

Josh felt overwhelmed by the situation. "She's right. Nicole could be anywhere."

Lindsey moved a piece of pancake around her plate with her fork as if trying to mop up all the excess syrup. "If only we knew somebody inside."

Josh looked at the light reflecting off the surface of his coffee. After a moment of contemplation, he said, "Maybe we do."

"Who?" Emilio sounded anxious for the answer.

Josh looked at his friend. "Carole-Jean Harris."

Lindsey's excited eyes fell back to an appearance of despair. "I meant someone sympathetic to our cause."

"Perhaps we can persuade her to be sympathetic to our cause," said Josh.

Emilio's eyes glared with anger. He pounded his fist on the table. "Yeah, we'll kidnap every living relative that she has! Then, we'll mail her a severed head every other day until she sets Nicole free!"

"No, no, no!" Josh held up his hand.

"Then what?" Emilio's question was burning with fury.

"I'll offer a trade," said Josh.

"What could you possibly give her that she'd want more than Nicole?" Lindsey looked at him as if his statement were the most absurd thing she'd ever heard. Her eyebrows turned down at the corners in an expression of worry. “No! No, Dad!” She reached for his hand.

Josh felt moved by her concern. He held her fingers. “Not really. Just as a ruse.”

“Carole-Jean would expect nothing less from you,” said Emilio. “She’ll be ready for anything.”

“I know. But it will be too tempting. She’ll at least go along with it, to try to flush me out,” Josh replied.

“Yeah, and when she does, she’ll spring her trap. It’s too risky.” Lindsey shook her head.

“Not if I’m nowhere to be found” Josh smiled.

“Where will you be?” Emilio narrowed his eyes, as if trying to guess the rest of the plan.

“Three miles away from the meet location.” One side of Josh’s mouth turned up. “Looking at the screen of a drone controller.”

Lindsey’s eyes opened wide. “Then, when you don’t show up, they’ll turn around and go home. Meanwhile, you’ll be following from a distance to see where they take Nicole.”

“You have a drone?” Emilio asked.

Lindsey answered, “Micah does—did. I mean, we still have the drone.” She looked at the table. “Just not Micah.”

“It’s a good idea. I’ll tell her that I’ll surrender myself as well, to sweeten the pot.” Emilio nodded. “Although, if it doesn’t work out, I’m keeping my idea for plan B.”

“It will work,” said Josh. “It has to.”

Junk walked into the dining area. “Good morning. I thought you folks would sleep until lunchtime, at least.”

"That was the plan," said Lindsey. "At least for me."

Josh replied, "We had some pressing business to discuss." He filled Junk in on the plan to rescue Nicole.

"You folks are going to need some help." Junk walked over to the coffee pot.

Josh said, "It's dangerous. A lot could go wrong. I couldn't ask you to get involved. But we have to go. If it hadn't been for Nicole driving the patrol vehicle away, we'd have all been killed or captured."

Junk brought his coffee to the table and pulled up a chair. "I felt bad about staying behind after what happened. Pigpen, too." He blew the steam from the top of his beverage and took a sip. "So did the girls, for that matter. I understand that it's risky, but if you'll have me, I'd like to come along."

Josh felt grateful. "We'd be happy to have you."

"What about Craig and the others?" Emilio asked. "Would they come?"

"I'll ask," Junk replied.

The back door of the barracks swung open. Anne-Marie rushed in. "I just got a text from Dana! She's in Yosemite with Tim and George. George is injured badly."

"What about Solomon?" Lindsey's eyes lit up.

"No. He's gone. He died on the tanker with most of the others." Anne-Marie lowered her gaze.

Junk stood up. "How did they get to Yosemite?"

"Her explanation was brief," said Anne-Marie. "But they found an abandoned house and hid out for two days. George caught a bullet in his shoulder.

They thought they had George stabilized, but he took a turn for the worse. They *borrowed* a vehicle and drove until they ran out of fuel. They're holed up in a ranger station next to a ski lift. The building had some first aid supplies, but they're low on food and have no money."

Anne-Marie looked at the others. "We have to go get them. George isn't going to make it otherwise."

Junk looked at Josh. "Think we could do both? Kim is a nurse. We can take some antibiotics up there. Kim can work on getting George back to health. The rest of us can try to spring Nicole."

Josh asked Emilio, "Are you okay with that?"

"I guess I'll have to be. We need all the help we can get."

***

By noon, the group finished their final preparations for the trip out west. Josh stocked the bed of the El Camino with food and provisions for an extended stay. It was possible that George would not be the only injured member of the team by the time the rescue mission was complete.

Kim loaded her Camry with her medical bag as well as weapons and various supplies for herself and Anne-Marie.

Junk and Pigpen stocked Junk's van with tents, sleeping bags, and the other necessities to set up a base camp. The body of the van was finished in gray primer while the front left quarter panel was a vibrant yellow, the hood, dark blue, and the passenger's door was maroon. Junk had enough fuel cans in his miss-match colored van to get all three vehicles to California. They'd have to barter for gas on the way back.

Pigpen smiled revealing his stained crooked teeth. "Lindsey, you can ride in the van with us. That way you wouldn't have to sit in the middle of the seat between Josh and Emilio."

She replied, "Thank you for the offer, but we're going to take turns sleeping in the back of Kim's Camry."

Josh walked over to Junk, who was placing a box of MREs in the van. "Craig isn't coming?"

"Naw. Said he'd better hang around in case any other survivors show up. Plus, him and Vivian will be the only ones left to keep an eye on things." Junk closed the sliding door and got in the driver's seat. "We've got plenty of us."

"Yeah. I appreciate your help." Josh walked back to the El Camino, got inside, closed the door, and started the engine.

"When are you going to call Harris?" Emilio buckled the passenger's side seatbelt.

"Nevada. That way, we're close enough to meet anywhere in California within 24 hours." Josh put the vehicle in gear.

"Think she still has the same number?"

"Yeah," said Josh. "If not, we'll still get a hold of her. She'll take the call. She won't be able to resist." Josh put the El Camino in gear and led the convoy toward the interstate.

***

The next two days were filled by a long, arduous, and uneventful cross-country road trip. The group passed through Carson City, Nevada on Friday morning. They were stiff and tired, but otherwise no worse for wear. Including his prior trip with Rev to bring Mackenzie to Kentucky, it was Josh's third such excursion. He'd still not recovered from his last trip.

For the final leg of the journey, Lindsey drove the El Camino while Josh navigated. Emilio was riding shotgun with Anne-Marie while Kim slept in the back seat of the Camry. Josh picked up his radio. "We'll pull to the side for a short break after this bridge up ahead."

The convoy crossed over the Carson River and stopped on the wide gravel shoulder. The landscape was flat and even for miles ahead and miles behind. However, to the west, the flatness ended abruptly as majestic mountains shot up suddenly, as if out of nowhere. Josh exited the vehicle and walked back to the Camry. Emilio stepped out of the back. "You going to make the call?"

Josh felt nervous as he activated the new burner phone and prepared to dial the number. "Yeah, this one is for all the marbles." Once his communications with Carole-Jean Harris were finished, this phone would be crushed into a million pieces and sown to the wind.

Junk and Pigpen stepped out of the van to stretch their legs as did the other road-weary travelers. Josh looked on at the small scrap of paper where he'd jotted down Carole-Jean's number. He entered the digits carefully. Then, he pressed the call icon. He held his breath as he listened.

"Hello?" Her dry and emotionless voice was unmistakable.

"Carole-Jean," said Josh.

"Who is this? How did you get this number?"

"You gave it to me. This is Joshua Stone."

She was silent for a moment, as if at a loss for words. "You've got some audacity. How can I help you, Mr. Stone?"

"I have a proposition."

"Go on, then. Let's hear it."

Josh proceeded to set the trap, offering his life for that of his sister's.

"What makes you think I have your sister?"

"Pardon me if I was mistaken. I'm sorry to have wasted your time. I'll let you get back to whatever it was that you were doing."

"No, no, don't hang up. Just give me a moment to look in my system," she said.

"I'll give you a few minutes to do that and call right back." Josh ended the call.

Josh felt as if he were performing for a live studio audience. All of his traveling companions watched him with bated breath.

"Why did you hang up?" Kim asked.

"To disrupt any tracking program she was running. She'll answer when I call back. Few things would make this woman happier than to see my head on a silver platter." Josh watched the minutes tick by before redialing the number. Finally, he did.

"Joshua, how nice to hear from you again. We have Nicole. Although not for long. She's been deemed unfit for rehabilitation. The UEA has marked her for termination. I must admit, I find your proposal tantalizing, however, it seems like a lot of effort on my part to trade one terrorist for another. What's in it for me?"

"I think we both know you'd rather terminate me than a hundred other patriots."

She laughed. "Even if that were true, I have to be a responsible steward of the resources to which I've been assigned."

Josh paused and looked at Emilio who gave him a nod. Josh replied. "Agent Emilio Vega will also turn himself in."

"Ah, Agent Vega! Your nefarious sidekick. I'm sorry to hear that he's still alive. But this certainly makes the deal a little easier to sell to my overseers."

"Don't play games with me, Carole-Jean. We both know you've been given carte blanche as the director of the UEA."

"Okay. I'll call you back at this number to tell you when and where to make the exchange."

Josh countered. "I'll call you back in twenty-four hours. I won't be keeping the battery in this phone. Don't forget, I'm very well versed in what the GU can do remotely with a cellphone."

"Very well. But don't try anything with me, Joshua. Otherwise, your sister's execution will go from a quick, nearly-painless beheading, to a long, drawn-out ordeal where she dies very, very slowly." Carole-Jean Harris ended the call.

"Beheading? Is she serious?" Lindsey looked at Josh.

Junk frowned grimly. “We’d heard rumors—over the Ham radio. But this confirms it.”

Pigpen pulled out a fragment of something which had been caught in his unkempt beard. He examined it as if considering whether to eat it or cast it aside. “I suppose it’s the GU’s way of winning hearts and minds for their new unity campaign.”

“Fear is a good motivator, I suppose.” Kim shoved her hands in her pockets.

Anne-Marie looked at the others. “Beheading? That’s barbaric!”

Josh hoped his plan would work. “We should get back on the road. We still have about another five hours of driving to get to George and the others.”

CHAPTER 20

And I asked, "What is it?" He said, "This is the ephah basket going forth. This represents their iniquity throughout all the land." The lead cover was lifted, and there was a woman sitting in the ephah basket. And he said, "This is wickedness." And he threw her back into the basket and then thrust back the lead stone over its opening.

Zechariah 5:6-8

Friday evening, the convoy arrived at the Badger Pass Ski Area inside Yosemite National Park. Josh and the team found everything abandoned, just as Dana had described. Kim and Anne-Marie took the medical bag and hurried to the small A-frame building marked *Ranger Station.*

Josh, Emilio, and Lindsey grabbed their AK-47s.

Pigpen exited the driver's side of the van. "What do you want me and Junk to do?"

Josh pointed to the A-frame building. "Check on the girls. Take some food and water with you. Dana and the others are probably famished. We're going to have a look around, make sure there aren't any other people using this location as a base of operation."

Junk held up his radio. "Give us a holler if you need us."

"Thanks," said Josh. "Keep your rifles near."

Josh led the team for a quick sweep of the area. "We can pull the vehicles up beneath that carport. It will make them more difficult to spot from the air." They walked around the parking lot, then up through the tall grass below the ski lift. "I bet this place is pretty in the winter with all the snow."

"I think it's nice even in the summer," Emilio said.

"What exactly are we looking for?" Lindsey asked.

"Signs of recent human activity." Josh said. "We don't want to be surprised by any other groups who might return from a scavenging trip in the middle of the night."

"Wouldn't Dana have seen them by now?" Lindsey inquired. "They've been here for two days."

"They've been in the ranger station. It's too small for all of us to fit in. Another group could have been coming and going in and out of the main building without Dana being aware of them." Josh scanned the area meticulously.

"So we'll be staying here?" Lindsey studied the large building. "Does it have hotel rooms?"

"No," Josh replied. "Which is good for us. It makes it less appealing to other groups as a long-term shelter. But it will serve our purposes well, if it's not inhabited, that is."

Josh, Emilio, and Lindsey finished checking the perimeter, then made their entry into the main building. Emilio pulled the door open. "The lock has already been broken."

Josh looked inside. The decor was dated but reminiscent of a grand timber-frame lodge. "If someone were living here, they'd have it secured by some other means."

Lindsey cautiously walked in and surveyed the interior of the building. "They have a snack bar that looks like it's been looted already. Equipment rental; we don't really need skis. Oh, there's a gift shop!" Josh and Emilio followed her in, continuing to scan the area.

Emilio pointed toward the front of the building. "Multiple entry points. It's a lot to guard. What about the little administrative trailer across the street?"

Lindsey looked at the sparsely stocked carousel rack of stuffed animals. "I like it here. Another way of saying multiple entry points is multiple exits. Getting hemmed up in a small space is worse than having a porous camp." She took a small black bear from the rack and pulled at his ears with her thumb and index finger, as if checking the quality of the stitching or perhaps simply enjoying the softness of its synthetic fur.

"She's right," Josh defended. "We're ten people including George, Dana, and Tim. If we were to get hit in that admin trailer, it would be like shooting fish in a barrel for our attackers."

Emilio pointed to the second level where seating for a coffee shop looked out over the bunny slopes. "Okay then, let's at least take the high ground."

Lindsey stuffed the small bear in her shirt and lifted her AK-47 to continue clearing the building. "Fine by me. Let's check it out."

Josh walked slowly up the stairs to the mezzanine. He led the team past the tables and chairs. He checked behind the counter and inside the back room where a small office was located. "Looks clear. I'm going to check on George. I'll tell everyone that we're going to set up camp here. You guys can move all of the tables and chairs. Tip the tables over on their sides against the railing. They might not stop a bullet, but at least they'll block the view from the floor below."

"10-4," said Lindsey. "The office has carpet on the floor."

Josh knew what she was hinting at. "Okay, you and the other girls can set up the office for your sleeping area."

"Thanks," she said.

Josh maintained awareness of his surroundings as he descended the stairs to the main floor, and out to the ranger station. When he walked inside, he saw George unconscious on a military cot. Dana,

Tim, and the others watched him quietly. "How is he?"

Dana glanced up with worried eyes. "Not good."

Kim said, "I cleaned and dressed his wound. I mixed the ciprofloxacin with some homemade saline solution and gave him an injection. Now we have to wait and see if his body responds."

Josh looked at the bottle of fish antibiotics next to the plastic cup on the table by Kim's medical bag. "You gave him fish antibiotics?"

"They're made in the same factory as human antibiotics," Kim said.

"Oh." Josh looked at George whose skin was pale. "Septic shock?"

"Yeah," said Kim. "I'm afraid so. The Cipro may not be enough, but it's all we've got."

"I was sorry to hear about Solomon." Josh squatted near Dana and put his hand on her shoulder.

She nodded. "Thank you. My condolences to you as well. We should have listened to your warnings."

Tim echoed the sentiment. "She's right. That's all George could say the whole time we were hiding out."

"I've had plenty of regrets of my own over the years. They're as worthless as a book of wet matches. Don't waste any more time on them." Josh looked at the others. "We're setting up camp on the second floor of the main building. Emilio and I can carry George's stretcher if it's okay to move him."

Kim stood up and began placing her medical supplies into her bag. "Just be gentle. We've done all we can for him at this point."

"Okay." Josh left the station to retrieve a load of supplies from the El Camino. After wagging them up the stairs, he enlisted Emilio and Lindsey to get George relocated. The others chipped in with getting the food, ammo, and bedding upstairs. Evening came and overwatch shifts were assigned. After two days on the road, Josh welcomed the opportunity to stretch out on his sleeping bag. Despite being directly on the hard tile floor, he slept soundly until it was his turn to keep watch.

***

Saturday morning, Josh checked the time on his watch. He rolled his feet to make less noise as he walked over to Emilio's sleeping bag. He nudged his old friend gently. "You're on deck, big guy," he whispered.

Emilio rolled over with his eyes swollen. "Okay. You going back to sleep?"

"No. I've got to go call the Wicked Witch of the West."

"Yeah, but that's like a five-minute job." Emilio sat up.

"I'm going to Sacramento."

"To make a call?"

"Yeah. She'll figure out what cell towers I'm pinging. Going to Sacramento will keep this place out of the search perimeter once we've made our move."

"We're not coming back here once we're done."

"I hope we don't have to," said Josh. "But I'd like to have the option." He looked over at George lying motionless on the cot. "In case we have people with injuries that need treating. Some things can't be done in the back of a moving vehicle."

"How far is Sacramento?"

"Seven hours, round trip."

Emilio slipped his feet into his boots. "You should let me tap one of the others for watch duty so I can come with you."

Josh shook his head. "No. They need you, for leadership. Dana's the only other one really qualified, and she's still pretty rattled by her ordeal."

"I'll come with you," said a feminine voice.

Josh hadn't noticed Lindsey standing behind him. "Are you sure?"

"Let her tag along," Emilio said. "You need a second set of eyes and ears."

"Okay." He turned to Lindsey. "Rifle and a sidearm. We're traveling light." Josh grabbed his gear and headed down to the El Camino.

Soon, the two of them were on the winding mountain road driving to Sacramento.

Lindsey reclined in the passenger's seat and got comfortable. She took the small stuffed black bear from her bag and placed him on the dashboard facing out at the road. Next, she opened an MRE and started her breakfast.

Josh glanced over at Lindsey. Her attachment to the stuffed bear reminded him how young she was. Not even twenty years old, and she'd had to endure so much. He felt a warm, fatherly love for the girl. "What's your bear's name?"

"Micah," she said without hesitating.

The unexpected answer hit Josh right in the heart. His eyes glossed up to the point that he could barely see the road. His lower lip spasmed and emotion overtook him. He wiped his eyes with the back of his sleeve. He swallowed hard and regained his composure. Once he felt confident that he could speak without melting into a bawling mess, he said, "That's a good name. I like it."

She smiled. She reached across the space between them and put her hand on Josh's arm. A single tear rolled down her cheek as she replied, "Me, too."

***

They arrived in Sacramento at 10:30 AM. "Are you going to pull over somewhere?" Lindsey inquired.

"Yeah. I'm going to go all the way through town and get on I-80. I'll put in the call from an exit off the interstate."

"Seems like more driving."

"Yeah, but it will help define the search parameters to look for a location that can be accessed via I-80."

"Which doesn't include Yosemite," said Lindsey. "Smart."

Josh took the third exit northeast of Sacramento. Since it was not an OASIS city, the conditions in and around Sacramento were harsh. He pulled into the parking lot of an abandoned office building at the edge of a residential neighborhood. The building had been severely vandalized. Most of the homes in view were either boarded up or left with doors wide open as if they'd been looted repeatedly. "Keep your eyes open. I'll make this call quick, and we'll get back on the road."

Lindsey held her pistol in her lap. "Okay."

Josh kept the engine running in case he needed to make a quick retreat. He placed the battery in the burner specifically assigned to calling Carole-Jean Harris. He stepped out of the vehicle and made the call.

Seconds later, she answered. "Meet me at Shoreline Amphitheatre in Mountainview, tomorrow morning at 11:00."

"No way," Josh replied. "You'll have my people locked in. They'll never get out of the city with my sister. I'm not doing this so you can have your cake and eat it too. If she doesn't have a guaranteed path of escape, we're wasting each other's time."

"Fair enough. What location better suits you?"

Josh looked at the map to find a semi-rural location near Mountainview. "Scott's Corner. There's a nursery right off the interstate. We'll have people looking for helicopters and people surveilling the immediate area for anything that remotely looks like an ambush. If you try to trap me, I'll walk away. If you want me and Agent Vega, you'll make sure nothing is happening in the area that spooks my team. Don't think you're going to arrest me and keep my sister also. It's either or."

"Very well. I understand."

"11:00 AM?"

"See you then." She ended the call.

Josh looked inside the car. "Can you drive back?"

"Sure." Lindsey slid over to take the wheel.

Josh walked around to the passenger's side and got in. "Right back the way we came." He removed the battery of the Harris burner and watched as Lindsey got on I-80.

For the ride home, Josh researched potential locations, weighing the pros and cons of each. After a half an hour, Lindsey asked, "Do you know where you'll launch the drone from?"

"Yeah. About two miles from the fake meet location is a park-and-ride lot for public transit. We'll be able to park there without raising suspicion. People sit in their cars at those places all the time, either to pick someone up who's getting off a bus or waiting for the next bus to come along because they just missed the last one.

"We can stay right there until they drive by us. Then, once they're a mile back toward Mountainview, we'll get on I-680 and follow them in."

Lindsey gave him a sly smile. "That's why you let Harris pick the first location. You think Nicole is probably being held in Mountainview."

"It's as good of a guess as any," said Josh.

***

They arrived back at camp just before 4:00 PM Saturday. Josh hurried in to tell Emilio the latest news about the plan. He found Tim, Anne-Marie, and Kim sitting at one of the tables, looking out over the gentle snowless hills of the ski area. Josh immediately looked at George's empty cot. "George is better?"

Kim turned to look at him with eyes red from crying. "No. He was too far gone."

"You did everything you could to help." Tim took her hand and pulled her head to his shoulder.

Josh lowered his gaze to the tile floor. "Where are the others?"

Anne-Marie pointed at a clump of pines. "Just beyond those trees. They're burying George. We had a short service for him. We would have waited for you, but we thought we might have to move quickly when you got back."

Josh felt sad. "No, we're here for at least another day. But that's fine. I understand. I'll walk out and say my farewells. He was a good guy."

"He really liked you," said Tim.

Anne-Marie added, "George thought highly of you."

"Thanks." Josh proceeded solemnly down the stairs. He was well acquainted with loss and sorrow.

CHAPTER 21

And thine ears shall hear a word behind thee, saying, “This is the way, walk ye in it,” when ye turn to the right hand, and when ye turn to the left.

Isaiah 30:21

Josh borrowed Kim’s Camry Sunday morning. The common make and model drew less attention than the El Camino. Kim’s vehicle had the additional benefit of including a back seat, which was helpful since Emilio and Lindsey had come along for the ride. Josh looked at the other vehicles in the nearly-empty park-and-ride lot but saw no occupants inside.

"We'd probably have a lot more company on a weekday," said Lindsey.

Emilio surveilled the surroundings. "I'm surprised they still offer public transportation this far out from San Francisco."

"It's essentially a high-end suburb of Palo Alto. Lots of middle management from the big tech companies live out here." Josh checked the time on his watch.

"Which is to say middle management for the Global Union since the CEOs of the biggest ones sit on the governing council," Lindsey added. "If any place in the world is going to still have a modern standard of living and pre-crash creature comforts, it's going to be this area."

"Yep." Josh got out of the car and walked around to the trunk. He opened it and took out the drone and its controller. He powered on the unit and sent it up. Once the small unmanned aerial vehicle was out of sight, he returned to the driver's seat to pilot the craft.

Josh sent the UAV toward the designated meet location, watching for suspicious activity along the route.

Lindsey looked at the camera monitor on the controller. "Is that a concrete plant?"

"Looks like it," Josh replied.

Emilio leaned over to watch from the passenger's seat. "Three black SUVs lined up by the road at the concrete plant. Do you think they all happen to be putting in overtime on a Sunday morning?"

"Not at all," Josh said. "But it's good, it gives us an out."

The team watched as the small aircraft streamed video feed of the entire trip to the plant nursery where the meet was scheduled to take place. Josh kept the drone high but zoomed in with the camera to look at the two black SUVs in the parking lot. "There they are."

"I wonder how long they'll wait to see that you're not going to show," said Lindsey.

"Not long." Josh took out the burner and placed the battery inside. He sent a text to Carole-Jean Harris. *I told you not to pull anything funny. I saw the SUVs at the concrete plant up the road from our meet. The deal is off.*

"Won't she be able to track our location?" Lindsey asked.

"No. She'll figure out which cell tower we pinged, but we'll be long gone by then. Plus, she expected us to be in the area for the exchange anyway." Josh held the phone up so Lindsey and Emilio could read Carole-Jean's response.

Those were my back-up security. You're a criminal terrorist. You couldn't expect me to trust you without properly providing for my own safety. Regardless, I'm a busy woman. I can't waste time like this. I'll give you and Vega until Wednesday to turn yourselves in to the nearest UEA office. Otherwise, your sister will die at daybreak on Thursday morning.

"She's lying about the SUVs." Lindsey lowered her brows.

"Of course she is." Josh returned his focus to the drone.

Emilio looked on. "Which Suburban do you think Nicole is in?"

"I don't know," said Josh. "The windows are blacked out on both."

"They're moving!" Lindsey pointed to the screen.

Josh watched the two SUVs pull out of the nursery parking lot. "They're taking two different routes!"

"We should have brought another team," said Emilio.

"Still, we only have one drone," Lindsey replied.

Josh handed the controller to Emilio. "Follow the vehicle going north. We have to get moving now, or it will be out of range." Josh started the engine and raced out of the parking lot.

"What makes you think she's in the vehicle heading north?" asked Emilio.

Josh accelerated up the on-ramp. "I'm making an educated guess. Harris is probably returning to her office somewhere near Mountainview or Palo Alto. The other vehicle is likely taking Nicole to a different facility."

"You better punch it," said Emilio, "they're moving fast."

"How fast can the drone go?" Lindsey inquired.

"It tops out at 45 miles per hour." Josh felt nervous that they were going to lose the SUV.

Emilio stared at the screen on the controller. "I can cut corners on the turns, but we can't keep up."

"Okay, stay with them as long as you can. When you start to lose them, take the camera up. If we can catch up with our car, we can follow from a distance." Josh pressed the pursuit.

Everyone was quiet for the next few minutes. Finally, Emilio said, "They're taking an exit. I won't be able to see them once they hit the ramp."

"Try!" said Josh. "Lindsey, pull up your maps. See what the next exit is."

Seconds later Lindsey replied, "I-580."

"Good," said Josh. "Emilio, which direction?"

"They went west, but I lost them."

"Okay. Just drop the drone in a nearby field where it's not likely to be found. Make a note of some landmarks. We can't stop for it now, but we may need it later." Josh waited until the final moment to slow down for the exit. He hit the brakes before the curve, then rapidly re-accelerated up the ramp.

Emilio powered off the controller and pointed out the window. "I parked it on the bank of a drainage ditch behind that Home Depot."

"Good enough." Josh watched the speedometer which was registering above 90 miles an hour.

"Is that it?" Lindsey pointed to a black SUV in the distance.

"We'll know soon enough." Josh pressed the gas pedal to catch up.

Moments later, Emilio exclaimed. "Government plates! That's them!"

Josh breathed a little easier and let his foot off the accelerator just enough to fall back a few yards. "We'll stay close enough to follow, but far enough to hopefully not be spotted." Traffic wasn't heavy, but there were plenty of other vehicles to provide cover for the Camry.

The chase continued for another hundred miles, taking the Golden State Highway south through Modesto and Turlock.

“You know where they’re headed, don’t you?” Emilio asked.

Josh glanced at the rearview to Lindsey who was navigating with her phone. “Chowchilla?”

“That’s what it looks like to me,” said Lindsey.

“How far is the prison from our camp at the ski area?” Josh asked.

Lindsey entered the information into her phone. “80 miles.”

“Let’s hope that’s enough of a buffer.” Josh followed from a distance until he saw the SUV take exit 167.

Emilio watched the SUV drive away. “Now what?”

Josh continued driving, getting in the right lane to take the next exit. “Now, we turn around and go get our drone. I have a feeling we’re going to need it.”

***

Monday morning, Josh ate a couple of granola bars while looking out over the ski slopes where tall grass was blowing gently in the wind. Tim walked up behind him. “Beautiful, isn’t it?”

“Yeah. This would be a nice place to come and relax.” Josh wadded the packaging from the first granola bar and pushed it into his pocket. “I don’t even know what that word means anymore. I heard you got that radio working in the ranger station."

"Yeah. I'm using Junk's inverter connected to the van for the power supply. Lindsey is using it to charge the drone right now, so I'm taking a little break. Everything else from the radio: receiver, antenna, mic, they all work fine. I picked up some chatter about Valley State Prison."

"What did you hear?" Josh paused from eating.

"Since we're so close to Chowchilla, I heard two guys from the area talking about the prison. One of them knows somebody who knows somebody who works there, so it's hard to say how reliable the info is."

"I understand, but what did they say?"

"One of them claims that Valley has been converted to an extermination camp—rows of guillotines, mass graves."

"Guillotines?"

Tim shrugged. "That's what they said."

Josh shivered at the thought. He couldn't imagine Nicole even having to contemplate such a brutal death. "Thanks. Do me a favor."

"Sure, anything."

"Don't mention the guillotines to Emilio, not just yet anyway."

"You got it. What are you guys going to do?"

"Put together a plan. But first, we have to take the drone down to the prison, try to get an idea of how many guards we'll be dealing with, general layout, that kind of thing."

"Once you have a plan, you can count me in," said Tim.

Josh looked him in the eyes. “Are you sure about that? You’ve been through a lot, with the ambush on the tanker, the escape, and everything.”

“So have you.”

Josh looked out at the ski lift. “Yeah, but she’s my sister.”

“After what we’ve been through together, we’re all family now. Dana feels the same way. You can count on all of us. Junk, Pigpen, Kim, Anne-Marie, whatever you decide to do, we’re all in.”

Josh felt humbled by the pledge of support. “I appreciate that. We can certainly use all the help we can get.”

Emilio walked up to Josh. “You ready to go? Lindsey is waiting with the drone down by the car.”

“Yeah.” Josh shook Tim’s hand. “Thank you, for everything. And keep listening to the radio. The least little piece of information could be the difference between victory and defeat.”

“I will.” Tim waved.

Josh hustled down the stairs to the Camry. “Is the drone charged up?”

“Ready to go.” Lindsey opened the back door and got into the car.

“Then let’s roll.” Josh got inside and started the engine.

Emilio sat in the passenger’s seat, put on his seatbelt, and closed the door. “Did you come up with anything to get us inside?”

Josh drove out of the parking lot and onto the winding mountain road which would take them down to the valley. “Aramark provides all the food and supplies to most of the prisons in California.”

"Yeah, as well as the rest of the country," said Emilio. "Are we going to boost an Aramark delivery truck?"

"We need something that can get us all inside the fence. Otherwise, it will be like storming the shores at Normandy." Josh turned the wheel sharply to take a hairpin curve.

"But if it's not a scheduled delivery, they won't let us in, even if they recognize the vehicle," said Lindsey.

Josh focused on the treacherous road before him. "We'll just have to make sure it's a scheduled delivery."

***

Because of the slow going down the mountain pass, it took two hours to make the 80-mile drive to Chowchilla. Josh found the small town in a state of near-abandonment. The businesses were all either boarded up, vandalized, or both. The houses, which looked to have been modest abodes before the collapse, now looked run down and neglected. Most had makeshift security features, such as two-by-fours nailed to the exterior of windows to make break-ins more of a challenge. Neighborhoods with major crime problems going into the collapse would have featured bars over the windows on most single-family homes. But, it was obvious that Chowchilla had been caught off guard by the meltdown. They'd had to make do with whatever they had on hand.

"Agricultural town." Emilio looked out the window. "My mom and pop must have traveled through a hundred places just like Chowchilla." He turned to look at Lindsey. "They were migrant workers."

Lindsey pointed to a drive-through testing site set up in the parking lot of the county health department and operated by the CDC. "They might not have much, but they've got testing."

Josh looked at the operation with curiosity. "I figured tests and vaccines would be reserved for the elites. I wonder how they managed that."

"Because these are the people harvesting crops for people at the top of the food chain," said Emilio.

"But they're all vaccinated," said Lindsey. "Why would they care if people touching their food have the virus?"

Josh replied, "They're tracking the mutations, making sure the virus doesn't stray too far from its intended design. And if it does, they want to know before it shows up on their plate."

Josh found the single grocery store providing necessities to the blighted community. "This looks like as good of a place as any to launch the drone." He pulled into the parking lot and drove to the side of the building.

"Mind if I pilot the first flyover?" Emilio exited the vehicle.

"Be my guest. But keep it high enough to avoid detection by the guards." Josh got out and opened the trunk.

Emilio quickly had the drone in the air and soaring toward the prison. Minutes later, he said, "I've got a visual."

Josh's heart skipped a beat when he saw rows of guillotines set up in the recreation area. He hoped Emilio wouldn't notice.

"This is a big operation. Must be hundreds of guards!" Emilio said.

Lindsey added, "Even if we successfully get inside, we'll never pull off a brute force attack. Not with nine people."

"She's right," said Josh. "This place is too big and too well guarded."

"What are those racks in the yard?" Emilio asked.

"Where?" Lindsey stared at the small screen.

"That's Valley," Josh interrupted. "It doesn't matter. Nicole is in CCWF, the installation to the south."

Emilio ignored Josh and zoomed the camera in. "Those are guillotines!" The iron devices were lined up in five rows of twenty. Every inch of the killing machines were painted black except the shiny metal blades which glistened in the sun. "We have to get her out of there! Right now!" Emilio turned to Josh.

"We have to not get caught." Josh saw that Emilio had lost his focus on operating the drone. He took the controller out of his hand and passed it off to Lindsey. "Can you take over?"

"Sure." She looked upset by the gruesome image but not nearly as shaken as Emilio.

"We need to go! Right now!" Emilio began walking toward the driver's side of the car.

Josh stood in his way. “No! You have to calm down. You read Harris’ text. We have until Wednesday.”

“That woman is a liar! I have to get Nicole out of that place.”

“What are you going to do? Storm the gates and hope they just let you walk out with her? We have to stick to the plan.” Josh stood in front of the car door.

“We don’t have a plan! You both said so two minutes ago!”

“We’ll come up with something.” Josh said a silent prayer asking God to show him a way.

Emilio pushed Josh out of the way. “I’m going right now.”

Josh could not restrain Emilio who was a much bigger individual. “Emilio! You can’t do this. Lindsey and I aren’t going to join you on a kamikaze mission.”

“Then stay here.” Emilio closed the door and started the engine.

Lindsey looked frightened, splitting her attention between piloting the drone and watching the altercation.

“Wait! I’ve got a plan!” said Josh.

Emilio glared at him. “You’re stalling.”

“No, really!” Josh held his hands up as he desperately tried to think of something. “Turn off the vehicle and let me explain.”

“Tell me right now, or I’m heading over there with guns blazing. I don’t care if they kill me, I can’t live with myself anyway if I sit back and do nothing for another second.”

Josh squinted, forcing his brain to come up with something, anything. He caught an image of the CDC van back at the testing center. "If we can't outfight them, we have to outsmart them. We need a really good con."

"You don't have any idea of what you're going to do." Emilio shook his head and put the vehicle in gear.

"Just hear me out!" Josh stood in front of the car. "The best con jobs sell people on something they *want* to believe. What do you think those guards want more than anything else?"

"I don't know, money?" Emilio huffed. "If you have a plan, let's hear it. Otherwise, I'm out of here!"

Lindsey joined the conversation. "Vaccines!"

"A lot of good that does us. Where are we going to get vaccines?" Emilio asked.

"We don't need vaccines," said Josh. "We just need a handful of hypodermic needles and some hazmat suits."

Emilio looked at him as if he were considering the viability of this still-unrefined scheme. "And maybe a CDC van?"

Lindsey added, "And maybe some sedatives—instead of the vaccine."

Emilio put the vehicle in park. "Do you think Kim has sedatives in her medical supplies?"

"Some, I'm sure." Josh kept thinking, developing the plan in his head. "But maybe we won't need a dose for every guard in the facility."

CHAPTER 22

Strengthen ye the weak hands, and confirm the feeble knees. Say to them that are of a fearful heart, be strong, fear not: behold, your God will come with vengeance, even God with a recompence; he will come and save you.

Isaiah 35:3-4

Early Tuesday morning, Josh held the flashlight beneath the dashboard of the CDC van while Emilio rewired the ignition to bypass the anti-theft device usually deactivated by the key chip, which they did not have. Lindsey stood guard, watching the county health department building where the drive-thru testing site had been set up.

Josh whispered to Lindsey, “See anything?”

“Still all clear,” she replied.

“How much longer?” Josh felt nervous.

Emilio kept working. “The days of shoving a screwdriver in the ignition and driving away are over. This is a complicated process. It takes time.”

Finally, twenty minutes into the operation, the engine started. “We’re good to go! Load up!” Emilio took the driver’s seat.

Lindsey got into the back. Josh sat in the passenger’s seat and closed the door. He called over the radio. “Dana, we’ve got the vehicle. We’re coming to you.”

“We’re here,” she replied.

Lindsey tossed hazmat suits from the back of the van to Josh and Emilio. Next, she began pulling one such suit over her clothes. Josh took out a new burner phone and placed a call to the prison. The operator answered. “CCWF.”

“Good morning, this is Doctor Ed Shelton from the CDC. May I speak to the administrator on duty?”

“The warden will be in after 7:00 if you want to call back. Is this about the personal protective equipment you guys were supposed to send us two weeks ago? They’re bringing women in from all over the country now. I’ve got more guys threatening to quit if we can’t protect ourselves from this new strain of the virus.”

“What’s your name?”

“Captain Anderson, Roger Anderson. I’m the shift supervisor.”

“I completely understand your frustration,

Captain. We're doing everything we can. Unfortunately, no one could have anticipated what the GU has been through recently. Lots of PPE was sent to the outer regions of the OASIS cities which were hit with the bombs. However, I'm in a position to help out your facility. I can offer you something better than PPE."

"I'm listening."

"I have a shipment of vaccines going from San Francisco to Fresno. It's only for their highest-ranking political figures and essential workers there. We've got a few extra vials in the shipment. Corrections officers are slated to be vaccinated in six weeks, but your facility is on the way for the Fresno team. They could make a quick stop and inoculate the guards you have on shift."

"Oh? That's great. When would you be coming?"

"Twenty minutes. The team would have to be in and out, so you'd have to get everyone together. Then, I need a secure room where we can administer the injections. Set up some chairs for your people to sit in while they're getting the shots. The CDC team would have to leave within fifteen minutes of arrival so they're not late getting to Fresno."

"I'm running a skeleton staff right now, fifty guys tops. All the prisons are short. We lock down at night anyway, so this is when we have the least amount of officers on duty. All my people are monitoring the blocks. Plus it's almost 5:00. The trustees will be getting breakfast together soon. They have to have guards to work. Maybe I could pull one guard at a time from each block to get vaccinated. But it would take at least an hour to rotate everyone."

"I completely understand," said Josh. "I don't want to ask you to jeopardize the safety of your facility. Valley probably has more flexibility since they're being re-tooled as a termination facility. I'll give them a call. You'll get your injections in about six weeks. In the meantime, I'll try to make sure you get that personal protective equipment in the next couple of weeks. Thank you, Captain Anderson. Have a pleasant rest of your day."

"Wait, wait, wait!" Anderson began yelling even before Josh finished his spiel.

"Yes, Captain?" Josh tried to hold back his grin.

"I'll…we'll make it work. Please, just come. I'll figure it out."

"Okay. The team should be arriving within the next twenty minutes."

"Thank you, Doctor."

Josh ended the call and looked toward heaven. "Thank you, Jesus!"

"That's it?" Emilio continued racing toward the pickup location for the rest of the team. "We're in?"

"We're in," said Josh with a look of satisfaction.

"Yes!" Emilio continued to the pickup location, which was 10 miles south of Chowchilla on the Golden Gate Highway. The location would also be the place where they would dump the van after the mission. It would indicate that the group had headed south when, in fact, the ski camp was to the east of the prison.

When they arrived at the abandoned gas station,

Lindsey tossed open the back door. “Get in! Hurry!” She handed out hazmat suits as Tim, Dana, Junk, Pigpen, Anne-Marie, and Kim got inside. Sidearms were concealed on their persons while folding-stock AK-47s were cached in duffle bags. The rifles would stay in the bags unless the plan went sour.

Junk was rather short, so he had to roll up arm and leg cuffs of his hazmat jumpsuit. “You sure these folks aren’t going to be armed?”

Josh replied, “The perimeter guards will have shotguns. I’m going to recommend they go first so we can sedate them and try to separate them from their firearms before a gunfight breaks out. The rest will only have tasers and pepper spray.” Using his knife, Josh made a small incision in his hazmat suit so he could get his hand inside to retrieve his Glock 18 pistol. He instructed the others to do the same.

Minutes later, Emilio turned off the main road. He followed the service road, which ran along the side of the colossal detention complex. The prison had 14 free-standing cell-blocks structures as well as several support buildings. He pulled up to the entrance of CCWF. “Okay, this is it.” The gate opened and he drove through.

The gate closed behind them and the guard controlling the gate pointed to the loading dock of one of the service buildings. “Everyone will be in there. I’ll be over as soon as I lock down the gate.”

“Okay.” Josh rolled up his window and motioned for Emilio to continue to the loading dock. Josh pulled his N-95 face mask over his mouth and put on his protective goggles. Next, he pulled the hood of the hazmat suit over his head and opened the door.

"Hi, I'm Doctor Carter," said Josh.

The captain waved but stood back. "I'm Captain Anderson, the person who spoke with your coordinator."

"Yes, Ed told me to ask for you," said Josh.

Kim, Lindsey, and Emilio came out of the van.

Anderson looked them over. "I assume you folks are vaccinated. May I ask why you need hazmat suits?"

Junk, Pigpen, Anne-Marie, Dana, and Tim came out behind them. They would be acting as part of a prep team, who would be cleaning the injection sites with alcohol swabs and handing out Band-Aids to apply after being vaccinated. They carried the duffle bags with the AK-47s.

Josh quickly replied. "Without protective gear, we could inadvertently carry viral particles to the next location we visit. Even people who are getting vaccinated could potentially get sick before the vaccine takes effect."

"Oh, I didn't realize that. How long for it to take effect?"

Being the team member with a medical background, Kim answered. "Two weeks for full effect. Your body develops antibodies during that time. Although, you'll begin to develop some level of immunity within a few days."

"We need to get started," said Josh.

"Yeah, sure." The captain led the team inside. The guard from the gate arrived, from his long sprint. He still held his shotgun and was breathing heavily. "I made it!"

"Good," said Josh. "We'll get perimeter guards taken care of first so they can get back to their posts." They walked up concrete stairs and through a pair of steel doors into a large receiving area. Pallets of supplies lined the floor. Along the walls were metal shelves with everything, from large bags of bakery mix and canned goods, to mop heads and gallon bottles of floor cleaner. In the middle of the room ten folding chairs were set up.

The captain made a call to the guards standing around. "Watchtower guards, you're up first. Shirts off."

Kim had only three needles. The third injection would be the team's cue to act. She walked up to the first one. "Why don't you take a seat? Some people have reported feeling a little dizzy for a few minutes, but it passes quickly." She injected the propofol into the first guard.

Josh took the man's shotgun and placed it on the floor behind the guard's chair. He continued doing that for the men in the line to get their injections.

Kim injected the third man. "There, that should do it."

The first guard nodded out, rolled forward in his chair, and plopped onto the floor, breathing with a labored snorting sound.

Anderson's brows snapped together. "Is that supposed to happen?"

Josh drew his Glock 18 and pointed it at the captain. "I need all of you to lie face down on the ground and interlace your fingers behind your head."

"What is this?" demanded the captain.

One of the perimeter guards spun around from sitting in his chair to grab his shotgun. POW! POW! Lindsey shot him in the head. Another of the guards bolted toward the exit. Josh fired his pistol three times, killing the man before he reached the door.

Pigpen and Junk walked behind the chairs, kicking the shotguns away from the guards. Anne-Marie and Tim followed behind, placing zip-tie restraints to the guards' hands and securing them to the chairs.

"I can't believe I fell for this." The captain looked around as if sizing up the situation. By this time, Emilio, Lindsey, and Dana already had the AK-47s out of the bag.

Josh replaced his 19-round magazine with a 33-round mag. "We need you to get on the ground. No one had to die. It's unfortunate that you've lost two of your people. Now please, face down.

"Not until I know what's going on here." Anderson shook his head.

"We're here for Nicole Stone. Once we have her, we'll leave."

"You won't kill anyone else or further disrupt the prison?"

"I'm not negotiating with you," said Josh. "I'm taking Nicole Stone with me when I leave here. The only variable is whether or not you and your guards are still breathing after we're gone."

The captain did as he'd been instructed. "Everybody down."

The team members quickly went around and zip-tied the remaining guards. Josh and Emilio stood the captain to his feet. “Get up,” Josh demanded. “Take us to the main control room.”

“Through those doors,” said the captain. Dana, Lindsey, Josh, and Emilio followed him down a hall to a large room with over fifty video monitors and four large computer screens.

“Where is Nicole Stone?” Emilio asked.

“I have to look her up in the system. We have over 3,000 inmates.”

Josh cut the restraints. “Pull anything, and you’re dead.”

The man sat at a chair and pulled up the information on the computer. “Block G, cell 37.”

“Pull up the camera,” said Josh.

The man did so and zoomed in on cell 37. Nicole could be seen sleeping on her rack.

“Open it,” Emilio commanded. “And all the access points between there and here.”

The captain complied.

Emilio tore a map of the facility from the wall. “Dana, come with me. Josh, keep an eye on us with the cameras. Make sure this guy doesn’t try to be a hero.”

“We’ll be here,” said Josh.

Emilio and Dana rushed out the door. Josh watched the captain carefully to make sure he didn’t try anything while watching Emilio and Dana sprint across the compound to Block G.

Lindsey watched as they entered the block. “They’re inside.”

Josh watched his sister crawl out of the rack wearily. “They’ve got her!” Soon, all the other inmates were whistling, or shouting, or banging on the bars. Nicole's cellmate also exited the cell, but Emilio turned with his AK-47 and held up a hand. He conveyed with no uncertainty that the woman should not follow them out of the block.

"Good enough." Josh pulled on the collar of the captain. "Let's go."

"At least let me close the doors." The captain resisted Josh's urging.

"Worry about that after we're gone." Josh pulled harder, dislodging the man from his chair.

"But I've got a loose inmate! She could make her way all the way to the warehouse, maybe even get a shotgun!"

"Not my problem." Josh shoved the man out the door. "Let's go!"

Josh and Lindsey escorted the man back to the warehouse space. Emilio and Dana soon returned with Nicole who looked thinner than usual and was clothed in an orange uniform. Josh embraced his sister. "How are you?"

"I've been better, but you're here now." She ended the hug. "Someone else is here."

"Who?" he asked.

"Mackenzie," said Nicole.

Emilio immediately began shaking his head. "No way. We gotta go."

Nicole grasped his hand. "We can't leave her. The only reason she's here is because she wouldn't give up any information about us."

Josh gritted his teeth, remembering the promise he'd made to Rev. "Where is she?"

"Bro, you can't be serious!" Emilio objected.

"Block C," said Nicole. "It's not that far."

Josh grabbed Captain Anderson by the collar. "Come on. I need one more person."

The captain moved forward with a begrudging attitude. "You said one prisoner and you'd leave."

"I'm exercising my right to alter the terms." Josh pushed him toward the control room. He looked at Tim and the rest of the team. "We need a few more minutes."

"Hurry! Please!" Anne-Marie stood holding a shotgun over one of the restrained guards.

Emilio, Dana, and Lindsey followed Josh and Anderson. Once inside the control room, Josh pushed the captain back into the chair. "C Block. We're looking for Mackenzie Thompson."

Captain Anderson entered the information. "Cell 12."

"You know the drill." Josh watched the cameras as the captain opened the access for Emilio, Dana, and Nicole to retrieve Mackenzie from her cell. Once again, the other inmates beat on the bars, yelled, whistled as Mackenzie walked free.

Lindsey pointed at the desk. "Did you see that? He just put his hand under the desk."

Josh looked beneath the surface to see a flashing red button. "He just triggered a silent alarm." Josh picked up his radio. "Emilio, you guys need to hustle. We've got trouble coming our way." Josh picked the captain up out of the chair and pushed him to the floor. "How do I turn it off?"

"I didn't do anything!" Anderson held his hands up.

"Yes you did. And if you can't tell me how to deactivate it, you're no good to me." Josh pointed his pistol at the man's head.

Emilio arrived a few seconds later. "What happened?"

"Anderson hit the panic button," said Lindsey.

"You're proving to be too much of a problem." Emilio raised the barrel of his AK.

"No! Please!" The captain covered his face.

It was too late. Emilio pulled the trigger and the man slumped to the floor.

"What did you do that for?" Josh yelled.

"This guy is a thorn in our side. He's going to get us killed if he hasn't already," said Emilio.

"I was trying to persuade him to shut off the alarm."

"Not possible." Emilio looked under the desk.

"Then maybe he could have called in and said it was triggered accidentally."

"Unlikely." Emilio studied the control panel. "Right here! Emergency release."

"It needs a key," said Lindsey.

Josh took the keys clipped to the captain's belt loop. "I bet it's on here. What do you have in mind?"

"All prisons are equipped with a cascading release function. It opens all the doors in the entire facility in case of a fire or other emergency." Emilio held out his hand for the keys. "Whoever responds to the alarm will have more problems than just us."

"3,000 inmates." Josh thought about the effect of what they were about to do.

"Many of whom are not criminals," said Mackenzie "Most are just enemies of the state, like me."

Josh handed the key to Emilio. “This one looks like it will fit.”

Emilio quickly inserted the key and turned the lock to activate the function. An indicator light above the key turned green. Josh looked at the monitors. All the doors were opening. “Let’s go! Some of these women may be less appreciative than others.”

The team ran back to the warehouse. “Back to the van! Hurry!” Josh shouted. Everyone rushed to the vehicle.

“What about the gate?” asked Lindsey.

Josh grabbed the guard who’d let them in. “Do you want to live?”

“Yeah!” He nodded adamantly.

“Then get up!” Josh lifted him to his feet and pushed him in the van. “Go! Go! Go!”

Tim stomped the accelerator, and the van sped toward the gate. Josh escorted the guard out and into the gatehouse. He cut his ties. “Open it!”

The guard quickly entered the commands for the electric gate and it rolled back. Josh took him back outside so he couldn’t do anything until they were gone. Josh entered the side door of the van and pulled it shut. “Let’s get out of here!”

Two prison patrol vehicles pulled in front of the van and blocked the road. “Where did these guys come from?” Tim shouted.

“Valley State, across the road.” Josh grabbed an AK-47 and pulled the side door open. He opened fire on the vehicles as did Emilio, Dana, and Lindsey.

Josh called out to Tim. “Keep driving. I think

they got the message."

Tim drove around the patrol cars slowly while Josh and the others remained ready to fire again. Josh looked back at the prison as Tim sped away. "The first of the inmates are coming out of the gate." He slid the side door shut and looked out the back window. "They're getting in the patrol cars."

"They'll be in the armory soon," said Emilio. "It will be a while before the GU peacekeepers get a chance to figure out what just happened."

Josh sat down with his back against the wall of the van. He looked at Emilio and Nicole holding each other after so much time apart. He felt happy for them and turned to Mackenzie.

"Thank you, for getting me out of that place," she said.

"You're welcome. Thanks for not giving them any information about us."

"I told you that I wouldn't."

"I know." Josh looked at the floor. "I guess I underestimated you."

The team arrived back at the abandoned gas station five minutes later. "Everybody out!" Josh pushed the door open. "Make sure you get everything."

The team members rushed to the vehicles. Six managed to fit in the Camry. Pigpen, Junk, Nicole, and Emilio got into the rear of the El Camino. Josh drove and Lindsey rode shotgun. Josh led the race back to the ski area.

Lindsey looked into the side view mirror. "We did it!"

"We're not out of the woods yet. If they send out

a chopper, they could spot us pretty easily."

"I can't imagine Chowchilla has a chopper." Lindsey took the small stuffed bear from the dashboard and held it in her hands. "Fresno either, for that matter. From what I hear, that place is a wasteland—picked apart by gangs and criminals. In fact, I'm surprised the captain even bought that story about taking vaccines to Fresno."

"He was desperate for a solution. He wanted to believe it." Josh looked up. The morning sun was coming over the mountains to the east. "Let's hope you're right about the helicopters. If so, I think we'll make it."

CHAPTER 23

And when he had opened the fifth seal, I saw under the altar the souls of them that were slain for the word of God, and for the testimony which they held: and they cried with a loud voice, saying, How long, O Lord, holy and true, dost thou not judge and avenge our blood on them that dwell on the earth? And white robes were given unto every one of them; and it was said unto them, that they should rest yet for a little season, until their fellowservants also and their brethren, that should be killed as they were, should be fulfilled.

Revelation 6:9-11

Josh looked out the large windows of the ski area building. He scanned the skyline for helicopters. Nicole came up to him. She was dressed in a tee-shirt and a pair of jeans given to her by Kim. She took his hand. “Thanks again for coming to get me.”

Josh smiled and kissed her on the head. “Of course. You look better.”

“Yeah, orange isn’t my color.”

“Did you get something to eat?”

“I ate two MREs.”

“I wish we had better food. We’ll have a feast when we get back.”

“Are you kidding? MREs are like fine dining compared to the slop they were feeding us inside. G Block was all people being held for termination, so we probably got worse food than the others.”

Josh turned to Nicole. “Micah didn’t make it.”

She looked at the floor and squeezed his hand. “I’m sorry.”

“Thanks.” Josh gently rubbed the back of her hand with his thumb. “What you did for us was brave—stupid and suicidal, but brave.”

She looked up at his eyes. “If I hadn’t taken the car, Emilio would have done it. Then he would have gotten caught. I knew I might not survive. I was okay with that. But I didn’t want to deal with wondering if he was dead or alive.”

“Just so you know, he’s been a complete wreck since you took off. I have been, too. It’s just that I’ve been so overwhelmed with grief…because of Micah.” Josh looked up again. “But because of your sacrifice, I was able to be by his side when he passed. I can't tell you how much that means to me."

She nodded. "You've done a lot for me. I'm sure I'd have been dead long ago if it hadn't been for you. I'm glad I was able to help."

Mackenzie walked up wearing street clothes given to her by Anne-Marie. "Any news?"

"Not yet. Junk and Pigpen are monitoring WNN." Josh pointed out the window to the small A-frame building. "Tim has a small Ham radio set up over in that ranger station. He's monitoring the available frequencies to see what he can set up. We'll remain on high alert for the next twenty-four hours."

"You don't think we're inside the search area?" Mackenzie asked.

"I suspect all of North America is part of the search area, which is why we're staying put for a few days," Josh replied. "But the GU is limited on the number of resources they can dedicate to looking this far away."

"Eighty miles? It really isn't that far away." Nicole stared up at the clouds.

"If we were inside the search area, they'd have something like 20,000 miles to cover. That's if we were right at the end of the search area. I think they'll search the immediate area, ten miles or so. Then, I expect they'll have peacekeepers patrolling the highways for a few days, pulling over anyone who looks suspicious. But Lucius Alexander has another pandemic on his hands, he's just lost multiple cities in a nuclear exchange, he's dealing with the onset of a global famine brought on by drought and the locusts… Don't get me wrong, he's Satan incarnate. I'm sure he's happier than a pig in a mud hole with all of this death and destruction. But he has to keep up appearances. It's a lot to manage. We're small potatoes in the grand scheme of things."

Emilio had joined the group while Josh was talking. He wrapped his arms around Nicole and held her tight. "That's why Alexander appointed Harris to hunt people like us. Carole-Jean, on the other hand, has all the time in the world to hunt you down."

"Thanks for the reminder." Josh frowned. "Keep an eye out. Call me on the radio if you hear choppers. I'm going to see if Tim has picked up anything on the Ham."

Josh took two MREs and walked down the stairs. He checked the sky before leaving the cover of the building to cross the field going to the ranger station. He sprinted the short distance and quickly went inside. He placed one of the MREs on the desk next to Tim. "Hear anything?"

"Thanks." Tim tore into the green plastic pouch. "The locals are in a tizzy. They've only apprehended a couple hundred of the escaped convicts."

Josh began eating the spaghetti dinner in his pouch. "Considering many of those women were probably there for Bibles or guns, I don't feel too bad about that."

Junk called over the walkie-talkie. "Josh, you best come hear this."

"Gotta go. Call me if you hear anything else." Josh rolled up the edge of his pouch and headed for the door.

"Thanks again for bringing me lunch," said Tim.

Josh hurried back to the main building and found Junk. "What is it?"

"Carole-Jean. She just gave a press conference. They've released photos of you, Emilio, Nicole, and Mackenzie. She's offering a twenty-five hundred-mark reward for information leading to any one of you. Of course, we don't have a television, so I can't say if the pictures are really you."

"They have all of our pictures on file. I'm sure she released accurate likenesses of us." Josh thought about the reward. "So, twenty-five hundred each?"

Pigpen snorted. "Yep. That'd be pertnear two-hundred thousand in old money."

Josh looked at the scroungy fellow out of the corner of his eye. "You figured the math on that pretty fast. You're not thinking of cashing in, are you?"

Pigpen laughed. "What in the devil would I do with a pile of money like that? Besides, I just risked my neck to get y'all free. It might not be the cleanest neck, nor the purtiest neither, but it's my neck—only one I got. And it's worth a devil of a lot more to me than two-hundred-thousand dollars."

"I suppose that will make me rest a little easier," said Josh.

***

Later that evening, the group listened to the

radio, sitting around several tables that had been pushed together. Lucius Alexander gave an address that was broadcast over WNN.

"This latest act of violence committed against the Global Union at a California correctional facility this morning emphasizes how important it is that we completely eradicate this lingering spirit of rebellion and defiance. I have signed an executive order granting extended authority to both the Unity Enforcement Agency as well as the Department of Global Security to eradicate groups like the one responsible for this attack.

"The order gives enhanced search and seizure powers to the UEA and the DGS allowing them more latitude in what can be considered probable cause and also nullifies previous ordinances which would have required a warrant signed by a judge. The order further protects UEA and DGS agents against civil and criminal liability while doing their jobs. We must insulate them from such frivolities and de-shackle them from bureaucratic red tape so they can successfully perform the duties to which we have assigned them.

"The UEA will begin raiding churches and home study groups which are not in compliance with the new unity mandates. Offenders will be readily assessed for suitability for reform. Those who do not show promise for such an extensive investment will be terminated. The challenges we face as a society are dire. None of you need to be reminded of that. We can no longer afford to have such a vicious enemy inside our own gates. I've been reasonable. I've been patient. But we are not seeing the desired outcome by offering the carrot, so it is time we switched to the stick.

Josh looked around at the group. "We may be here a little longer than I originally planned."

"How long can we last?" asked Nicole.

"We have maybe four weeks of provisions," said Junk.

"Then we should probably ration our food stocks to make it five," said Josh. "It sounds like they are committed to hunting us down. It's not a good time for a cross-country road trip."

***

Over the next four weeks, Tim was able to track the activity of the Unity Enforcement Agency via the Ham radio. Josh used the information gleaned from the radio to piece together a map showing where the UEA was operating. Josh identified what he assumed to be ten teams which seemed to operate in a given geographical area for roughly one week at a time. Activity would heat up in certain areas for about five or six days, then completely stop. Cycles of raids seemed to start on a Monday and run their course by the following Friday or Saturday. He guessed that Tuesday would be the best time for the group to set out on their path home.

However, the trip would be more complicated getting home than it had been coming out west. In addition to the UEA raids on churches, patriot groups, and home Bible study groups, the Ham radio transmissions were reporting on checkpoints set up on the major interstates, often near state borders and interchanges where interstates intersected.

Having depleted their food resources, the caravan set out on a Tuesday in late August. Taking the scenic route back meant that the normal two-thousand-plus-mile trek from Yosemite to the cornfield outside of Kokomo, Indiana would come in well above twenty-five-hundred miles.

Josh was down to his last fifteen ounces of silver. With a price on his head, other team members would have to handle the bartering. In addition to looking for gas stations that would trade for silver, they also had to purchase food. With the threat of the UEA, fewer and fewer merchants were willing to exchange goods for anything other than global marks. Looking for trading partners would add more time to the already long trip.

Before setting out each day, the team needed a place where they knew they'd be able to stop for the night, pitch a tent, and camp without the threat of encountering peacekeepers, UEA raiders, or DGS agents. Planning each leg of the journey home was tedious and allowed no room for error.

***

It took the team five days to reach Ellington, Missouri. A few miles outside of the town, they found an abandoned summer camp to stay the night. The camp was primitive but had ten small cabins with four pairs of bunk beds in each. The camp also had a bathhouse but the power was off, so those were essentially useless. The next morning Josh was up early. He rolled up his sleeping bag from the thin vinyl-covered mattress. He'd slept well with the security of walls and a roof, plus even a thin mattress was better than the hard ground of the previous four nights. He tiptoed to leave the cabin trying not to wake Emilio, Nicole, Dana, Lindsey, and Mackenzie who all shared the cabin with him.

Morning had come and the clouds to the east were radiant with hues of fluorescent orange, and hot pink. Tim was awake. He sat on one of the picnic tables out front of the cabins eating a package of cookies. "Red sky in the morning…"

"It's more pink than red," said Josh as he approached the table.

"Yeah, well, regardless of the color," said Tim. "I think we should stay put for a few days."

"Why do you say that?"

"I picked up some Hams talking in the area."

"On the handheld?" Josh pointed to his walkie-talkie.

"Yeah. UEA is doing some raids in southern Illinois."

Josh lifted his shoulders. "We could cut down through Kentucky. It wouldn't be that far out of our way."

"DGS is patrolling the Mississippi—looking for people fleeing the raids. They're watching all the bridges, even got helicopters flying up and down the river watching for people trying to cross on small watercraft. My guess is they'll be watching the western tip of Kentucky also."

Josh thought for a while. "We could go farther south to get around the troubled spots. We could cut down through Arkansas, then back up through Tennessee and Kentucky. Of course, we'd be expending more fuel, and it's getting harder and harder to find. Not to mention, we're almost out of capital."

Tim finished his cookies and slapped his hands together to knock off the crumbs. "We could also go out of the frying pan and into the fire. South is the opposite direction we need to get to. We could potentially get stuck farther away from home." He looked around at the tranquil surroundings. "If we're going to be stuck somewhere for a few days, this place is better than most."

"Yeah, it's the first place since Yosemite that's had a roof." Josh looked back to the clouds, which were now more of a fuchsia color. "Especially if we're going to get rain." He turned back toward the simple camp cabin. "I'll talk it over with Emilio and Dana, but you're probably right. Maybe we should stay here until things cool off."

He made less of an effort to be quiet upon returning to the cabin. Emilio rolled over. "Time to get moving?"

"I'm not so sure about that." Josh relayed what Tim had heard over the radio.

Lindsey was deep inside her sleeping bag, but her eyes were open and she listened in on the conversation. "How much food do we have?"

"Two days," said Josh. "We could send a team into town and try to purchase something."

"I saw one grocery store when we drove through," said Emilio. "Chances are slim."

"I'll have a look inside the common building. I'm sure they have cooking supplies in the kitchen," said Josh.

"I'll go," said Lindsey. "If you need someone to make a trip into town."

"Thanks. I'll let you know." Josh left the cabin and crossed the grounds toward the common building. He ran into Junk and Pigpen.

"Mornin'," said Junk.

"Good morning," Josh replied.

"Tim said wes might be hangin' around here for a spell." Pigpen stuck his hands inside the bib of his grubby overalls.

"Yeah, possibly. I was going to check out the kitchen." Josh nodded to the main camp building. It was a simple structure. The board-and-batten siding was of dark stained wood. A common dining area was covered and screened in.

"Got a padlock on the door," said Junk.

"Oh, you've already been over there?" Josh asked.

"Fixin' to fetch the bolt cutters." Pigpen pointed to the van.

"Okay then. I guess I'll meet you guys over there." Josh walked slowly, taking in the peaceful scenery as he crossed the open area to the common building. He enjoyed the cool morning air. The last few days had been uncomfortably hot, so he expected this one to be no different.

Junk returned with the bolt cutters. Josh stood back while he did his thing. Snap! The lock dropped to the ground. Josh opened the door. "I suppose it's a good sign that the lock was still on it. Maybe we'll find food."

Josh and Pigpen rummaged through the kitchen while Junk went in search of other items of interest. Josh examined the contents of a wire shelf. "Cooking oil, seasonings, hot sauce, cornmeal…"

Junk came into the room holding a pair of fishing poles. "All you're missin' is a mess of catfish."

Pigpen asked, "They got a pond round here?"

Josh pointed toward the back of the property. "The creek runs into Clearwater Lake. I saw it on the map. It's less than a quarter-mile downstream."

Pigpen looked under the cabinets. "Got three number 10 cans of baked beans and some coffee!"

"Shoot!" exclaimed Junk. "We can hole up here plumb through the winter. What else you got down there?"

Pigpen took out the cans. "That's all."

"It's a start," said Josh. "Particularly if we can pull in some fish from the lake."

"I'll be happy to contribute to that effort," said Pigpen. "I didn't ever get to go to no camp growin' up. Always thought it'd be fun. I reckon this is my chance."

"Let's go dig us some worms, then," said Junk. "Might find some things to eat on the way down to the river."

"Like what?" Josh asked.

"Wild carrots, if you can tell the difference between them and hemlock. They look a lot alike, but wild carrots have got little hairs on the stems.

Hemlock will kill you. We can also find, clover flowers, plantain, dandelion; you can eat 'em raw or cook 'em up like collards."

Pigpen seconded the motion. "If you had you a piece of hog fat to drop in the pot with 'em, you'd have some of the best eatin' money could buy."

"Okay then," Josh waved at the peculiar fellows as they walked out the door. "Whatever you guys find, we'll eat it." He hoped he wasn't committing to any overly eccentric foods.

Josh made his way back to the cabin. He retrieved his Bible and went to sit on the picnic table. After only a few minutes of reading, Lindsey came up and sat next to him. "I'm not disturbing you, am I?"

"Not at all." He looked up. "How are you doing?"

"Fine, I guess. Any idea how long we'll be here?"

Josh sighed. "When the UEA starts a campaign in an area, they're typically there for at least a week. Then, when they move, they usually go to another spot in relative proximity. That's been their pattern so far."

"The people they are scooping up. Are they being taken to those death camps like the one we saw with the guillotines?"

Josh looked at his Bible. "The ones who refuse to enroll in the re-education programs, I'm afraid so."

"Do you think this is the Fifth Seal?" she asked.

"I do."

She shook her head. "I thought we'd be gone

before this. I suppose that was just my American entitlement attitude."

"Why do you say that?"

Lindsey lifted her shoulders. "In China, if you're caught going to an underground church, they'll sell your organs on the open market. In much of the Middle East, you can be stoned or decapitated. In North Korea, they'll put you in a concentration camp or send you to work in underground mines until you die. I mean, that whole, Jesus-is-going-to-come-get-me-before-anything-bad-happens doctrine didn't apply to Christians in those parts of the world. But I guess I thought we would get a pass, because we were Americans."

He took her hand. "If it makes you feel any better, you weren't the only one who thought that."

"What about the kids? I mean, people with kids, don't you think a lot of them will cave to the demands of the GU so they don't lose their children? I couldn't possibly imagine what that would be like, knowing that you're being hauled off to some death camp and that the GU is going to put your son or daughter in a re-education foster center where they'll be taught to be atheists."

Josh considered the scenario. Losing Micah the way he had almost seemed a blessing compared to what Lindsey was contemplating. "Poor people."

Lindsey stood up, as if consciously putting an end to her introspective analysis. "But once again, I'm sure this is something Christians in other parts of the world have been dealing with for decades." She walked away as suddenly as she'd come.

Josh said a silent prayer for his suffering brothers

and sisters in the new UEA death camps as well as those around the world. Then, he returned to his studies.

***

Later that night, they had a nice meal of fried catfish, baked beans, and steamed wild greens—without the hog fat. For the remainder of the week, the team caught bass, bluegill, catfish, and shell crackers; they collected dandelion, wild carrots, plantains, and clover flowers. They tried to make the best of their time at the primitive summer camp—even with the backdrop of all the persecution going on around the world.

On the following Monday, Josh, Tim, Emilio, and Dana revisited the idea of continuing the journey back to the compound outside of Kokomo, Indiana. However, more UEA raids were being conducted in Western Kentucky and Tennessee, so they stayed another week at the abandoned summer camp.

CHAPTER 24

Come, my people, enter thou into thy chambers, and shut thy doors about thee: hide thyself as it were for a little moment, until the indignation be overpast.

Isaiah 26:20

By the grace of God, the team arrived back at the compound in mid-September, eight weeks after the action to free Nicole and Mackenzie. They pulled into the gravel drive early on Tuesday afternoon. Josh looked forward to sleeping on his bunk in the trailer. "We made it." He cut the engine and smiled at Lindsey.

"Yeah." She took the stuffed bear off of the dashboard and opened her door.

"What's wrong?"

"Nothing." Her downcast eyes told another story.

"I know it's hard to come home to all of Micah's stuff when he's not here. It's tough for me, too. But we'll get through it—together." Josh stepped out of the El Camino which had rolled in on fumes.

She held the bear tightly and grabbed her rifle. "Thanks."

Tim exited the back of Junk's van and stretched. "I'll take your radio and get it charged up if you like."

Josh handed him the walkie-talkie. "Sure, thanks."

Emilio and Nicole had carpooled with Kim and Anne-Marie for the final leg of the journey. Dana approached them. "We've got an extra room in the house if you guys want it."

Emilio nodded. "That would be great. The RV belongs to Mackenzie, so we'd be homeless otherwise."

Mackenzie helped with bringing some of the gear out of the back of the van. "You wouldn't be homeless. You guys busted me out of the slammer. Letting you bunk with me would be the least I could do."

Nicole hugged her. "We appreciate the offer, but…"

"I know, it's a house." Mackenzie looked at Josh and Emilio. "If you guys still have my dad's rifle and pistol around, do you think I could have them?"

Josh was surprised but happy to see Mackenzie taking an interest in firearms. "Yeah. I've got his

AR-15. I think Emilio has his pistol. I'll get those to you after we get settled in."

"Thanks. No hurry." She looked at Nicole. "Could you work with me? With shooting, I mean. I know how to pull the trigger, but I'd like to get proficient—at least with the rifle."

"Yeah." Nicole looked at Emilio then back to Mackenzie. "Sure. I'll work with you."

Junk and Pigpen came stomping out of the barracks after carting a load of gear inside. "Looks like we got robbed," said Junk.

Pigpen added, "Rascals didn't take everything, but we're missing a lot. Three-quarters of our food, most of the ethanol."

Emilio looked at Nicole. "Wait here. I'm going to check on our belongings in the RV."

"We should check, also," Josh said to Lindsey.

Josh and Lindsey sprinted around to the back of the barracks. Josh opened the door. "At least the trailer is still here."

Lindsey went to the bedroom. "We had two AKs stashed under the bed. More ammo also. Someone has been in here."

Josh checked his bunk area but saw nothing missing. "I stashed a couple of rifles and some ammo out in the cornfield. It should still be there, as long as no one has plowed."

Lindsey walked to the front of the trailer where Josh was. "Still, it just burns me."

"We have to count our blessings considering no one was here to watch over the compound."

She put her hands on her hips. "Isn't that what Craig was supposed to be doing?"

Josh walked out of the door. He looked across the barren field. Craig's house was now in view without the vibrant green stalks to act as a partition. "He had his place to worry about."

"I think we should go ask him if he knows anything." Lindsey started toward the stubs of the corn stalks which had been gnawed to the ground by the locusts.

Josh motioned for Lindsey to stop. "Hang on. We should take Dana with us since neither one of us knows him that well."

"Okay." She fell in behind him.

Josh found Junk and Pigpen out front of the barracks. "Where's Dana?"

Pigpen pointed toward the road. "Walkin' over to see Craig."

"Thanks." Josh motioned for Lindsey to tag along. "Let's try to catch up with her."

The two of them cut across the empty cornfield to meet Dana.

She turned when they got close. "Hey, what's up?"

"That's what we're trying to figure out," said Lindsey.

Josh slowed his pace when he reached Dana's side. "It doesn't seem likely that looters would have hit our section of the compound and left anything."

"I agree." Dana walked up to Craig's door and knocked.

Craig opened the door. "You guys are back! I was so worried. Come in!"

Dana led the way through the door. “A bunch of our stuff is missing from the other side. Do you know anything about it?”

“Yeah, I carted most of it up here…to keep it safe. In case you came back. It’s just me, Vivian, and the kids, so I had no way to protect your stuff over there.” Craig signaled for them to have a seat on the sofa. “Wow! It’s so good to see you. I was praying for you guys.”

“Thank you for that,” said Josh.

“Great, so we’ll go get the El Camino and come back,” said Lindsey. “So we can haul everything back to the barracks.”

“Okay, sure.” Craig gave an affirmative nod. “But why don’t we take care of that tomorrow? I’m sure you guys are beat—from the trip.”

“Actually, we’ve been sitting on our tails for the better part of a week,” said Dana. “I think we’d all feel better if we went ahead and got it taken care of now.”

Craig gave a saccharine smile showing his teeth. “It’s going to take me some time. I have to sort everything out. I’ve got your stuff down in the basement—with my stuff.”

Lindsey lowered her brows. “So you were praying for us to come back, but you hoped God wouldn’t pay you any mind, right? You’d pretty much written us off, comingled our supplies with your own.”

Craig looked hurt. “I don’t think that’s a fair characterization at all, Lindsey.”

“Okay then, we’ll see you tomorrow.” Lindsey got up abruptly and walked out the door.

"Hang on for a second." Josh was too late. She was already gone.

Dana stood up. "I guess we better go. Things suddenly feel a little awkward."

Josh didn't know what to make of Craig's behavior. Being a guest on his property, he was inclined to give the man the benefit of the doubt. However, he got up from the couch to walk out with Dana.

"I'm sorry you feel that way," said Craig. "Maybe…maybe we need to talk about an arrangement. My previous agreement for you folks to stay here was with Solomon. Obviously, he's not around, so…"

"You folks?" Dana turned around. "I thought we were all in this together."

Craig held his hands up. "We are, we are. But, this is supposed to be a mutually beneficial situation. Solomon promised that my family would never want for security and provisions—as long as he was here. He always held up his end of the bargain."

"Okay, nothing has changed," said Dana.

"A lot has changed." Craig's eyes looked apologetic. "You guys don't really have the ability to keep up your raiding missions. We don't have any corn to produce ethanol or to grind into meal."

Dana looked very surprised by Craig's implications. "Yeah, but the locusts hopefully won't be around again next year. We can start a new crop."

Craig stuffed his hands in his pockets and dropped his gaze to the floor. "Hopefully."

“We’ve got seed corn,” said Josh.

“*I* have seed corn,” said Craig, as if to clarify his position as landlord. “Why don’t we do this—why don’t I dispense supplies to you guys as the need arises. That way, I can keep an accurate account and make sure none of us gets in a position where we have to do without.”

Josh took a deep breath to avoid saying something he’d regret. “Okay, right now, I need the two AK-47s and the boxes of ammo that were taken from my trailer. It wasn’t part of any communal supply.”

“Can I get those for you in the morning?” Craig asked.

“No, one of them belonged to my dead son, and I want them both. Right now!” Josh’s voice got louder.

“Just try to relax.” Craig held his hands up. “No need to shout. You’ll frighten my kids.”

“Okay, so don’t go rummaging through my personal property when I’m not home, and if you do, don’t make me beg to get it back. Then, I’ll have no reason to raise my voice and disturb your children.”

“I’m going to go get your belongings. I’ll be right back.” Craig left the living room.

“This isn’t going to work out,” said Josh.

“Could we all relocate to your place in Kentucky?” asked Dana.

“Absolutely.” Josh gritted his teeth while he waited.

Craig returned minutes later with two large ammo cans and the two folding-stock AK-47s.

"Here you go. Tell the others that I'll bring back their rifles in the morning. I was just trying to keep them safe."

"Sure." Josh handed one rifle and one box of ammo to Dana. "Can you carry these for me?"

"Yeah, no problem."

Josh led the way out the door without another word to Craig.

When they arrived back at the barracks, Dana explained the situation to the rest of the group. Emilio fumed. "Let's just go in there and take what's ours. He can't stop us."

Josh pointed at his friend. "No! Absolutely not! For starters, he has kids in there. Secondly, this is his place. He's free to do whatever he wants with it."

"But not with our stuff." Lindsey stood with her arms crossed.

"We'll get our stuff back. I'm not going to let him get away with anything, but I'd like to do it without a gunfight," said Josh.

Junk ran his hand through his unkempt hair. "We coasted in on fumes. We need some time to brew another batch of fuel. I can't imagine Craig has enough ethanol stashed in his basement to get three vehicles all the way to Kentucky."

Josh frowned. "We need to bring the trailers and RVs. Fifty gallons should get us there. How long to distill that much?"

Junk looked at his grimy associate. "At least a week for it to ferment. Ten days would be better."

"Another three days to run the still, that's going full steam around the clock," said Pigpen.

Josh nodded, "Alright, we'll bide our time until we're ready to go. Everyone, I need you to act as if Craig's arrangement is acceptable. We don't want to tip our hat that we're planning to leave. We're in a tight spot here. Over the next two weeks, we'll go along to get along. Hopefully, we'll be able to get him to hand over most of our supplies."

"And if we don't?" asked Anne-Marie.

"We have supplies," Josh answered.

Kim inquired, "How do you know that your place hasn't been looted?"

"We have them stashed deep inside a cave," Josh replied.

"We might have enough to get us through the winter," said Nicole. "But with eleven of us, that's going to be about it."

"We'll be taking some supplies from here," assured Josh.

"Even if that means by force?" Tim asked.

"It won't come to that," said Josh. "But if that's the only way…"

All agreed that the plan was solid and that it provided the best path forward considering the circumstances.

***

The next morning, Josh awoke to the sound of someone knocking on his trailer door. He grabbed his pistol and looked out to see Craig. Josh opened the door. "Hey, Craig."

"Good morning Josh. Vivian made some of her famous fried apple pies. I brought them as sort of a peace offering. Mind if I come in for a minute?"

Josh held the door for him. "Sure."

Craig handed a foil package to Josh. "I didn't mean to get off on the wrong foot. I dropped off a load of supplies at the barracks before I came over. It's a large portion of the supplies that were here when you folks left two months ago.

"I hope you'll try to see things from my side of the fence. That's a long time for a group to be gone in our current environment. I honestly didn't expect you guys to come back."

Josh opened the foil and took one of the small pies. "That's understandable, but you see our side, I'm sure. We had a rough trip home and then to find most of our supplies missing, it was unsettling. We shouldn't have to beg to get it back."

"I know, I know. I should have been more understanding. I really hope we can make this work. I've been thinking, if you guys can pull off a couple of raids against the government, that should get us through the winter. Then, we can plant in the spring and hopefully get the operation back to normal."

"It might be a while before we can go out on a raid. Things are kind of hot right now." Josh enjoyed the fried pie, knowing that Craig wouldn't be profiting from any more of the group's raids, or their labor either, for that matter.

"Yeah, sure. Take your time. We've got enough to see us through for a while. In all fairness, I did hang on to a few extra supplies for my family. After all, this side of the compound has a lot fewer mouths to feed since that debacle in San Francisco."

Josh hid the anger that he felt flare up at Craig's lack of decorum over the lost lives. "Sure, Craig. Listen, I appreciate the fried pies. I'll share them with Lindsey. Like I said, we had a tiring trip, and I'm still trying to get settled. We'll talk in a few days."

"Sure." Craig looked disappointed, as if Josh should have offered him coffee or something. "Stop by anytime. I'm always around."

"I'll do that." Josh painted on a fake smile and let the man out the door.

"Have a blessed day, brother."

"You, too." Josh closed the door.

Lindsey came out of the bedroom. "You handled that so much better than I would have. I can't stand that guy."

Josh handed her one of the fried pies. "Here. These were probably made with our supplies."

She looked at the fresh-made treat for a second before succumbing to her hunger. "These are pretty good."

Josh slipped on his boots. "I'm going over to the barracks to see what he dropped off."

"Sure. I'll be around in a while." She held the door open for him.

Josh found Dana making an inventory of the small load of supplies that Craig had brought over. "How are we looking?"

"Scoundrel!" she exclaimed. "We had at least ten times this much stuff. I got in his face about it. He said he'd bring another load over this afternoon but claims this is more than half of it. I'm keeping a log of what we have and what we use from now on. I should have started one a long time ago."

"Yeah, but you were busy trying to take down the New World Order," said Josh.

"Can't fight if we can't eat." She continued writing information in the spiral-bound notebook.

"I'm going to see how Junk and Pigpen are doing. See you later." Josh walked over to the large grain silo. He found Junk and Pigpen working by a large vat. "Craig didn't haul off our corn, did he?"

Junk laughed. "No. That snake don't want to do no work. That's why he wants us to hang around."

"Is all the corn still good?" Josh asked.

"Got some mold on it," said Pigpen. "But it ain't rotten. We can still use it."

Junk continued crushing the corn in the vat using something he'd made which resembled a giant metal potato masher. "Might not win no moonshine awards for taste, but it'll get us where we're going."

"And we'll have enough?" asked Josh.

"We'll have plenty," replied Pigpen.

***

Craig brought another small load of supplies later that afternoon, as he'd promised. The group spent the next two weeks recuperating from the mission and prolonged journey home. They also stowed the items they intended to take to Kentucky inside the travel trailer and RVs. They packed a little at a time so not to look like they were preparing for a big move.

Finally, on Thursday, October 3rd, they filled up their gas tanks with the freshly brewed ethanol, stowed the rest of their belongings, and got ready to roll out on the following morning.

Josh walked over to Mackenzie's RV where Emilio was helping her to check the fluids. "Think it will make the trip?"

Emilio shrugged. "If it were the normal four-hour trip down 65, I'd say no problem. But the back-roads route we're taking to stay off the radar—it's a gamble."

"We'll take it slow, especially going up hills. We're all loaded to capacity." Josh squeezed Mackenzie on her shoulder. "But don't worry. We'll make it."

"Have you talked to Tim about the radio chatter?" Emilio asked.

"I just came from there. He hasn't heard anything that should cause us any concern." Josh heard a vehicle pull into the drive. "I better go check that out."

Emilio placed the dipstick back into the oil reservoir of the RV. "I'm coming, too."

Josh rounded the corner to see that Craig had stopped by. He was near Junk's van, speaking with Junk and Pigpen. Josh and Emilio quickened their pace to close the distance between them and Craig.

"Josh, Emilio, good to see you." Craig held out his hand.

Josh didn't accept the gesture. "What's going on?"

"I was looking out my window and to my surprise, I saw Junk and Pigpen loading a bunch of distilling equipment into the van. I came by to find out if they were planning on going somewhere."

Junk looked a little nervous. "I told him that stuff around here's been going missing. The van is as secure of a place as any to keep stuff locked up."

Craig paid no mind to Junk's response. "In fact, I've seen a lot of scurrying about today. You folks aren't planning on heading out, are you?"

"I can't see how that is any of your business," said Emilio.

Craig lifted his eyebrows. "The supplies I gave you, those are sort of a down payment toward the agreement I made with Josh and Dana. You folks promised me that you'd be holding up your end of the bargain…as prosperous tenants."

Josh held his hands up. "Wait a minute. Those supplies were ours. And I made you no promises about anything. No one is going anywhere right now. So why don't we all take a breath and try to cool off? We can talk about this at a later time."

Craig pointed at Junk's van. "I want to be clear. All the equipment at the compound belongs to me. If you're planning to leave, the still needs to stay here."

Pigpen lowered his brows. "Junk and me built that still! Out of parts we scavenged or paid for out of our pocket!"

"As part of your service to add value to the compound—which belongs to me," said Craig.

Emilio stepped closer to Craig, towering over him. "You better take Josh's advice and get on back over to your side of the field before you have an accident."

"Are you threatening me? On my own property?" Craig looked up at him.

"No one is threatening anyone." Josh stepped between the two. "But please, take my advice before this situation deteriorates." He gently escorted Craig to his truck.

Craig got in and closed the door. "If you're leaving, please don't take anything that doesn't belong to you."

"There's no threat of that," assured Josh as he kept in front of Emilio.

Emilio stepped around Josh as Craig drove away. "I should have pounded the snot out of that little weasel."

"Twelve more hours and you'll never have to see him again." Josh turned to face the barracks. "Come on. Let's finish up with the RV, get something to eat, and hit the rack. Tomorrow is going to be a long day."

CHAPTER 25

For this we say unto you by the word of the Lord, that we which are alive and remain unto the coming of the Lord shall not prevent them which are asleep. For the Lord himself shall descend from heaven with a shout, with the voice of the archangel, and with the trump of God: and the dead in Christ shall rise first: then we which are alive and remain shall be caught up together with them in the clouds, to meet the Lord in the air: and so shall we ever be with the Lord. Wherefore comfort one another with these words.

1 Thessalonians 4:15-18

Josh awoke to the sound of Lindsey's voice before dawn on Friday morning. "Dad, wake up!"

He turned to see her holding her rifle. "What is it?"

"Helicopters." She pointed up.

Josh sprung from his bunk, grabbed his rifle, and ran to put on his boots. "Get some magazines!"

She pulled on her tactical vest. "Do you think they're here for us?"

The sound of spinning rotors passed low over the trailer.

"I don't know yet, but it's not a good sign." Josh stuffed loaded magazines into his vest after zipping it up. He grabbed his radio and pressed the talk button. "Emilio, are you seeing this?"

"Yeah, I'm watching. I've spotted at least three different choppers so far. What do you make of it?"

Josh switched the safety off of his rifle and looked out the window. "I hope I'm wrong, but it could be that Craig figured out a way to make our relationship profitable."

"I should have shot him in the head yesterday!" huffed Emilio. "You better get over here to the house. That trailer won't even slow a bullet down."

"I'm not sure the house will be much better." Josh looked out. "Those are Blackhawk gunships. It's too dark to see what they're outfitted with, but we can assume air-to-surface rockets and miniguns. We're not going to win that fight with AK-47s."

"We have to try," said Lindsey.

Josh pressed the talk key again. "Okay. We'll come to you. Mackenzie, are you up?"

"Yeah, what's the plan?"

"Leave your RV, stay between the barn and the RV to keep out of sight, and come to our trailer." Josh looked outside again. "We're going to make a run for the house."

Anne-Marie called over the radio. "What about us? Should we all go to the house?"

Junk replied over the radio, "You and Kim come to the barracks. We might not want to have everyone piled on top of one another if they start shooting."

"Junk is right," said Josh. "Let's not make it too easy for them."

A knock came to the door. Josh looked out. "That's Mackenzie. Let's move!"

Lindsey followed him out the door. Josh was impressed to see Mackenzie wearing a chest rig filled with magazines and holding her rifle as if she actually knew what she was doing with it. "On my mark."

"Ready when you are," said Mackenzie.

"Go!" Josh led the sprint across the open space to the house. Suddenly, bright spotlights from a low-flying helicopter shone down on him. A voice boomed out of a loudspeaker. "Drop your weapons and surrender. This is your only warning."

Rat-tat-tat-tat-tat! Gunfire coming from the house peppered the helicopter and managed to hit the spotlight. Josh turned to wave the girls on. "Come on! Faster!"

They continued the dash to the house where Nicole was standing with the door open. Josh made it inside as did Mackenzie and Lindsey.

Tim stood inside with his rifle ready. “What are we going to do?”

“We’ve got nothing,” said Dana.

Josh looked outside. “It’s about three-quarters of a mile to Deer Creek. It has trees all up and down the creek.”

Emilio shook his head. “Trees with no leaves on them. And absolutely nothing for cover between here and there.”

More gunfire rang out from the barracks. Three helicopters flew low over the metal barn buildings returning fire as they came over. The bright light of the muzzle flashes illuminated the dark kitchen area of the house where Josh and the others were standing. He looked out the window watching the bullets rip through the thin sheet metal like cardboard. “If we stay here, we’re dead anyway.”

Another volley of gunfire came out of the barracks after the choppers had gone. The Blackhawks came around for a second round. This time, they fired rockets at the building from where the gunfire had originated. A series of small blasts blossomed up into fireballs which lifted glowing smoke and ash toward the sky.

Dana looked out. “Josh is right. We’re dead anyway.”

“Junk, are you guys okay?” Josh called over the radio.

No answer came. He made another call. “Kim, Anne-Marie, Pigpen, anybody, pick up!”

The radio remained silent.

“If we’re going to move, we should do it now,” said Emilio.

Josh looked at the remaining members. "Everyone ready?"

Nicole pressed the butt of her rifle into her shoulder. "Ready as I'll ever be."

Josh nodded. "Two teams. One lays down cover while the other moves. There's another farm between here and the creek. It's the only thing that will offer any kind of cover or concealment. Once there, we'll try to maneuver around the buildings to catch our breath. But as you can see, not much stands in the way of a Hellfire missile.

"Emilio, Nicole, Dana, Tim, you're team one. We'll put down cover and you guys try for a hundred-yard dash. Use anything for cover—a fence post, a stump, don't be picky. You have to give us some cover once you're three-hundred feet out."

"Let's do it!" Emilio led his team.

Josh looked up. "God, please! Get us out of this mess!" Then, he aimed at the first helicopter he saw and began shooting. Mackenzie and Lindsey joined him at firing upon the choppers. The aircraft flew out of range and began to get into formation for an attack.

"Let's go!" Josh led the charge out of the house.

"Shouldn't we be waiting for Emilio to cover us?" Lindsey followed behind.

"In a perfect world, yeah. But they're going to level that house on the next pass. We don't want to be in it." Josh ran as hard as he could.

Bullets ripped across the open field as the Blackhawks passed over. Josh saw Tim fall face-first onto the ground. Despite the agony, he felt for his teammate, he kept running. After flying over, the helicopters launched rockets at the now-vacated house. The explosion illuminated the ground around Josh, but he dared not turn to look at the destruction.

Emilio and Dana shot at the helicopters as they flew away, but it was like a child throwing pebbles at an elephant. Josh watched the Blackhawks form up in a phalanx before the farm which was their intended midpoint for the sprint to the creek. The choppers hovered low over the ground.

Ropes dropped out of the side. Soldiers rappelled out of the helicopters. Josh watched them stream out like a line of ants. Their numbers seemed unending. Realizing that they were now rushing toward the threat, Josh slowed his jog, coming to a complete stop.

Lindsey caught up to him. “What are we going to do?”

Josh looked behind him at the smoldering ruins of the compound. He was already tired from running. Even if he turned back, he had nowhere to go. He turned once more to look at Emilio, Nicole, and Dana. Emilio held up his hands as if asking for instructions.

Josh motioned for Emilio’s team to walk back to his position. They did so. Defeated, Josh let his rifle hang at his side. He put his hand on Emilio’s shoulder when he arrived. “Emilio, I want you to know that I love you like my own brother. I know you said that prayer a while back. I hope you meant it. I’d urge you to search your heart right now, make sure your faith is sincere. This is looking like the end of the line—for all of us."

Nicole began crying softly. Lindsey did also.

Next, Josh turned to Mackenzie. "Your father loved you very much. I can't imagine how disappointed he would be if you don't make it to Heaven."

She dropped her gun and covered her mouth with her fist. She blinked out a tear and turned away from Josh.

Josh continued. "I mean it, Mackenzie. You've come a long way. I think you've discovered that many of your beliefs were based on a lie. But this one, the one about there not being a God, this is really the only one that matters. Please, while you still have time."

The soldiers closed in on the group. Josh looked up. "God, I don't know what is getting ready to happen, but I chose to trust you. For those of us who believe in you, we know that we will be delivered in the next life, if not in this one. For those who haven't yet believed upon the blood of Your Son, Jesus Christ, I pray that you will grant them mercy, give them one more chance. Please, God!"

"Drop your weapons! Facedown! On the ground!" The soldiers held their weapons' lights trained on the group, ready to cut them down if they refused to comply.

Josh let his rifle fall to the barren dirt at his feet. He held his hands in the air and slowly lay down in the empty field. A soldier quickly restrained his hands. "Get up!"

Once the group was relieved of their guns and zip-tied, one of the soldiers called over the radio. "We've got six."

"Do you have the four bounties?" The responding voice was familiar. It was the voice of Ethan Combs, the former ATF agent who had set up Patriot Pride as a sting operation.

"Roger that, Top," the soldier replied.

Combs said, "Good. Then we don't have to sift through the remains looking for them. Walk them back to the compound. I've got a transport vehicle waiting. Then, you boys can load up in the choppers and go enjoy some well-deserved R-and-R. Your first three bottles are on me."

"Thanks, Top." The soldier shoved Josh forward. "Come on. Let's move."

Lindsey walked next to Josh. "What's going to happen?"

"In the end, we're going to see Jesus, and Micah, and your mom, and my wife. No matter what happens between now and then, keep your focus there. Can you do that for me?"

She smiled through the tears. "Yeah, I can do that."

Combs stood waiting for the arrival of the detainees back at the compound. He shook his head at the sight of the conquered team. "My, my, look what the cat dragged in. Josh, you've lasted longer than I ever imagined that you would." He pointed at Lindsey. "Where do I know you from?" He snapped his fingers. "You're Christina's kid! Boy! That nut didn't land far from the tree, did it?"

Ethan looked the group over. "Here's my two escaped convicts." He started to put his hand on Nicole's arm.

"Don't touch her!" Emilio raged.

"And you must be Josh's sidekick from his DHS days." Ethan had a satisfied grin on his face. "Well, you folks sure got me a nice bonus, so let me express my deepest gratitude."

"What are you going to do with us?" Josh asked.

Ethan lifted his shoulders. "I'm dropping you off in Indianapolis. Your biggest fan is waiting for you there."

"Carole Jean?" asked Josh.

"Yep," said Ethan. "She wants to personally congratulate you for your impeccable effort before you're shipped off to a termination center. And let me say, you really have outdone yourself. It's almost a shame to see you die—almost." He motioned to the soldiers. "Get them in the van."

Josh stepped up into the rear of the van and took a seat at the front. A thick window with heavy metal grate inside the glass separated the prisoner transport section of the vehicle from the front.

The others were loaded into the back and the doors were shut. The small window to the driver's seat was the only light source. Josh watched the driver take the wheel while Ethan Combs got into the passenger's seat. The glass was thick, but Josh could still hear Ethan's voice. "Let's go cash in our chips, Henry."

Lindsey sat on the hard metal bench next to Josh. She put her head on his shoulder and wept softly. Emilio sat across from Josh. Nicole's hands were bound behind her back, like everyone else's, so she nuzzled her face against Emilio's shoulder as if it were their final moments together. Dana sat next to Lindsey, and Mackenzie sat next to Nicole. Both looked dejected and hopeless.

Josh watched out the window as the van drove down the road. Morning was coming, showing the devastated landscape left behind by the locusts. He took solace in the fact that he would soon be home, finished with this broken world. It held nothing for him. He would miss no part of it. Yet he did not relish the thought of his final moments, looking up at a guillotine, its fearsome blade glistening in the sun. But at least it would be quick.

No one said much on the short one-hour ride to Indianapolis. Josh could see the towering skyscrapers of downtown.

"Do you hear that sound?" asked Dana.

"Yeah, it's like a horn from a boat," said Nicole.

"More like a trumpet," Lindsey said.

"What? I don't hear anything," said Emilio.

"Yeah, me either." Mackenzie looked at the others.

Just then, Josh remembered. "Today— it's Yom Teruah!"

"What's that?" asked Nicole.

"The Feast of Trumpets!" Josh felt excited as he tried to explain. "Rev taught me about how Jesus's crucifixion was the fulfillment of the Jewish Passover, then how the resurrection fulfilled the Feast of First Fruits. Next, the coming of the Holy Spirit fulfilled Pentecost. Rev speculated that the rapture might occur as a fulfillment of the Feast of Trumpets!"

Just then, the van seemed to leap up then fall back to earth, as if running on a roller coaster. Emilio's eyes opened wide. "I didn't hear any trumpet, but I sure felt that!"

Josh looked out the front window. The road ahead was undulating like a wave on the ocean. He could hear Combs screaming at the driver. "Watch out! That overpass is coming down!"

The driver slammed the brakes. "Earthquake!"

The van felt like it pitched skyward once more, but this time, Josh did not feel it come back down.

He saw Stephanie, standing amidst a peaceful vapor. Her arm was around Micah. Lindsey was running; her hands were free from the zip-tie restraints. She held them outstretched toward Micah. Josh hugged Stephanie. "Where am I?"

A thundering voice behind him said, "You're home, Joshua."

He turned to see a brilliant figure, bathed in pure brilliant light, with eyes burning like white-hot flames. Josh's strength left him, and he collapsed to his knees, undone by the perfection and magnificence before him. While he could not take his eyes away from the stunning glory in front of him, he was suddenly aware of all of his brothers and sisters who had been caught up as he had been, and of those who had been resurrected from their graves, like Stephanie and Micah.

CHAPTER 26

And I beheld when he had opened the sixth seal, and, lo, there was a great earthquake; and the sun became black as sackcloth of hair, and the moon became as blood; and the stars of heaven fell unto the earth, even as a fig tree casteth her untimely figs, when she is shaken of a mighty wind. And the heaven departed as a scroll when it is rolled together; and every mountain and island were moved out of their places.

And the kings of the earth, and the great men, and the rich men, and the chief captains, and the mighty men, and every bondman, and every free man, hid themselves in the dens and in the rocks of the mountains; and said to the mountains and rocks, Fall on us, and hide us from the face of him that sitteth on the throne, and from the wrath of the Lamb: for the great day of his wrath is come; and who shall be able to stand?

Revelation 6:12-17

Emilio opened his eyes. He turned his head away from the morning sun. The metallic taste of blood was in his mouth. His shoulder ached. He looked around. The back doors of the van were open, and he was outside of the vehicle, a few feet away. He tried to get up, but his hands were still restrained behind his back. Reality seemed to move in slow motion. His heart beat like a hammer, but it seemed at a glacial pace. His ears rang. He realized the van was laying on its side. He saw the jagged edge of the crumped front quarter panel protruding outward like a dagger. He tried to inch himself over to the shard of metal but toppled over from disorientation. Blood was running into his left eye, and he could do nothing to clear it—not until he got to the sharp break in the fender. He pushed himself up to his knees with his forehead on the crackled and uneven asphalt.

Finally, he turned backward and sawed at his thick plastic restraint. Gradually, his senses returned. He became mindful of the sounds and smells around him. He could hear screaming. The scent of burning rubber wafted by his nose. The rubble from the collapsed overpass only yards away was littered by cars which had been on the interstate when the earthquake brought it down. Some vehicles had landed right-side up, while others were sideways and still others completely inverted.

Emilio pressed his restraints harder against the serrated edge of the busted quarter panel. The zip-tie snapped and fell away. Emilio used his shirttail to wipe the blood out of his eye. He felt a long gash just below his hairline. Still dizzy, he steadied himself with the front wheel of the van, which was now located at the top of the vehicle. He looked around the front of the van. He could see that Agent Combs and the driver were still inside, but the shattered glass obscured their forms too much to be able to ascertain whether or not they were conscious. They didn't seem to be moving.

Emilio lifted himself to look in the driver's side window which was broken out. The driver was slumped down toward the passenger's side, restrained by his seatbelt from falling farther. Emilio slowly pressed the airbag out of the way to see the man's face. His eyes were open. However, Emilio could easily see that the man's head was turned much too far to the left. His neck had been snapped by the impact, despite the airbag's best efforts.

Ethan Combs was also either dead or unconscious. He could see the barrel of an M-4 rifle lying on the passenger's side window which was at the bottom of the sideways van. Emilio lowered himself into the front of the van in an attempt to retrieve the weapon. He was a wanted criminal, and he didn't stand a chance of escape without a gun.

Agent Combs' weight was pressed against the butt of the rifle. Emilio squatted down in the tight space. He tried to pry the weapon from beneath Combs. He pressed the man's body with his knee while pulling at the gun.

Suddenly, Combs' hand moved. His eyes opened. Blood was trickling out of his nose. He drew a pistol from an in-the-waistband holster. Emilio grabbed Combs' hand and wrapped his thumb around the barrel of the gun for a better grip. He pushed the muzzle away from himself. Agent Combs pulled the trigger twice. Emilio could feel the heat from the discharge. The slide snapped his thumb backward, but he held tightly with his remaining fingers. He wrestled with Combs for the pistol, turning it toward Combs' chest.

"No! No!" Agent Combs grunted.

Emilio pressed the weapon against Combs, using the man's body as a vice so he could free one hand to manipulate Ethan Combs' finger which was occupying the interior of the trigger guard.

"No!" Combs continued to fight, but he was no match for Emilio's strength and determination.

Using his index and middle fingers, Emilio applied pressure to Combs' index finger. POW! He inched the barrel closer to Combs' heart. He pushed his trigger finger again. POW! Combs' grip fell limp and Emilio pried the pistol from his hand. He tucked the pistol in the back of his pants then pulled the rifle from under the weight of the dead man's mass. Before crawling out of the van, Emilio pulled a knife from Combs' pants pocket and a flashlight from the glove compartment. He hurried to crawl out of the cauldron of death.

When he emerged, he looked for any law enforcement vehicles that might be responding to the incident. He stood up on the side of the van to get a long-range view. The streets were completely buckled, impassible for anything less than a monster truck. The destruction from the quake went on as far as the eye could see.

Any police vehicles in the immediate area had troubles of their own. No one was in a position to come after him. Emilio lowered himself down from the van. He quickly went to check on the others. The knife was ready to liberate Nicole and the others from their restraints. He hoped they'd survived the crash. He bent down to look into the back of the van.

Mackenzie lay face down on the sidewall of the vehicle. The others were gone. Emilio looked around. "Nicole!" He called again, "Nicole!" He desperately probed the surrounding area. *How far could they have possibly been thrown?*

He widened the search area and kept calling. "Josh! Nicole! Where are you?" No one answered, and he could locate none of their bodies. He looked back at the van. He returned to see if Mackenzie was alive.

He checked her pulse. "Hey, wake up." He cut away her restraints.

She opened her eyes. She had an abrasion on her chin. She touched it and winced. She focused on Emilio. "What are you doing here?"

"We had a wreck. It was a massive earthquake or something. I was thrown from the van. So were the others. I can't locate any of them."

She managed to sit up. "No, I mean, why didn't you get raptured with the rest of them?"

He shook his head. "You don't believe in that stuff."

She rubbed her head. "I didn't believe in a lot of things. But my dad has been warning me about this for most of my life. Josh was right. Feast of Trumpets. They're gone. And everything that's happened so far is going to look like a picnic compared to what's coming."

"Don't say that. They're around here. We'll find them. You'll see."

"Combs and the driver, are they dead?"

Emilio flashed the pistol tucked under his shirt. "They are now. And it's bad out there. No one is coming after us. Come on, help me look for the others."

She crawled out of the van and surveyed the damage. "They're gone, Emilio. Jesus took them."

"Are you going to help me find them, or not?"

"Nope." Mackenzie stared out at the heap of smoldering ruins which had been downtown Indianapolis only minutes earlier. "Are there any more guns in the van?"

"I don't know. I'm trying to find my wife."

"It's a lost cause." Mackenzie hoisted herself up onto the van and down through the driver's side window.

Emilio resumed his search for Nicole and the others. Occasionally he looked up to see how much progress Mackenzie had made. Eventually, she emerged from the van. She was covered in blood but held a shotgun, plus several magazines. She climbed back down and brought the magazines to Emilio. "Here. These won't do me any good. I found another pistol on the driver." It was tucked into her jeans. She began walking.

Emilio tucked the mags into his waistband and kept searching for Nicole. Minutes later, Mackenzie looked as if she might soon be out of earshot. "Where are you going?" he called out.

She turned around and yelled, "To Kentucky. But first we have to find our way around this mess."

Emilio stared at plumes of smoke and dust rising out of the fallen city. Deep down, he knew that Mackenzie was right. He finally believed everything Josh had tried to tell him. He wished he could go back in time, only one hour. He so wanted to call out to Jesus and repent. He desperately wished he could be with Nicole, but it was too late. Or was it? Perhaps God would still show him mercy. Sure, he'd missed the rapture—and the next three and a half years would be horrific, but maybe he didn't have to miss Heaven altogether.

He knelt and placed the rifle on the ground. He crossed his hands and looked to the sky with deep regret, like a boy who'd missed the school bus by only seconds. "I'm sorry, Jesus. I'm sorry I've been such a stubborn skeptic. But, if you'll give me another chance, if you'll forgive me, I'll believe—with my whole heart."

At that moment, Emilio felt a weight lift from his chest. He could breathe more freely. The sorrow of missing Nicole was as sharp as ever, still cutting him to pieces inside. However, he had hope. Whatever the Great Tribulation had in store for him, he would endure it, for he would have the power of the Messiah to bring him through. Emilio whispered a sentence to himself, which he recalled from one of Josh's Bible studies, "Lo, I am with you always, even unto the end of the world."

Continue the adventure with the follow-on series

The Kingdom of Darkness, Book One: Tribulation

DON'T PANIC!

Inevitably, books like this will wake folks up to the need to be prepared, or cause those of us who are already prepared to take inventory of our preparations. New preppers can find the task of getting prepared for an economic collapse, EMP, or societal breakdown to be a source of great anxiety. It shouldn't be. By following an organized plan and setting a goal of getting a little more prepared each day, you can do it.

I always try to include a few prepper tips in my novels, but they're fiction and not a comprehensive plan to get prepared. Now that you're motivated to start prepping, the last thing I want to do is leave you frustrated, not knowing what to do next. So I'd like to offer you a free PDF copy of *The Seven Step Survival Plan.*

For the new prepper, *The Seven Step Survival Plan* provides a blueprint that prioritizes the different aspects of preparedness and breaks them down into achievable goals. For seasoned preppers who often get overweight in one particular area of preparedness, *The Seven Step Survival Plan* provides basic guidelines to help keep their plan in balance, and ensures they're not missing any critical segments of a well-adjusted survival strategy.

To get your **FREE** copy of ***The Seven Step Survival Plan***, go to **PrepperRecon.com** and click the FREE PDF banner, just below the menu bar, at the top of the home page.

Thank you for reading *The Beginning of Sorrows, Book Three: Upheaval*

Reviews are the best way to help get the book noticed. If you liked the book, please take a moment to leave a review on Amazon and Goodreads.

I love hearing from readers! So whether it's to say you enjoyed the book, to point out a typo that we missed, or asked to be notified when new books are released, drop me a line.

prepperrecon@gmail.com

Stay tuned to **PrepperRecon.com** for the latest news about my upcoming books.

Can't get enough post-apocalyptic chaos? Check out my other heart-stopping tales about the end of the world as we know it.

The Days of Noah

In an off-site CIA facility outside of Langley, rookie analyst Everett Carroll discovers he's not being told the whole truth. He's instructed to disregard troubling information uncovered by his research. Everett ignores his directive and keeps digging. What he finds goes against everything he's been taught to believe. Unfortunately, his curiosity doesn't escape the attention of his superiors, and it may cost him his life.

Meanwhile, Tennessee public school teacher, Noah Parker, like many in the United States, has been asleep at the wheel. During his complacency, the founding precepts of America have been systematically destroyed by a conspiracy that dates back hundreds of years.

Cassandra Parker, Noah's wife, has diligently followed end-times prophecy and the shifting tide against freedom in America. Noah has tried to avoid the subject, but when charges are filed against him for deviating from the approved curriculum in his school, he quickly understands the seriousness of the situation. The signs can no longer be ignored, and Noah is forced to prepare for the cataclysmic period of financial and political upheaval ahead.

Watch through the eyes of Noah Parker and Everett Carroll as the world descends into chaos, a global empire takes shape, ancient writings are fulfilled, and the last days fall upon the once-great United States of America.

Black Swan: A Novel of America's Coming Financial Nightmare

America's financial doomsday. A wayward son.
The epic struggle to survive.

Country music icon Shane Black is this year's headliner for the New Year's Eve bash in Times Square, but when violent riots break out, he'll need more than a six string to escape the maelstrom.

After decades of abuse as the world's reserve currency, the US Dollar's day of reckoning is at hand. Without a functioning monetary system to purchase basic goods, society rapidly descends into abject chaos. Protests, looting, and bloodletting take the place of civility in a country which is coming unhinged.

Thrust into an apocalyptic gauntlet of terror, Shane must resort to savage brutality to get out of Manhattan alive.

Seven Cows, Ugly and Gaunt

In ***Book One: Behold Darkness and Sorrow***, Daniel Walker begins having prophetic dreams about the judgment coming upon America for rejecting God. Through one of his dreams, Daniel learns of an imminent threat of an EMP attack which will wipe out America's electric grid and most all computerized devices, sending the country into a technological dark age.

Living in a nation where all life-sustaining systems of support are completely dependent on electricity and computers, the odds of survival are dismal. Municipal water services, retail food distribution, police, fire, EMS and all emergency services will come to a screeching halt.

If they want to live, Daniel and his friends must focus on faith, wits, and preparation to be ready . . . before the lights go out.

Cyber Armageddon

Cyber Security Analyst Kate McCarthy knows something ominous is about to happen in the US banking system. She has a place to go if things get hectic, but it's far from the perfect retreat.

When a new breed of computer virus takes down America's financial network, chaos and violence erupt. Access to cash disappears and credit cards become worthless. Desperate consumers are left with no means to purchase food, fuel, and basic necessities. Society melts down instantly and the threat of starvation brings out the absolute worst humanity has to offer.

In the midst of the mayhem, Kate will face a post-apocalyptic nightmare that she never could have imagined. Her only reward for survival is to live another day in the gruesome new reality which has eradicated the world she once knew.

Ava's Crucible

The deck is stacked against twenty-nine-year-old Ava. She's a fighter, but she's got trust issues and doesn't always make the best decisions. Her personal complications aren't without merit, but America is on the verge of a second civil war, and Ava must pull it together if she wants to survive.

The tentacles of the deep state have infiltrated every facet of American culture. The public education system, entertainment industry, and mainstream media have all been hijacked by a shadow government intent on fomenting a communist revolution in the United States. The antagonistic message of this agenda has poisoned the minds of America's youth who are convinced that capitalism and conservatism are responsible for all the ills of the world. Violent protest, widespread destruction, and politicians who insist on letting the disassociated vent their rage will bring America to her knees, threatening to decapitate the laws, principles, and values on which the country was founded. The revolution has been well-planned, but the socialists may have underestimated America's true patriots who refuse to give up without a fight.

ABOUT THE AUTHOR

Mark Goodwin holds a degree in accounting and monitors macroeconomic conditions to stay up-to-date with the ongoing global meltdown. He is an avid student of the Holy Bible and spends several hours every week devoted to the study of Scripture and the prophecies contained therein. The troubling trends in the moral, social, political, and financial landscapes have prompted Mark to conduct extensive research within the arena of preparedness. He weaves his knowledge of biblical prophecy, economics, politics, prepping, and survival into an action-packed tapestry of post-apocalyptic fiction. Having been a sinner saved by grace himself, the story of redemption is a prominent theme in all of Mark's writings.

"He brought me up also out of an horrible pit, out of the miry clay, and set my feet upon a rock, and established my goings." Psalm 40:2

Made in the USA
Columbia, SC
27 August 2020

18175243R00170